TWISTED LAWYER

The Rise of Sterling

Book 2 of the Preston Sterling Series

A NOVEL BY

TRENT PARKLE

Twisted Lawyer, The Rise of Sterling

Trent Parkle

ISBN: 979-8-218-37732-8

To my lovely wife: You are the true love of my life. Thank you for inspiring me to be the best man I can be. To my children: You fill my heart with love.

Disclaimers: This is a work of fiction. Any resemblance to real people is coincidental. If you think you resemble one of my characters, I hope you are pleased with the resemblance. If you are not pleased, please read my disclaimer.

This book references legal issues. This book does not constitute legal advice. It is not a textbook. Do not use my book as a blueprint for your life. You will end up in prison.

Chapter 1

A year after getting kicked out of the Army for adultery, Preston Sterling had to admit that his life was finally heading in the right direction. A year ago, his life was different. Much more chaotic. He had faced a string of setbacks. First, and most devastating, his girlfriend broke up with him. Then, in a related matter, his wife left him. Then he lost his commission in the US Army JAG Corps as a reservist, and finally he lost his civilian job as a prosecutor. Basically, there was nowhere to go but up so he should not be surprised that he was doing better. Sterling was now feeling pretty good about his life.

Divorcing his wife was by far the best thing that ever happened to him. She was no longer a good partner. This became abundantly clear after she stole the memory card from his digital camera and sent it to the Army prosecutors via FedEx. The memory card contained some compromising photos. Although CPT Sterling considered them to be very tasteful keepsakes, the Army determined that the pornographic photos constituted proof of adultery.

His wife's hope had been to get him convicted of adultery in a court martial. She almost succeeded. She was, and is, a spiteful woman. The Army charged him with adultery. Both his wife, and his girlfriend, testified against him in high profile court-martial. Thanks to the zealous advocacy of his attorney, LTC Peterson, CPT

Sterling's court-martial was dismissed following a suppression motion. When the military judge found out the Army's trial counsel used stolen evidence against

CPT Sterling, the case against him came to a grinding halt.

The Army trial counsel got the last laugh and used an administrative process to kick CPT Sterling out of the Army. As soon as the ink was dry on his discharge paperwork, he made the long drive from the out-processing center at Ft. Bragg, NC to his home in Tacoma, WA. Initially, he planned to return to his job as a Deputy Prosecuting Attorney in Pierce County. He soon discovered that the wheels were already in motion to fire him from his civilian job. Preston Sterling avoided being fired by offering his resignation, which was quickly accepted by the elected prosecutor.

Preston found himself broke and unemployed. He faced a pending divorce and a custody battle. And yet, a year later he was in fairly good shape financially. Having borrowed $5,000 from his parents to start a law practice last year, he opened a law office working out of a run-down strip mall on the outskirts of town.

He managed to settle his own divorce case and won joint custody of his two children. The week-on, week-off, custody arrangement gave him personal time to explore his own interests, and also time to be a dad. His free time gave him opportunities to date young, fit, and beautiful women, which tended to annoy his ex-wife. He didn't see a downside to upsetting her since he wasn't in the mood to repair their broken relationship.

His growing law practice focused on criminal and military law. Making lemonade out of lemons, he used the publicity generated from his court-martial as a marketing tool. He starred in a cheesy self-made TV commercial in which he wore a dark suit and tie underneath a tan flak jacket and a Kevlar helmet. The background featured the courthouse at Ft. Knox. The camera panned to attorney Preston Sterling who jumped on top of a dark desk making it appear he was in the courtroom. He then yelled "When the military tried to court-martial me, I blew up their case!" He then pulled the pin and threw a dummy grenade which, thanks to some decent CGI, appeared to blow up the courthouse. He then pointed to the camera and said, "As your attorney, I can do the same for you!" His name and phone number then appeared at the bottom of the screen, then the background faded to the stars and stripes waiving in the wind.

That commercial ran on TV for nearly a month before the State Bar Association ordered him to take it down. They claimed that the advertisement tended to show the legal profession in a less than flattering light and seemed to encourage domestic terrorism. Additionally, the commercial appeared to be a promise that he would win his client's case, which was unethical. He took down the commercial, paid a fine and accepted a letter of reprimand. But the business he generated from that advertisement was priceless! In his experience there is no such thing as bad publicity.

His military clients appreciated having a lawyer who himself had the guts to take on the giant military legal machine. They assumed correctly that he would fight for their rights as zealously as he fought for his own rights. They didn't expect him to win all the time, but they always knew he had their back.

Business grew quickly. He paid back the loan from his parents in less than six months. Six months after that, he signed a lease on a downtown office suite at the Wells Fargo building in downtown Tacoma, WA. During his time in the strip mall, he had lost out on some high paying clients who were skeptical of the merits of an attorney who worked out of such a rundown office. His new downtown office should help to convey a sense of dignity and status. He was ready to make it to the big time!

Chapter 2

Looking at the building directory on the ground floor of the Wells Fargo building in Tacoma, Preston enjoyed seeing the newly engraved brass tab which read "Floor 7, Law Office of Preston Sterling." He had considered calling his practice "Preston Sterling and Associates" but his faith in his fellow attorneys was hovering near an all-time low. He thought it unlikely that he would want any associates working for him.

Preston Sterling had become something of a lone wolf, no longer willing to work and play well with others. He could be professional and even courteous with opposing counsel, but that was an act. It was a required part of the legal profession. If he ever wanted to settle cases for his clients, he knew he needed to convey respect and appreciation to get the best deal. Attorneys, even opposing counsel, are people. People treat others much the same as they are treated. That said, Sterling harbored a rebellious streak which competed with his desire to get along well with others. On any given day, it was not clear which divergent trait would claim dominance.

Sterling avoided the temptation of getting his own receptionist. The lone wolf part of him hated to share anything, or anyone, but the terms of the office lease included a receptionist serving the entire seventh floor. This allowed him to split the cost with the three other lawyers, and two psychologists who had offices on the same floor. The receptionist could also sign for delivered packages and certified mail, making her services a good value.

His office suite was small, but it had a large window and at least a partial view of downtown. To mask the limited size of the office, he purchased a glass office desk. Light was able to pass through clear material. The desk did a decent job of creating the illusion of using "less" to make the office look like "more." He learned this trick by reading a design magazine he purchased at a Barnes and Noble just a block from his office.

Hanging up in his office, framed on a wall, was a copy of the Army Times newspaper which ran a story following his victory at Ft. Knox last year. The front cover read, "Adulterous Captain Gets Off." Preston found the title amusing, although it was probably not at all what the writer intended. Yes, he avoided a conviction following a court-martial, and in that sense, he got off, but he preferred the other meaning.

Chapter 3

For the most part, Preston Sterling's clients were decent people who made mistakes. They were often military servicemen facing a court-martial, or maybe some kind of administrative sanction. Some of his clients had charges in civilian court. Sterling also had some clients who were simply unsavory.

His least favorite clients were child molesters. He took their cases because they were willing to pay a lot of money for his services. Demographically, sex offenders are distributed roughly equally in all socio-economic groups. The ones who have money know that a conviction will cost them their jobs and send them to prison. They are desperate for a way out and Sterling had no qualms about profiting from their desperation. Although he truly despised them, they kept the lights on at his practice, so he took their cases.

Preston's recently earned reputation as being somewhat of a counter-culture rebel with a law license opened doors for him. Tacoma was known for having a gang problem. The most notorious of the gangs were the Hilltop Crips. The Crips battled the Bloods for control of the drug trade in Tacoma. The crips gained control of the Hilltop area of town. They became so synonymous with the gang lifestyle in Tacoma that the public tended to refer to all gang members as Hilltop Crips.

The Crips had a hierarchy. Their hierarchy was not unlike the military rank structure. The leader is something like a general, both groups have lieutenants to assist higher bosses, and both have foot soldiers who take orders from above.

The Crips needed attorneys. Sterling's status as an attorney who had been prosecuted by the system gave him credibility. He represented some of the gang members, mostly those charged with low level drug possession cases, but also some clients charged with the more serious charge of delivery of a controlled substance. The gang members, for the most part, were good clients. One thing Sterling liked about the gang is that they aways paid in cash and they paid up front. He never had to send them an invoice. He also enjoyed the look on the faces of the 7th floor's other tenants when a pack of Crips came to his office for a consultation.

Taking cash payments from Crips presented some problems. Banks are required to report cash deposits of over $10,000. Despite what he had seen on TV crime shows, depositing a series of deposits of $9,999, even if spread out over a few days, still triggered mandatory reporting to the IRS. Sterling didn't mind paying taxes on cash to keep the IRS happy, but his clients didn't like it when Sterling's books reflected so much cash coming in from the gang. If the gang had more cash available than their job history would support, then the IRS could target the gang and send them to prison much like they did to Al Capone back in the day.

Sterling came up with a foolproof system to avoid making problems for his gang clients. He simply cooked the books. He kept the name of his clients 100% accurate so that the bar association would be satisfied that his client list matched his ledgers, then he reduced the actual payment amount he claimed to just a small fraction of the actual cash payment he received. Even better, he would often claim he did such work for free, as part of his commitment to give back to the community. The local bar association kept track of "pro bono" hours. With any luck he would get an award for his efforts to help the disadvantaged members of society. It was the kind of PC bullshit that had become popular, and it should be sufficient to address the billing issues.

This then created a new problem. Cash kept piling up. He had to get creative with ways to pay for high dollar items with cash. Obviously, he couldn't buy a new car in cash. But he still wanted to make a splash in the legal community. He managed to keep his cash on hand down to a manageable level by getting creative with his vehicle purchase.

He bought a 2007 Mercedes G-Wagon at an insurance auction. It was a flood damaged vehicle that had been ruined in nearly every way. It had body damage from being swept down the Green River when a mentally disturbed suburbanite mom tried to drown herself and her kids. The kids died but the mom survived. The insurance company just wanted to get rid of the vehicle, and for good reason.

In addition to carrying the stigma of being the murder weapon used to drown innocent children, the vehicle was a mess mechanically. The electronics were shorted out and the ECU's were destroyed. Every interior surface was either covered with mud, mold, or both. At least the engine and transmission were mostly intact. To the insurance company, and to most normal people, the vehicle was a complete loss. Only a fool would spend good money to buy the trashed SUV, then also spend the money needed to fix it.

Preston paid $8,500 cash for the sad looking G-Wagon with a flood salvage title. Over the last few months, he rotated body shops making sure to spend less than $10,000 at any given place. In a couple months, he could replace his old Camry with a nearly flawlessly repaired German luxury SUV. He would roll up to the fancy society events looking like the most successful lawyer in town. And it would really piss off his ex-wife when he picked up the kids in a G-Wagon.

Chapter 4

Returning to his office from the morning court docket, Preston Sterling was ready to be done for the day. Unfortunately, it was not even noon yet. He had spent two hours in District Court waiting for his client to be arraigned on a DUI. His client's matter only took about 10 minutes. The rest of the two hours was devoted to waiting for the judge to call his client's name. The judges tended to schedule 30 or more cases on both the morning and afternoon dockets. There was no other way for the judges to handle the massive volume of cases they were expected to process, but it was a huge waste of time for the lawyers.

Passing through the building's common area on his way to his new office, he smiled at the shared receptionist, Kathleen. She was older, but reliable. She seemed to enjoy working at the reception desk. Sterling never saw her when she wasn't smiling. After a tough day in court, he appreciated her upbeat demeanor. Kathleen greeted him and handed him a pink phone message slip. He thanked her and without reading it, made his way to his office.

The light making its way through the large window in his small office lifted his spirits. He took a seat in his black leather desk chair and leaned back. He put his feet on the glass desk. His attention turned to the pink slip given to him by the receptionist. The phone number had a prefix he did not recognize, but the name of the caller brought back memories. LTC Mark Peterson requested a call back. The box "urgent" had been checked on the message.

Over a year ago, LTC Peterson represented Sterling (then known as CPT Sterling) during his court-martial at Ft. Knox, KY. It was LTC Peterson who engineered the suppression motion that earned CPT Sterling his freedom against the charge of adultery. Within the legal community the outcome was widely criticized as a miscarriage of justice. The dismissal generated more outrage than appreciation even among Sterling's friends back home.

The successful outcome didn't help the reputation of Sterling's attorney either. Some had even speculated that if LTC Peterson hadn't represented CPT Sterling in such a zealous manner, "Lieutenant Colonel" Peterson might now be known as "Colonel" Peterson. Representing Sterling may have cost him a promotion. Sterling was toxic that way, at least at that time.

Except for representing clients, Preston Sterling had largely turned his back on the military. He didn't chat with old friends. He didn't send Myspace friend requests to catch up with Army buddies. The feeling was mutual. No one from his unit wanted to be associated with Sterling and that included his lawyer. LTC Peterson didn't enjoy representing CPT Sterling, mostly because Sterling was a terrible client. His ongoing infatuation with his accuser clouded Sterling's judgment, nearly costing him a dismissal. LTC Peterson's zealous representation of Sterling speaks volumes as to his professionalism and ability to separate the dislike of the client from the requirement to provide zealous advocacy.

Sterling was curious as to what would merit a call from his former lawyer. Turning back to the pink slip, he decided to make the call. He picked up his new iPhone, ready to navigate the screen to find the call function. Sterling's perception was that the new device was overly complicated and overpriced. He paid $500 for the iPhone. Somehow, he got caught up in the hype. It was the new "must have" electronic gadget among his peers. In Sterling's mind, it made more sense to buy a computer and a cheap cell phone, but now he was stuck with the thing. Maybe he would grow to appreciate it, but he doubted it. He couldn't help but think Apple was going to go down in flames based on this newest offering.

He punched in the number on the pink slip. Three rings later, a voice answered, "This is LTC Peterson." Sterling responded, "This is CPT Sterling, or um, Sterling. I got a message that you called. How have you been?"

LTC Peterson answered, "I'm fine Sterling, but this is not a social call." Getting right to the point he continued, "A friend of mine is in trouble, and he needs a lawyer. He lives in Dupont and he is facing a court-martial out of Ft. Lewis. I want you to represent him."

"Sir, I appreciate what you did for me, but I have bills to pay. I don't do pro-bono work." Well, not *actual* pro-bono work, Sterling thought to himself. LTC Peterson answered back, "I never said it was a pro-bono case. He has money. My friend is a West Point graduate. He is a Lieutenant Colonel in charge of a Special Forces unit. He got busted for some misunderstanding about importing enemy weapons from Iraq to the US."

"OK, no big deal," responded Sterling. "So, he packed up a few confiscated AK47's along with the American gear, right? It's not like he brought back RPG's or something." There was a long pause on the other end of the line. Breaking the silence, Sterling asked, "What did he import from Iraq?" LTC Peterson answered, "RPG's. Launchers and grenades." Sterling shot back, "Why the hell did he do that?"

"Look, just chat with the man. He is a good person. Real GI Joe American hero type of guy. He needs a good attorney, and despite your questionable romantic interests you are an excellent attorney. Plus, you owe me," said an exasperated LTC Peterson. This was a not-so-subtle dig at Sterling for having dated his own paralegal, while married, and on active duty, which then landed Sterling in the middle of a court martial.

Well played, Sterling thought to himself. LTC Peterson did an effective push/pull persuasion, appealing to Sterling's ego as well as the recognition of owing a debt to LTC Peterson. Sterling said, "Yes, I will meet with the guy. No guarantee that I will take the case. Then again, there is no guarantee he will want to hire me after I tell him my fee." LTC Peterson laughed and said, "Fair enough. Good to see you landed on your feet." Sterling couldn't help but answer back, "Lucky for me I had an excellent attorney."

Chapter 5

The following day, Sterling set aside 30 minutes for a consultation with LTC Michael Carter. Sterling was pretty sure he was simply going to take the meeting as a courtesy. He was unlikely to take the case. The meeting itself was a favor that Sterling owed to his former lawyer. Considering that Sterling owed his existing freedom to the hard work of his lawyer, it was merely a down payment on making things right.

LTC Carter checked in with reception ten minutes prior to the 9:00 am meeting time. This was a good sign. So many of Sterling's clients arrived late, or simply blew off the appointment. It was refreshing to have a potential client take his own case seriously.

Sterling usually played the power game by making his clients wait. It didn't matter what time they showed up for an appointment, he would make them wait. This was a show of dominance meant to convey that Sterling was a busy and important lawyer. However, since LTC Carter was courteous enough to be early, and was a friend of LTC Peterson, Sterling made an exception and immediately went to the reception area to retrieve his potential client.

LTC Carter arrived wearing his Class A uniform, adorned with four rows of awards stacked perfectly in order of precedent. On his right sleeve he wore a combat patch signifying one or more prior deployments to an overseas hot spot. On his left sleeve he wore the special forces patch with the three lightning bolts crossing a sword. Above the patch were special tabs listing "Special Forces" "Ranger" and "Airborne." LTC Carter had been around, and based solely on an examination of his uniform, Sterling knew he was dealing with a real soldier as opposed to a desk jockey.

LTC Carter stood confidently and purposefully. He looked Sterling in the eyes and both men unconsciously measured up the other. Sterling saw in front of him a man pushing 50, with a chiseled jaw and a weathered face. His full head of short, salt and pepper hair gave him a distinguished look. He appeared to be in excellent physical condition, not just for a man of 50, but for a man of any age. Sterling couldn't help but think he was looking at version of himself in ten years. At least he hoped he would hold up as well. Sterling reached out a hand and introduced himself. He invited LTC Carter back to his office. The man had an easy grace about him as he followed Sterling down the hallway.

Sterling invited LTC Carter to have a seat in one of the client chairs on the other side of the glass desk. Before having a seat, LTC Carter took a moment to examine Sterling's efficient and upscale new office. He noticed the framed copy of the Army Times hanging on the wall. LTC Carter seemed to search his memory, then the flicker of recognition crossed his eyes. "Oh, you are *that* Sterling. The CPT who fucked his paralegal, pissed off his wife, then got his ass in a sling over it." Sterling smiled, and said, "Yes, that pretty much sums up who I am."

"You are not serving a prison sentence in Leavenworth, so I guess it worked out OK for you." Said Carter casually. LTC Carter's expression and demeanor did not convey criticism or confrontation. Sterling knew this type of warrior. He is a man who has seen and done far too much to worry about offending the over-sensitive among us. Far from taking offense, Sterling found the directness to be refreshing. As a defense attorney, he was accustomed to people lying to him, especially his own clients.

Knowing he could skip the pleasantries, Sterling invited LTC Carter to explain what brought him here. Carter started by explaining that he and LTC Peterson graduated from West Point together, so he reached out to his JAG buddy seeking legal help. LTC Peterson was not available to assist, but recommended Sterling as an excellent attorney with something of an axe to grind against the Army. Carter explained he was facing a court-martial. Charges had already been "preferred" by the Army prosecutor, and his client feared the charges would soon be "referred" to a general court-martial. The Army was accusing him of illegally importing weapons from Iraq, failing to declare weapons, and a general charge of abusing his authority to facilitate each of the charged crimes. Sterling took a moment to remember that the "preferral" of charges precedes the "referral" of charges in the military legal system.

Preston Sterling asked a general question, "What is your take on the charges?" It was an open-ended question designed to let LTC Carter take control of the discussion. Without a hint of guilt or shame he replied,

"Would you like to know if I did it? Do you want to know if I brought RPG's to America from Iraq? Because the answer is hell yes I did!" LTC Carter had a big grin on his face.

Sterling wasn't expecting his client to so openly, and proudly admit to doing what the Army suspected he had done. Sterling hoped there was more to the story, otherwise he could only help his client enter a guilty plea. Not that he was a stranger to representing guilty clients.

LTC Carter went on to explain that he was on his fifth combat tour in the last six years. His Special Forces unit was tasked with securing high value fixed locations in north-central Iraq. Assisting his SF unit was a company of airborne infantry soldiers from the 82nd Airborne Division. While he trusted the training of his Special Forces Teams, not everyone in an SF unit is on an A-team. Many soldiers in his unit were support personnel thrust into assisting with the mission. Similarly, the infantrymen sent to help his unit generally lacked specific training on using enemy weapons.

That lack of training on enemy weapons became apparent when he found his unit tasked with defending a prison on the outskirts of Mosul, Iraq. Like Special Forces, airborne infantry units of the 82nd Airborne are considered "light" infantry. They lacked heavy weapons such as artillery, tanks and Stryker transports. Adapting to the environment, LTC Custer worked with the local leaders to round up enemy weapons. The locals were the best source of information as to where the insurgents were stockpiling munitions.

A favorite weapon of the Ba'athists and other Pro-Hussein forces was the RPG (rocket propelled grenade). LTC Carter and his unit managed to confiscate nearly 200 launchers and over 1000 rockets with various warheads. They didn't destroy the confiscated arsenal. They used them to supplement their own light weapons. In defense of fixed positions, a couple hundred insurgents armed with RPG's could easily overrun SF teams, no matter how well trained the SF might be. To level the playing field, LTC Carter's men defended the prison with confiscated RPG's.

S-2 (intelligence) spread word that an attack would likely come soon, maybe in the next couple days. Insurgent scouts were spotted taking photos of the prison, then running off into the hills. Despite having some idea that an attack might be coming, LTC Custer did not expect it to come so soon. Shortly before sunrise the next day, a soldier pulling guard duty spotted movement approaching the prison and sounded the alarm. LTC Custer's men were barely in position when 500 insurgents attacked the wall. The prison would have been overrun without the use of RPG's to slow the enemy's progress and to take out the technicals (pickups with mounted machine guns in the bed) favored by the insurgents.

The defense of the prison came at a high cost. In the heat of battle, an infantry soldier struggled to match the correct launcher with the correct rockets. Some people assume that there is only one model of RPG, but this is incorrect. There are many similar models and many similar rounds.

The Iranian made RPG 7 launcher was able to hold the rocket from a confiscated RPG 16. However, when the American soldier pulled the trigger, the warhead activated without initiating the rocket. The result was that the warhead cooked off like a hand grenade with its pin removed. The infantry soldier holding the launcher waited for the rocket to shoot the warhead out of the launcher only realizing too late that he was at the center of the explosion. This happened twice during LTC Carter's command, and he was committed to ensuring better training. No amount of talking points can demonstrate the difference between launchers as effectively as physically holding an actual example. At the end of their deployment in Iraq, LTC Carter ordered the RPG's to be loaded into the Conex bound for his home unit at Ft. Lewis, WA.

Sterling asked him, "So you are in trouble for loading live warheads into the Conex for transport back to the states? I guess that would be dangerous." LTC Carter replied, "No, I ordered my guys to drill out the rounds and empty the explosives from the warheads. I then had them cut large holes in the launchers with a welder. We rendered the RPG's completely inert prior to loading them up in Iraq."

Despite being a former JAG attorney, Sterling failed to understand what crime had been committed. He asked, "Then what happened? Did some of the RPG's end up in a pawn shop off base?" Impressed, LTC Carter's face lit up, "Yes, that is exactly what happened! My supply sergeant didn't have an easy way to enter the enemy gear into the inventory database. Enemy RPG's don't correspond with any of the codes we use to update our records. Since the supply sergeant wasn't able to code the items, he decided he could sell the weapons to a pawn shop, and no one would find out."

Sterling had some familiarity with the Army's inventory process. While awaiting his court-martial a year ago, he had been stripped of his duties at the JAG office and forced to help HQ with inventory of non-sensitive, low value items. It was meant to humiliate CPT Sterling, and it worked.

LTC Carter went on to explain that a well-meaning off duty Military Policeman (MP) was shopping at the pawn shop off post. He noticed the RPG and grenade. Both seemed out of place, and he reported the matter to Army CID (Criminal Investigation Division) who determined that the launchers and grenades were illegally imported contraband. The pawn shop willingly gave up the name of the supply sergeant who sold the launcher and grenade. Hoping to strike a deal, the supply sergeant was quick to point the finger at LTC Carter for ordering the weapons to be brought back to Ft. Lewis from Iraq.

Special Agent Smith of CID could feel himself salivating at the prospect of putting steel bracelets (handcuffs) on a Lieutenant Colonel. He had only recently earned the title of "Agent" and was anxious to handle a big case. Thinking they were trading up, CID enthusiastically recommended offering the supply sergeant immunity in exchange for his testimony against LTC Carter. He forwarded the case to the Army prosecutor for review.

The JAG office considered their options and granted the supply sergeant immunity if he offered truthful testimony during trial. What was missing was any input from LTC Carter. CID didn't interview him prior to seeking charges. They hoped that LTC Carter would be caught off guard and unable to prevent the inevitable search warrant for the remaining launchers and grenades still held in the supply room on post.

Sterling wasn't terribly surprised. It had also been his experience that CID agents get so excited about the half the case they do know that they don't bother to explore the half they don't know. Usually, the JAG office reviewing referrals from CID does a good job of understanding the strengths and weaknesses of cases, but this one must have slipped through the cracks.

Chapter 6

Major Trevor Rankin knew that he had a good chance of earning a promotion to the rank of Lieutenant Colonel. He had enough time in the grade of Major to qualify for promotion. All he needed was a solid annual evaluation. If he could earn a top block, reserved for the top 25% of Majors, his promotion was all but assured. When he reviewed CID Agent Smith's report about a Special Forces Lieutenant Colonel illegally importing RPG's from Iraq, he knew the trial gods had smiled upon him.

This was the type of case that could garner him attention even beyond his chain of command. This is type of case that CNN would love to cover. He assumed that like himself, everyone was tired of these hot shot Special Operations types playing fast and loose with the rules. Guys like that thought they could get away with anything. These combat warriors got all of the glory, but it was guys like him who kept the Army running. MAJ Rankin might not wear a combat patch on his shoulder, but like his mother always told him, "The Army is too smart to send its best and brightest into harm's way."

CID's report included photos of the launcher and the grenade confiscated from the pawn shop. Actually, MAJ Rankin's copy of the report only had black and white copies of the photos, but from what he could see, there was little doubt as to the illegal nature of the items. Based on this evidence, he secured a search warrant from Judge Anderson to take possession of the remaining launchers and grenades still held in the property room of the SF unit at Ft. Lewis. In all, CID confiscated five launchers and nine grenades, including the launcher and grenade from the pawn shop.

MAJ Rankin's case was coming together nicely, and he was proud of himself. He was coordinating a slam dunk prosecution of a rogue officer. He selected the charges himself. One count of illegally importing weapons from Iraq, one count of failing to declare dangerous weapons held in storage, and a count of abuse of authority to facilitate each of the charged crimes. The last of the three charges came together when LTC Carter's subordinates also struck up immunity deals to testify that LTC Carter had ordered them to load up the contraband in Iraq in preparation for shipping the items to America.

Chapter 7

Preston Sterling really wanted to believe LTC Carter. He gave every indication of being a credible person and he was likeable. If this case went to trial, likability would play a large role in determining whether the verdict was guilty or not-guilty. Jurors side with people they like. Evidence would also be important in determining whether his client got convicted, but in a close call, he wanted them to like his client.

Most clients in an initial consultation with a lawyer present only the information which is favorable to their position. It is like dating. Both parties want to look attractive to the other. Sterling had not reviewed any discovery, not even a police report, and therefore he had a hard time evaluating the case. He was not going to make the mistake of becoming so overwhelmed with the half he knew that he disregarded the half he didn't know.

On the surface, this seemed like a case Sterling could get dismissed before it ever made it to a jury. Time is money so if this was a quick case with little effort needed, he could justify a $10,000 fee. But if this case consumed his life by sucking him into the black hole of litigation, he would be unable to take on other cases, potentially for months. Maybe he should charge $50,000. Maybe more.

"Did you have a chance to get a legal opinion from Trial Defense Services on post? You have a right to a free attorney. It is a benefit you have earned." Sterling was curious what the defense JAG had told him. LTC Carter replied, "Yes, I met with them for a quick consultation. They offered to help get me the best possible plea bargain." Sterling laughed, then realized LTC Carter wasn't joking. Sterling knew that LTC Carter was not seeking a plea bargain and Sterling agreed.

Stealing the initiative, LTC Carter told Sterling, "Look, I am not a rich man, but I've socked away a solid amount of my paycheck that I couldn't spend while in the desert, plus TDY, and hazard pay. I am willing to pay you $20,000. This seems like a good case to me, and you should be able to win. But if we go to trial and lose, I will still pay you." Sterling pointed out that attorneys can't take criminal matters on contingency anyway, so promising to pay no matter the outcome is not a carrot, it is a requirement.

Not wanting to get bogged down in the details, Sterling told LTC Carter, "This looks like a good case to me as well. Keep in mind that I have not seen any of the government's evidence. Frankly this whole matter has me curious as to how we ended up here. It makes no sense to me that you would be charged with a crime. I would like to be your attorney. And I accept your offer of $20,000. As soon as you write the check, I am your lawyer."

Chapter 8

The next day, Preston Sterling set off early so he could attend the morning docket in Pierce County District Court. He had two clients that day and thankfully both matters were set in front of Judge Jamison. As far as judges went, Sterling couldn't complain about appearing in front of Jamison. He was generally considered to be a fair and pragmatic man who ran an efficient docket.

Sterling had a client from each of his two disparate client bases represented today. Jamal Watkins had originally been charged with Possession of Controlled Substance-Cocaine. Sterling managed to get the felony reduced to a gross misdemeanor of PODP (Possession of Drug Paraphernalia). The recommendation was a sentence of two days in jail, with credit for two days served, no probation and a $43 conviction fee. Not a bad outcome, and it would keep him on good terms with the Crips.

Jamal Watkins entered the courtroom a couple minutes late, and he looked like hell. Sterling had seen him a couple times before during client meetings and there had been a steady decline in his client. Sterling knew his client was high. By the looks of him, he probably hadn't slept in days. Sterling approached his client and asked him to step out into the hallway. Jamal initially didn't recognize his lawyer but by the time they were in the hallway he remembered that he was supposed to enter a plea today. Sterling confirmed with

Jamal that he still wanted to enter a plea. Jamal insisted that they resolve the matter as quickly as possible. Sterling agreed, not wanting Jamal to lose the favorable plea agreement from the prosecutor. Walking his client back into the courtroom, Sterling made a plan to get his client out of court as soon as possible.

When Judge Jamison entered the courtroom from the back entrance reserved for court staff, his bailiff announced, "All Rise," and everyone stood for the judge. Judge Jamison quickly followed up with, "Please be seated." The judge started the docket and asked if there were any matters ready to proceed, Sterling jumped up and said he was ready on the Watkins matter. The judge invited Sterling to approach counsel table with his client. The judge then took a moment to collectively advise the room full of defendants of their important rights. It was a standard part of the routine.

Judge Jamison truly wanted to protect the rights of everyone in his courtroom. He asked for everyone's attention, and explained, "Each of you have important rights. One of those rights is that you do not have to enter a plea of guilty. Instead, you have the right to have the prosecutor attempt to prove each charge beyond a reasonable doubt. That would mean going to trial. You could have a trial in front of a judge or a jury. Either way, if you are convicted of a crime following trial, you would have the right to appeal that conviction. You are presumed innocent, and you have the right to remain silent. I have a couple warnings for you. If you are not a US citizen, a conviction to certain crimes could result in immigration consequences, possibly including deportation. If you are a US citizen, a conviction to certain crimes could make it hard for you to travel outside of our country." Midway through the instructions, Sterling noticed his client's eyes shutting, seemingly drawn downward by an unstoppable force. Sterling took an elbow and nudged Jamal in his ribs. Jamal opened his eyes just in time.

Turning his attention to Jamal Watkins, the judge asked, "Mr. Watkins, do you have any questions about your important rights today?" Sterling's client answered, "No, your honor." Sterling breathed a sigh of relief. It was going well so far. Just a couple questions remained for his client to answer. The judge asked the prosecutor to read into the record a summary of facts from the police report. The prosecutor read into the record that a police officer observed Jamal Watkins engage in a hand-to-hand exchange in a neighborhood known for drugs. Officers contacted Jamal and he attempted to swallow the crack. An officer grabbed him by the throat preventing him from swallowing the hard rock. The item later tested positive for cocaine.

Judge Jamison asked Sterling if he had any challenge as to the sufficiency of the facts for purposes of the plea. Sterling advised the court that he had no challenge. The court found probable cause for the original charge of possession of a controlled substance, and accepted the prosecutor's amendment to a lesser charge. The judge turned to Jamal and asked, "Mr. Watkins, as to the amended charge of Possession of Drug Paraphernalia, what is your plea?" Jamal looked at Sterling. Sterling nodded and whispered, "Guilty."

Jamal took his attorney's lead, and said, "Guilty, your honor."

The plea went through without any hiccups. The judge followed the recommendation and Jamal was free to go. After the plea, Watkins thanked his lawyer, which rarely happens, and excused himself explaining that he needed to get back to work. Sterling had a pretty good idea of what kind of work Jamal would be doing. Likely it involved standing on a street corner selling drugs.

His other case was a bit more complicated. Specialist Terrence Walker had been charged with 4th Degree Assault-Domestic Violence. After a night of drinking with his Army buddies who serve with him in his Stryker brigade, Walker went home and got into an argument with his wife. The argument escalated and Walker punched his wife in the stomach. She called the police. The police interviewed both parties. They read Walker his Miranda warnings, and an embarrassed Walker admitted to everything, noting that this wouldn't have happened "If she would have just listened to me." A judge issued a restraining order at the arraignment.

Walker violated the restraining order almost immediately by going to see her at work and trying to reconcile. She called the police. Walker later told law enforcement that as a man, he just really needed to prove to his wife that he loved her, and no piece of paper could keep them apart. Unimpressed with his display of affection, the officer arrested Specialist Walker for Violation of a Domestic Violence No

Contact Order. The only thing Walker did right was to hire Sterling.

Sterling convinced Walker to start mental health counseling sessions immediately in order to address his anger issues and impulse control problems. Naturally, Walker resisted the idea of treatment, explaining to Sterling that he didn't need treatment, he just needed his wife back. Sterling didn't try to fix his client, he simply agreed with Walker, and pointed out that by pretending to learn from his treatment sessions, he could impress his wife. If she set a motion to drop the protection order, he could then move back into his house. If he could convince her of his sincerity, she would probably be more willing to ask the prosecutor to drop the assault charge. This plan appealed to the manipulative part of his client's view of the world.

After Sterling succeeded in delaying the case for five months for his client to demonstrate progress in counseling, Walker largely complied with treatment. He got his wife to file a motion to recall the no contact order (NCO), which the judge granted, then he moved back into his home. But now the delay which Sterling relied on to show his client's progress became a liability. Sterling knew that the honeymoon phase could only last so long before his client would inevitably screw it up. Sterling needed to settle the case quickly.

He managed to get the prosecutor to dismiss the charge of violating a domestic violence protection order. He hoped to get the prosecutor to reduce the assault charge to something less stigmatizing, like disorder conduct, but the prosecutor held firm. Sterling did get her to agree to recommend no jail and no probation.

There was one last detail he needed to address. A conviction for Fourth Degree Assault-Domestic Violence would trigger gun restrictions. In 1968, the US Congress passed the Firearms Control Act. This act stripped convicted felons of their gun rights, but left exceptions for law enforcement and military. In response to underenforcement of the law, and to fix the gaping holes left in the law, congress passed the Lautenberg amendment in 1990. This act broadened the crimes which would trigger loss of firearms rights, to include some non-felony domestic violence offenses. It also eliminated the exceptions for law enforcement and the military.

Military personnel who found themselves charged with domestic violence cases in civilian courts would sometimes accept a plea offer from the prosecutor, thinking that if they avoided jail, they were getting a good deal. They would later learn that they lost their gun rights. The ability to lawfully possess a firearm is a requirement of military service. The unfortunate soldier who thought he got a good deal in court suddenly found himself discharged from the Army.

Sterling managed to save the careers of at least a dozen soldiers since he opened his practice. It could be a delicate dance. This case was one of those times. The actual plea bargain that Sterling secured for his client was a plea to Fourth Degree Assault-Domestic Violence. The prosecutor would recommend no jail and no probation and would dismiss the No Contact Order violation. When Sterling arrived with his client to enter the plea, Sterling attempted to renegotiate. He asked the prosecutor to drop the domestic violence tag, and let his client plead to a simple assault.

Pretending to be a well-meaning but imperfect lawyer, he appealed to the prosecutor's sense of fair play, arguing that his client shouldn't pay the price for Sterling's oversight. The prosecutor initially bristled at Sterling's attempt to back out of the original deal. Sterling took full responsibility, insisting that he had forgotten about the firearms implications of the plea, noting that he owed it to his client to at least try to save his career.

By this time in the cycle of the case, the prosecutor had mostly moved on to other matters, thinking that this one was in the bag. She fell for Sterling's charming smile and his fake appeal to her better nature. She agreed to drop the DV (domestic violence) tag, thereby allowing Sterling's client to avoid losing his gun rights, which in turn allowed him to keep his job in the Army.

Sterling thanked her and promised to let the judge know that she had been fair and professional. It was a formula he had used before with great success. Thanks to the constant turnover at the prosecutor's office, it was never more than a few months before a new attorney would take her place, thus allowing Sterling nearly unlimited opportunities to tip the scales in his clients' favor.

Chapter 9

Sterling was anxious to get moving on the LTC Carter case. He figured there was a solid chance he could intervene before the Article 32 hearing could be set. The Army prosecutor might even be grateful that Sterling had the courtesy to save him from an embarrassing ass kicking in court. Surely if the prosecutor knew what a turd sandwich he was going to serve up to the jury, he would drop the case like a hot potato.

Sterling dialed the number for MAJ Rankin. The prosecutor answered and Sterling introduced himself and explained that he is representing LTC Carter and would like to discuss the case. MAJ Rankin seemed anxious to start off on the wrong foot and said "Somehow that just figures. An arrogant neanderthal like LTC Carter found an even bigger dirtbag to be his lawyer. Don't think for a minute that the JAG community has forgotten you and your escape from justice last year. This is a small world."

Sterling had never met this guy and already didn't like him. His first instinct was to tell MAJ Rankin to go fuck himself. Sterling's next thought was to tell MAJ Rankin about all the reasons why the case against LTC Carter was a heaping pile of shit. Sterling took a breath and counted to ten inside his head. It didn't take long before his need to seek instant gratification yielded to a far more diabolical plan to gut the prosecutor, at least in a legal sense. Sterling vowed that he would not only win the case, but he would also make MAJ Rankin lose. In the first few seconds of dealing with this prick, Sterling already wanted him to suffer the humiliation of a high-profile loss.

Thinking back to his youth, he remembered the famous boxer Muhamad Ali's strategy of "rope a dope" in which Ali would feign imminent defeat and lean against the ropes. He would let his opponent unleash punch after punch and Ali would lean back, block the blows that he could and absorb the rest. Ali would appear to have lost all hope, which only encouraged his opponent to hit harder, unleashing a barrage of punches hoping for the knockout. Eventually his opponent would run out of energy. Then Ali would spring forward off the ropes like a phoenix rising from the ashes. His exhausted opponent would be unable to fend off the relentless attack and Ali would score a decisive victory.

"Um, hello, Sterling, are you still there?" asked MAJ Rankin. Snapping out of his daydream Sterling responded, "Yes, sorry, I was just thinking about this case. I'm going to file a Notice of Appearance and a discovery demand." MAJ Rankin shot back, "Sounds good. Do you want to schedule a guilty plea now or should we go through the formality of a court-martial?" He laughed to himself, pleased to show off a level of bravado. Typically, this would be an appropriate time for the defense attorney to laugh as well, in an effort to humor the prosecutor. Sterling did not laugh. He again exercised restraint and simply offered, "Heck of a case you have here MAJ Rankin."

Chapter 10

MAJ Rankin was nearly overcome with glee. Someone needed to put Sterling in his place, and he was just the man to do it. Sterling was supposed to be a fearsome adversary in court, but MAJ Rankin couldn't see how that was possible. Any half-assed attorney right out of law school would at least try to offer some mitigating information about his client. Not that it would matter. MAJ Rankin was ready to reject any request for leniency, but he expected Carter's attorney to at least make an effort.

He was mentally prepared to reject any argument that LTC Carter's stellar combat record afforded him some consideration. MAJ Rankin disliked LTC Carter and the special operation types like him. LTC Custer and his war mongering probably did more to foster hatred among our enemies than any other US soldier stationed in Iraq. His attacks on insurgents received praise back home, but MAJ Rankin knew that diplomacy was only path forward. Guys like LTC Carter destroyed any hope of negotiating an honorable peace in Iraq and Afghanistan.

Despite the impossibility of persuading MAJ Rankin to show some mercy, part of him held it against Sterling for not trying. MAJ Rankin needed defense attorneys to placate his ego and recognize his position of power, but Sterling didn't even pretend to submit to his authority.

MAJ Rankin had nothing but contempt for Sterling, and now the trial had become a rare two for one. He would convict LTC Custer and embarrass Sterling. He wasn't sure what he had done to deserve such good fortune, but he wasn't going to question it. Better yet, Sterling clearly knew he was beaten. He can't remember the last time a defense attorney had so little to say.

Chapter 11

Reflecting on the phone call, and reviewing the discovery sent to him by the JAG office, it didn't take long for Sterling to measure up MAJ Rankin. The prosecutor is arrogant, rude and unprepared. Sterling surmised that MAJ Rankin had never seen the actual launchers. The photographs of the launchers weren't even part of the discovery file. The CID agent had photocopied the actual photos then included the black and white photocopies in his report. The copier used to prepare the CID report seemed to have been a holdover from the Reagan era. The resolution was horrible. He could barely confirm that the items in the photocopies were launchers and grenades, and it was impossible to see the damage done to the items in the course of LTC Carter's men rendering them inert.

Preston Sterling knew that the best way to destroy the government's case against LTC Carter was to do nothing. He needed to play "rope a dope." He had to make MAJ Rankin believe that the case was not just strong, but unassailable.

He ran his strategy by LTC Carter. Most clients get concerned when their attorney doesn't file motions and doesn't seem to be interested in completing witness interviews. LTC Carter agreed that the less MAJ Rankin perceived a threat, the less likely he was to discover that his case was a loser until it was too late. Sterling was already doing a good job of baiting the hook. They needed to keep this fish on the line until they could reel him in.

LTC Carter said he had another reason to avoid forcing the government to do too much extra investigation. He asked Sterling, "Since you are my lawyer, anything I say to you remains confidential right?" Sterling replied, "Yes, unless you are planning a future crime. Other than that, anything you tell me remains confidential." LTC Carter followed up with, "So if I have already committed a crime that would still remain confidential?" Sterling was a bit surprised, but assured his client that past crimes are still protected by attorney-client privilege.

LTC Carter nodded his appreciation and said, "When I was in Iraq, part of my duties involved giving cash payments to tribal leaders in order to win their support. We are talking about a lot of money. So much money that we didn't count it, we weighed it to come up with estimates. Some of the cash might have found its way into some shoe boxes I sent home to myself. I just don't need the government looking too closely at my finances."

"Not a problem. Let's get through this trial. If they ever try to bring up new charges, I will file a motion to dismiss for lack of proper joinder. But most likely, if they haven't found anything yet, they are not going to find anything," said Sterling. LTC Carter replied, "Thanks Sterling."

Sterling advised his client to waive the Article 32 hearing, which is the military's version of a preliminary hearing. Sometimes defense attorneys demand an Article 32 hearing as a tool for collecting discovery. The government would be required to make a showing of sufficient evidence for an Investigating Officer to recommend whether or not the case should proceed. In this case, the last thing Sterling wanted was a chance for the prosecutor to review his case. If MAJ Rankin found out his case was untenable, he would be forced to dismiss, but might look around for something else to charge. LTC Carter agreed to waive the hearing.

Sterling added, "There is one thing I would like you to do. I would like you to request that a military attorney assist us in defending this case. Specifically, I would prefer you get the JAG who promised to help you secure the best possible plea bargain. My guess is that they will grant your request to assign an attorney. Even though you have private counsel, given your rank and the potential jeopardy of a conviction, they will likely assign you a JAG defense lawyer to help us."

LTC Carter was skeptical, and for just a moment wondered if Sterling thought they should actually pursue a plea. What Sterling had in mind was far better, but devious. Sterling suggested that they bring on a JAG defense attorney as co-counsel in order to create disinformation. LTC Carter and Sterling would pretend to have huge concerns about the case and ask the JAG defense counsel to quietly float the idea of a plea up to MAJ Rankin. The idea was to keep MAJ Rankin trapped in his bubble of overconfidence. If MAJ Rankin caught on to the weakness of his case, he might back down too early. Sterling hoped that by keeping the JAG defense attorney ignorant of their plans, his part in the deception would be completely sincere, although unknown to him.

LTC Carter was truly impressed. "You are one twisted fucking lawyer, you know that, Sterling? It reminds me of the kind of mind games we used on the Taliban in Afghanistan. To get under the skin of the Tali leadership, and to gain the support of the locals, we photoshopped Taliban leaders having sex with goats. We then dropped leaflets out of helicopters spreading the images over villages near Kandahar. The locals didn't know much about photoshop, so they thought it was real. It created distrust of the Taliban, at least among the locals who disfavored that kind of animal abuse." Sterling cringed, unable to stop his mind from imagining the poor goats. Sterling wasn't sure that the comparison had merit, but it seemed like a compliment, so he just smiled politely at his client.

He continued, "I hate to make your job too easy, but would it help you to know that I secured a written legal opinion regarding the status of the launchers?" Sterling replied, "It depends. When did you get the opinion, and who wrote the opinion?"

LTC Carter explained that he got the opinion after getting back to the states, but prior to his supply sergeant selling the launcher at the pawn shop. An Assistant US Attorney wrote the opinion. LTC Carter promised to get Sterling a copy. Basically, the US Attorney determined that the weapons were now at most "former weapons" having been rendered inert. Nor were they capable of easily being returned to operational status. They were, essentially, no more dangerous than scrap metal. Sterling offered his view that a written opinion from a federal prosecutor would be persuasive but not dispositive. Also, he had concerns about giving MAJ Rankin the legal opinion too soon. Sterling offered, "Let me figure out a way to get MAJ Rankin to fall into the trap."

Chapter 12

Sterling arrived early for LTC Carter's arraignment at the aging courthouse. Ft. Lewis is a large Army post, south of Tacoma, WA. Vast sums of money flowed into expansion and improvement of the post during the war on terror. None of that money seemed to have trickled down to the courtroom. Instead of inspiring confidence in the legal system, the general atmosphere conveyed a sense of despair.

Trial Defense Services had granted LTC Carter's request to assign a JAG defense attorney to his case. CPT Taylor Jane sat at the defense table with Preston Sterling and LTC Carter. She appeared to be no more than a year out of law school. She was thin, with dark hair and stunning blue eyes. She looked good in her Class A uniform. The single medal on her chest reflected that her only accomplishment thus far in the Army was to graduate from the JAG basic course. Her overall package really worked for Sterling. She would be the perfect conduit for the disinformation he would have her unwittingly deliver to MAJ Rankin. Her youth and inexperience ensured that she would not figure out that she was being used as a messenger. Sterling relied on her ability to sell the deception with sincerity.

MAJ Rankin sat alone at the table designated for the Trial Counsel (Army prosecutor). An unusually large group of spectators attended the hearing, occupying four rows of benches behind the attorneys. Most wore military uniforms. They were probably lawyers or paralegals who were curious about this case. Those in civilian clothing appeared to be journalists. No doubt MAJ Rankin had contacted the media hoping for some coverage of what he thought would be his crowning achievement as a lawyer. MAJ Rankin assumed that when this case got to trial, the media would get to see him take down a Special Forces Lieutenant Colonel.

Waiting for the judge to take the bench would typically be the time for opposing counsel to discuss any last-minute details, or even discuss possible resolutions short of trial. Sometimes opposing counsel would engage in friendly conversation setting aside their adversarial roles until they were on the record. But this was not a typical case. MAJ Rankin's confidence in his case left no room for compromise. His open hostility discouraged polite conversation. He didn't invite a discussion with Sterling, and none was offered.

Judge Richard Anderson took the bench a few minutes later. Staring down from his elevated position at the center of the courtroom, he asked MAJ Rankin if he was ready to proceed with arraignment. He responded, "Yes your honor, MAJ Trevor Rankin present on behalf of the government" he glanced behind him to make sure the journalists caught his name. He was pleased to see them scribbling furiously into small notebooks. The judge next turned his attention to Sterling and asked, "Mr. Sterling, are you and your client ready to proceed?" Sterling, LTC Custer, and CPT Jane stood. Sterling responded, "Yes your honor, we are ready."

Judge Anderson read the charges while the three remained standing. "Mr. Sterling, what is your client's plea?" Sterling responded, "As to all charges and specifications, my client pleads not-guilty." Judge Anderson's permanent scowl took on an added tone of irritation. "Mr. Sterling, there are three charges, and none of the charges have multiple specifications. Would you like to change your plea?" Sterling knew what the judge was doing. The judge had been taught in judge school that if a charge had only one specification, that it was proper to simply enter a plea as to the charge. Pleading not-guilty to charges and specifications would therefore be redundant. The way Sterling worded the not-guilty plea wasn't wrong, just unnecessary. Judge Anderson wanted to set the tone right away, ensuring that the case would be handled the judge's way.

Sterling responded, "No your honor, my client would not like to change his plea. His plea is not-guilty as to all charges and specifications." Now clearly frustrated, Judge Anderson looked to CPT Jane and asked her if she would be able to take a moment and discuss the matter with her co-counsel. CPT Jane agreed, leaned over, and whispered something in Sterling's ear. Sterling pretended to listen to her. He already knew what she was going to tell him.

Sterling looked up at the frustrated judge and said, "Your honor, there are three charges, each with a single specification. That means there are both multiple charges, and multiple specifications. I want to be perfectly clear that my client is entering a plea of not-guilty as to all charges and specifications."

Turning red in the face, Judge Anderson pretended to write something in the file. In reality he needed a minute to focus on his composure. He wasn't used to being challenged, especially not in his own courtroom. The military attorneys would never get away with this kind of behavior. He would be able to complain to someone in their chain of command and demand that the offending attorney receive a reprimand. Sterling didn't have a chain of command, so the judge had little recourse. Sterling wasn't committing contempt of court, and Judge Anderson knew he just needed to move on, but he wasn't happy about it.

CPT Jane wanted to run away. She wondered to herself if it was too late to withdraw as co-counsel. Unlike Sterling, CPT Jane appeared in front of this judge often and did not want to offend the man. It was a generally accepted practice to convey a sense of respect for the judge and opposing counsel. Sterling, as usual, had a different approach. His goal was to provoke the judge. He wanted the judge to be off balance, emotional, and prone to bad decision making. This could present an opportunity for appealable rulings. But his real audience was MAJ Rankin. Sterling wanted to quickly put the prosecutor at ease and make him believe he was in control of the case.

MAJ Rankin thoroughly enjoyed watching the exchange between Sterling and the judge. MAJ Rankin would go out of his way to curry favor with Judge Anderson. If he could get the judge on his side, it would be like having two prosecutors teaming up against LTC

Custer and his idiot attorney, and one of those prosecutors would be wearing a robe.

The judge selected a trial date two months out and set cutoff dates for filing motions. He then asked Sterling if his client would be seeking a trial in front of a panel (a jury trial) or a judge-alone trial. Sterling advised that his client would be seeking a jury trial. Judge Anderson couldn't help but breathe a sigh of relief knowing that his job would be limited to making legal rulings rather than ruling on the merits of the trial. He already wasn't enjoying this civilian attorney.

Chapter 13

MAJ Rankin took as much time as possible before clearing out of the courtroom. He wanted to allow time for Sterling and LTC Custer to leave. In contrast, he really didn't have a particular problem with CPT Jane. She seemed like a decent person, but he wasn't stalling just for an opportunity to chat with her. He wanted to see if any of the media wanted to speak with him. He turned on his heel hoping one of the reporters would ask him for a comment.

Before he could take his second step, CPT Jane blocked his retreat. She apologized to him and wanted him to know that she did her best to correct Sterling when he messed up entering the not-guilty plea, but that he just wouldn't listen to her. MAJ Rankin told her that he saw her trying to help and assured her that it was not her fault. She thanked him, and said "Maybe not today, but as soon as possible, I would like to chat with you and just see if there is anything we can work out. If I can get a reasonable plea offer communicated to LTC Custer before Sterling screws this all up maybe we can save ourselves a trial." She gave him a smile that reflected her frustration with being assigned to the case.

MAJ Rankin thanked her and said he would see what he could do. He was lying. He had no intention of offering any kind of plea bargain. The only offer would be "plead guilty and argue the sentence." But just the fact that she wanted to discuss a plea now, with trial two months away, told him that the defense was scared. "Hell, even Sterling's co-counsel knows the case is slam dunk winner for me," he said to himself. Inadvertently, a smug, self-satisfied grin crossed his lips.

This had already been a great day, and now MAJ Rankin would make it a little better. The reporters were still waiting in the back of the courtroom hoping to get an interview with the prosecutor. He feigned surprise when they asked him for a statement. "Oh, well you know, there isn't much I can say about the case while it is pending. I just want your readers to know that this case is about more than just the illegal importation of extremely deadly weapons by a rogue officer with no regard for the law. This trial is about what we stand for as a country. We are a system of rules and if we lose sight of that, then we are just as bad as ISIS. Ultimately, this trial is about justice." The reporter then asked him to confirm that she had his name spelled correctly, "It is

Major Trevor R_A_N_K_I_N, right?" "Yes Ma'am," responded MAJ Rankin.

Chapter 14

"Bad as ISIS" read the cover of the Seattle Times. Below the headline was a photo of a serious looking MAJ Rankin. He was outside when the photo was taken, with the courthouse in the background. He had his arms crossed, and he had removed his garrison cap (hat). He was clearly posing for the photo. Sterling guessed he removed his hat so that the photo would better show his face. His failure to wear headgear outside is a violation of AR 670-1 (Wear and Appearance of Army Uniforms), but that was the least of MAJ Rankin's problems. The article in the paper quoted MAJ Rankin as saying this trial is about justice in the pursuit of a rogue officer who illegally imported weapons of mass destruction. Anyone reading the article would assume that LTC Carter was guilty of the crime before he even had a trial.

Sterling laughed to himself when he read the article. MAJ Rankin had exceeded all expectations. There was no way for him to back out of the case now. He was in too deep. He had tied the future of his career to the outcome of this case. The only way this could turn out well for him would be to deliver convictions on all counts. As it was, he would undoubtedly catch some grief from the judge for his comments to the media.

Sterling called a meeting of the defense team. They met at a Mexican restaurant in Lakewood, not far from post. It was easier for Sterling to meet off-post since he no longer had a military ID card. The Army had taken that away from him last year when they discharged him and stripped him of his commission as an officer.

LTC Carter arrived at the restaurant driving a fairly new Range Rover. Not very subtle for a guy who has shoe boxes full of cash, thought Sterling. LTC Carter entered the building and scanned the restaurant, finding Sterling in the back booth. He sat across from Sterling who passed the newspaper to LTC Carter. Before looking at the paper, LTC Carter asked if the men could trade places. LTC Carter didn't like the idea of having his back to the patrons. Sterling didn't object, and they made a quick swap. If something went down, Sterling would rather have LTC Carter do the fighting.

Now feeling comfortable enough to focus, LTC Carter grabbed the newspaper. He read it quickly then looked up at Sterling. They traded smirks. LTC Carter said, "Well, that worked well." They moved on to a discussion of when they should have CPT Jane approach MAJ Rankin about a plea offer. The plan to defend the case by not defending it was working so far, but they had to keep up the illusion that MAJ Rankin was in control. Before they could formulate a plan, CPT Jane arrived in a white Jeep Wrangler. The mud on the fenders suggested she actually took the vehicle off road.

Both men watched CPT Jane as she approached. She was pleasant to look at in her Class A uniform, and now she was sporting the more casual Universal Camouflage Pattern (UCP). The pixilated uniform was fairly new for the Army, and was phasing out the BDU (Battle Dress Uniform) which had been in service since the late 80's. The uniform obscured her thin, attractive frame but her blue eyes remained as stunning as ever. She looked more settled and confident than when they saw her at the courthouse the day before. She smiled and took a seat next to LTC Carter. Sterling started to move the newspaper over to her, but she stopped his hand and said, "I've already seen it. This is outrageous!" Both men agreed with CPT Jane's assessment.

Sterling then asked, "What should we do about it?" CPT Jane responded, assuming he wanted her feedback. "Maybe this is a perfect opportunity. He knows he has a strong case, but by now he surely knows that he messed up. That media interview was not only unwise, but it was also an ethical violation. All of that pre-trial publicity of the case could taint the jury pool. Maybe it wouldn't rise to the level of supporting a dismissal, but now we can discuss a better plea offer." LTC Carter and Sterling shared a quick look. Sterling was impressed with her analysis of the prosecutor's media interview, but it was how she immediately pounced on the possibility of a plea bargain that caught their attention.

"Do you think MAJ Rankin would be up for a discussion about a plea bargain," asked Sterling. CPT Jane replied, "Well, I was hesitant to say anything to you until something materialized, but yesterday after court I mentioned to MAJ Rankin that we should talk about ways to resolve the case. He seemed receptive to that idea yesterday. Now that he stepped on his own dick, I bet that moved the needle in our favor." CPT Jane apologized for her language. Both men waived off her apology.

Sterling had simultaneously underestimated her, and at the same time nailed his evaluation of her. She was smarter than he gave her credit for, but also Sterling was right to use her for disinformation. He thought she would need some encouragement to explore a plea offer, but she was already laying the groundwork. She had a head start on giving MAJ Rankin a false sense of security. But the fact that she did that behind Sterling's back validated his view that she should be used as a decoy. He couldn't trust her to know the true hell that MAJ Rankin was bringing upon himself.

Sterling nodded and advised her that it does no harm to see what the possibilities are in terms of settlement. He looked at LTC Carter and explained that defense attorneys have an ethical duty to communicate plea officers to their clients. He said to his client, "We will keep you in the loop." LTC Carter nodded, pretending to appreciate the option of pleading guilty. It was all a game that he and Sterling were playing for the benefit of CPT Jane. She was the only one kept in the dark about their true strategy.

The team next discussed the need to review discovery, including the prosecutor's witness list. The attorneys discussed how they should react to MAJ Rankin's publicity stunt. Sterling volunteered to file a motion to dismiss LTC Carter's case based on prosecutorial misconduct. He would have preferred for CPT Jane to handle the motion but he needed her to stay on good terms with MAJ Rankin. From what Sterling knew already, the prosecutor tends to personalize everything and if CPT Jane filed the motion, he would be mad at her. Sterling needed CPT Jane to be the good cop, even if she didn't know that was her role.

Getting the case dismissed as a result of the motion would be a great outcome, but Sterling knew that the judge was much more likely to give MAJ Rankin a half-hearted rebuke on the record, then determine that the prosecutor's statements did not materially prejudice the defense. Sterling couldn't remember any military case having been dismissed because of a prosecutor's pre-trial comments. Given that Sterling already managed to irritate this judge, he had no confidence his client would earn a dismissal.

Sterling focused on the likely outcome of the judge denying the motion to dismiss. It might further bolster MAJ Rankin's confidence in his case. They had two months before trial, and they needed MAJ Rankin to stay on track.

Business concluded, Sterling invited his client and CPT Jane to join him for some lunch. Both declined. Both had work they needed to get to. They excused themselves, leaving Sterling sitting by himself at the table. None of them had ordered anything, and Sterling didn't like the idea of using the restaurant for business without compensating them in some way. Sterling ordered a plate of nachos and a Modelo. No sense in passing up a chance for some good Mexican food and a beer.

Chapter 15

Jamal Watkins violated the #1 rule of being a drug dealer: Don't get high on your own product. He found himself with too much time on his hands and too much crack to resist. His attorney, Preston Sterling, who was bought and paid for by the Crips, managed to keep him out of prison and back on the streets, at least for now. He was supposed to be out earning money for the gang, but he was well behind on his sales, and he was coming up short on his inventory. He claimed that the cops had frisked him and took his stash, but no one else seemed able to corroborate his story.

When he came up short a second time, and again pointed the finger at law enforcement for stealing his drugs, any remaining credibility vanished. Eventually, his addiction took over entirely and he just quit working. He was in trouble, and he knew it. The Crips weren't known for sympathy, and they lacked a drug rehabilitation program for their employees. He owed them a lot of money and a lot of product.

Jamal spent little time focusing on repaying the Crips. His priority was getting money to pay for crack. Unable to earn money selling drugs, his main source of income became stealing catalytic converters and selling them to the scrap metal dealers. He also did his best to steal copper wiring from local building projects.

The Crips did not forget about Jamal. They needed to send a message about what happens when someone steals from the gang. They escalated their efforts to find Jamal. When it became too dangerous for him to be out in public, he lost his only sources of income. He quickly found it hard to buy drugs and his body reacted poorly to going cold turkey.

Hiding out in his sister's rundown but tidy apartment, he lay shaking on the couch as he experienced withdrawal symptoms. His sister made sure to bring him some water, but there wasn't much else she could do for him. She hoped he could outlast the withdrawals and get sober long enough to move away. Hopefully somewhere far away and out of the reach of his gang.

A loud pounding on the door got her attention. She ignored the sound, hoping it would go away. She wasn't expecting company but given that her brother was obviously hiding out at her apartment, she had a good idea who was on the other side of the door. Similarly, Jamal didn't say a word, just hoping the knocking would stop.

"Latisha, open the fuckin' door before I put my foot through your ass!" said Reginald (Reggie) Link, a midlevel lieutenant with the Crips. "Jamal is not here" offered Latisha. Reggie yelled back, "Bitch, why you know I'm looking for Jamal if Jamal ain't there? Nuts, good point thought Latisha. As she moved to the door, Jamal said in a loud whisper, "Latisha, don't open that…" Latisha opened the door and Reggie, along with a man the size of an NFL linebacker, pushed past Latisha. The big man moved surprisingly fast and within two seconds was at the couch, and in one more second, he was lifting up Jamal by the neck.

Reggie lifted his plaid button-down shirt with his left hand, and with his right hand removed his .38 caliber Smith and Wesson revolver. Revolvers are favored by assassins because they don't eject the shells, and therefore leave less evidence for the police to recover. Jamal's body convulsed uncontrollably as he tried to breathe. He wiggled his body, trying hopelessly to shake his way out of the grip of the man with the giant hand around his neck. Reggie nodded almost imperceptibly to the man, who slowly lowered Jamal enough to where his toes could touch the floor.

Reggie placed the gun in the middle of Jamal's forehead. Jamal's eyes crossed as they both tried to track the gun above, and to the middle of his field of vision. Reggie, in a low voice, growled at Jamal, "You owe us a lot of money. No one steals from us and lives to talk about it." Jamal responded in a scratchy voice barely able to find its way through his restricted throat, "No, the police did a pat down, they got it all. There was nothing I could do!" Reggie said, "Jamal, don't give me that bullshit. You are a strung-out junkie. We both know where the crack is, you smoked it all." A frightened Latisha screamed, "Noooo! Don't shoot him. He can earn it back for you." Reggie looked over at Latisha. His fight wasn't with her.

"Is that right Jamal? You can earn back the five large you stole from us?" asked an incredulous Reggie. "Ya ya that's right. I know a guy. I can get your money." Figuring they could always kill him later,

Reggie said, "Oh that's real good Jamal. Now go get me my money. We'll keep an eye on Latisha for you. If you are not back here in two hours, you and your sister both gonna eat a bullet. Before I shoot her, I might have some plans for Latisha, so you better get your ass movin'."

The big man released his grip on Jamal's throat. Coughing and trying to catch his breath, Jamal ran out of Latisha's apartment. No one followed him. He didn't know where he could get $5,000 in two hours. He lied about knowing someone. He would have said anything at that point just to avoid getting shot. And now they had his sister.

Jamal knew that leaving this world behind wouldn't be a huge loss for him. They might as well kill him. There were times he wanted to die anyway. But his mama would never forgive him if he let something happen to Latisha. For that matter, he couldn't live with himself if anything happened to her.

Through the foggy mush that had become his drug withdrawn brain, he struggled to formulate a plan. He wasn't exactly the type of guy who could get a bank loan. No one would voluntarily give him money. Then, like a vision, it came to him. He knew someone who got paid in cash. A man who would be unlikely to put up a fight. He liked his attorney pretty well. But desperate times called for desperate measures.

Jamal stopped by his own apartment just a short distance away. Inside a box of cereal in the cabinet he had stashed a .22 pistol. It wasn't exactly a bazooka, but it would be enough firepower to get that attorney to cough up some cash. Hopefully it would be enough money to save himself and his sister. Maybe even enough extra to get out of town.

He had been to his attorney's office twice, and even in his uneven mental state he had a good idea where he was going. It was getting late in the afternoon and most of the building's security officers would be leaving for the day. In their place a single guard would pull the night shift. Most of the office workers would be gone as well, which was good. Jamal didn't want witnesses to ruin his plan. He hoped Sterling would still be in his office.

The downtown business district was a two mile walk from Latisha's apartment and Jamal set out quickly on foot. He couldn't afford a taxi and he didn't have a bus pass. Tucking the gun into his waistband behind his shirt Jamal walked briskly to the Wells Fargo building. It was time to see Sterling. Jamal didn't have a backup plan. Either he got the money from Sterling, or he and Latisha were both dead.

Chapter 16

Sterling was working late again. He worked late on most nights, except during the weeks he had his kids. On kid days he did his best to spend the evenings with them, uninterrupted by work. For the most part he succeeded. This was not a kids night for him, so he saw no point in going home early.

He put the finishing touches on the Motion to Dismiss due to Prosecutorial Misconduct. MAJ Rankin was arrogant enough to think that his media comments were completely appropriate, but even he probably expected that his comments would draw a response from LTC Carter's attorneys. The dismissal motion was straightforward enough, but, like CPT Jane opined, it was not likely to be granted. It would be hard to prove that the media comments actually prejudiced LTC Carter's defense. Even so, it would be fun putting in writing some of the shortcomings of MAJ Rankin. Writing this kind of motion was almost therapeutic.

Sterling hit the print button and the HP laser printer hummed away. Sterling signed the original, then scanned it into the HP to make copies for the court, the court file, and the prosecutor. He figured he better also print a copy for his client and his co-counsel. He placed the motion and the copies in a manilla folder before placing the file into his briefcase.

He looked out the window, letting his mind drift. He wondered if he wasn't giving his co-counsel enough credit. She was competent, and she might even enjoy being part of watching MAJ Rankin choke on the bait they had been dangling. Sterling decided that he would need to bring her up to speed at some point, but not yet.

A firm knock on the door re-focused his attention. Turning his chair slightly, he looked at the outer door leading to the "Law Office of Preston Sterling." Sterling saw the outline of a man standing on the other side of the frosted privacy glass next to the door. Sterling got out of his chair and walked through his small waiting area. He placed his eye on the peep hole. Outside the door stood a vaguely familiar, although disheveled, figure. Without opening the door, Sterling barked out, "What do you want Jamal?" Sterling didn't mind working long hours, but he tried hard to maintain boundaries. Without boundaries, his clients tended to assume he was their personal on-call lawyer available 24/7.

"Hey Sterling, sorry to come late but it is an emergency. The cops keep harassing me and I got a warrant out for my arrest," said a convincingly nervous Jamal. "Yes Jamal, that is what happens when you deal drugs. Come back during office hours," said Sterling. Jamal replied, "I got cash and I need to hire you now!" That got Sterling's attention. He didn't want money walking away, and cash was the best kind of money.

Sterling started to open the door for his incoming money, and Jamal. The door opened no more than a few inches when Jamal pushed hard, knocking Sterling back. "What the fuck Jamal! Are you some kind of stupid?" Said Sterling. An angry Jamal shouted, "Shut the fuck up! This is a straight up robbery bitch. I want your cash."

Sterling's time in the military didn't require much training in self-defense. He had served as a JAG, and prior to that as a psychological operations specialist making propaganda, but never in a combat role. He knew how to shoot a gun pretty well, but his gun was locked up in his Camry in the parking garage. A rare and unfortunate mistake on his part. Recognizing that his in-court persona tended to inspire in other people a desire to harm him, he enrolled in Krav Maga classes almost a year ago. Although not Jewish, he liked the style of martial arts employed by the Israeli Defense Force (IDF). He appreciated its focus on real life scenarios and its brutal efficiency.

Sterling moved toward Jamal hoping to employ overwhelming aggression. Grabbing Jamal's left wrist with his right hand, he positioned his hips slightly passed Jamal's hips, then placed his right foot passed Jamal's heel. Rotating his body forward and to the left, Sterling spun Jamal, letting Jamal's weight complete the rotation. Jamal found himself on his back with the wind partially knocked out of him. The move caught him by surprise.

Jamal bounced up off the floor faster than Sterling would have imagined possible. Before Sterling could block it, Jamal's fist caught Sterling in the eye, knocking Sterling back against the wall. Trying to maintain the initiative, Sterling countered by thrusting a fist into Jamal's nose. The crunch of bone and cartilage rendered a satisfying crackling sound and Jamal's nostrils spewed blood on Sterling's new carpet. Sterling was reasonably pleased with his ability to fight the gang banger, but then any hope for victory was dashed as Jamal reached behind his back producing a handgun.

"Play time is over motha fucka! Hand over the cash!" Even with a gun pointed at his head, Sterling was reluctant to give up his money. He managed to say, in a generally convincing manner, "I don't keep cash in the office." Jamal knew Sterling was lying. "Where was you going to put the cash you thought I was giving you tonight? I know you got cash here!" Sterling let his adrenaline take a pause long enough to appreciate the peril of his situation. Sterling had not yet installed a wall safe in his office, so he hid money in envelopes buried inside client files locked inside a filing cabinet. Sterling estimated he had about $10,000 on hand.

"Ok, Jamal, you got me. Give me a moment. The cash is in the file cabinet. Let me grab the key," said Sterling. "Move your ass Sterling! Let's go!" Shouted Jamal, blood still draining out of his nose and sticking to his shirt. Sterling opened the wood cabinet, finding the key hidden behind various legal pads and sticky notes. Sterling opened the file cabinet and grabbed envelopes full of cash.

Not trusting Jamal to just take the money and go, Sterling pretended to accidentally juggle the envelopes and they fell on the floor to Sterling's right. Cash fell out of the envelopes onto the carpeted floor, immediately catching Jamal's attention. Jamal took his eye off Sterling for a moment, then leaned down to pick up the money. Sterling pushed Jamal off balance and ran for the door.

Jamal wasn't going to let his attorney get away. Who knows what the Crips would do to him if they knew he tried to kill their favorite lawyer. He rotated his arm upward and got off a shot that splintered the door next to Sterling's ear. Sterling crouched down, running a zig zag pattern down the hall heading for the stairs. If anyone was watching it would have appeared comical especially since no one was chasing him. Jamal thought about running after Sterling but prioritized picking up the money. Quickly opening each envelope, he confirmed they contained stacks of cash. He grabbed all of the envelopes and threw them in the black plastic bag lining Sterling's garbage can. He spun the top of the bag and twisted the top into a knot, then ran out of the building.

Sterling's heart was racing as he made his way to his Camry parked in the lower level of the Wells Fargo building. Sterling was out of breath from his sprint out of his office, but physical exertion wasn't the only thing causing his heart to pound in his chest. Sterling had never been shot at before. He hadn't even been in a fight since elementary school. He understood that his gang clients are dangerous people, but he never perceived them to be a threat to him. As their lawyer, he believed they were on the same team.

Sterling reached inside his glove compartment and grabbed his gun. He wished he had the gun handy earlier. Adrenaline still coursing through his system, he found himself feeling angry and violated. He let that strung out thug Jamal get the drop on him. Maybe Jamal was tearing up his office right now. Sterling got out of his car, slipped the gun into his belt, and buttoned his jacket to hide the weapon. He didn't need security cameras showing an armed intruder entering the building. Although he was fairly sure no one heard the retort of Jamal's small caliber gun, Sterling was not going to risk running into the lone security guard while he had his gun out.

Inside Sterling's office, Jamal was nowhere to be seen. The money was gone but otherwise his office was unmolested, other than the bullet hole in the door and the blood on the carpet. Sterling locked his office and returned to his car. He drove home confident that when the rush of adrenaline subsided, he could formulate a plan to address this attack.

Chapter 17

Jamal was running short on time. He managed a run/walk for two miles hoping to save Latisha. His body was hardly in good shape, so he needed frequent breaks between sprints. His diet consisted of whatever he could scavenge from dumpsters, except on the few occasions Latisha cooked him food. Mostly he focused on crack. His body wasted away steadily. Prior to his drug addiction he was in fairly good shape, even muscular. Those were better days.

The two-hour limit on saving his sister had almost expired when an exhausted Jamal knocked on the door of Latisha's apartment. Reggie opened the door. His face registered shock at seeing Jamal. Not so much shock at Jamal's obviously broken nose and bloody shirt, but shock that Jamal returned. Reggie noticed that Jamal was holding a black garbage bag. Reggie asked, "What do you have for me Jamal?"

Jamal started to untie the plastic bag but before he could finish, Reggie grabbed the bag from his hands. Jamal reach for the bag and said, "I have your money, let me just take out your $5,000." Instead of handing the bag back to Jamal, Reggie emptied the contents of the bag on Latisha's small round kitchen table. Jamal followed and watched Reggie remove the cash from the envelopes and count the cash. Again, Jamal had surprised him. Reggie counted $11,000 in total.

Reggie said, "Damn, Jamal! You really did it. Latisha and I didn't even have a chance to get acquainted." Jamal gritted his teeth and replied, "Hey, you got your $5,000. Give me the rest and leave Latisha alone." Reggie counted out $1,000 and threw it to Jamal. "Here is your finder's fee." A desperate Jamal replied, "But you said I needed to get you $5,000. The rest is mine." Reggie responded, "You are lucky your dumb ass ain't dead. Now get the fuck out of here before I change my mind." Hanging his head, knowing that this wasn't a negotiation, Jamal took his $1,000 and scurried out of the apartment. Halfway down the hallway he shouted, "Latisha, I will give you a call."

Chapter 18

The next morning Sterling arranged for a cleaning service to remove the blood from the carpet. The effort was only partially successful, and Sterling knew he would need to replace a section of the carpet, not just for aesthetic reasons, but also so that the landlord wouldn't raise questions about Sterling's clientele. The bullet hole in the door couldn't be sanded away, so he would need a new door too.

Sterling didn't report the robbery to the police. Calling the police on his own client wasn't a good way to develop a reputation as a zealous advocate, plus calling the police on a Crip was never a good idea if self-preservation was a priority. But Sterling did need to deal with the problem.

Losing the money offended him greatly. He also wasn't pleased to be sporting a rather large black eye, which looked worse today than yesterday. The bigger problem was one of perception. If word got out that Sterling was an easy mark, every down and out thug would consider following in Jamal's footsteps. Sterling dialed a private number connected to a pager. A few minutes later a familiar voice called him from a burner phone.

Buster King was a combination Chief Financial Officer, consigliere, and HR department for the Crips. He was the one who handed Sterling anonymous looking envelopes full of cash as payment for legal services. Sterling started the conversation by answering the phone, "Law Office of Preston Sterling, this is Preston Sterling speaking." Sterling was a cautious man, and if for some reason the Feds had his phone tapped, the recording was supposed to immediately stop if the conversation was for legal advice with an attorney. On the other line, Buster waited 10 seconds before saying, "Sterling, what's up?"

Sterling explained the situation to Buster about how Jamal robbed him and stole about $10,000 cash from Sterling, then tried to shoot his own lawyer. "$11,000," came the reply from Buster. "Wait, how do know I lost $11,000? Even I don't have an exact count of what I lost," asked Sterling. Buster explained that Jamal is no longer a member in good standing with the Crips. He was using the company product and owed them a lot of money.

Buster noted that his people had counted the money that Jamal brought them to repay the debt, and said it came to $11,000. Jamal didn't say where he got the money, but it all made sense now. Buster apologized to Sterling and promised that if they knew Jamal got the money from Sterling, they would not have accepted it. Sterling was skeptical but thanked him anyway. Buster told Sterling that Reggie let Jamal keep $1,000 so if Sterling could find Jamal before he spent it all on crack, there might be something left. "That's not what I had in mind Buster," said a frustrated Sterling.

"We can make this right. You want us to take care of the problem?" asked Buster. "No Buster, I am calling as a courtesy. I will take care of my own problem. I just don't need any interference from my trusted friends and clients. I need to know there will be no hard feelings between us," replied Sterling. Buster said, "I like a man who takes care of his own business. But I don't need no legal hassles. What do you have in mind?" Sterling replied, "I am not going to have him arrested. I'm going to kill him." Buster laughed and said, "You are one twisted fucking lawyer! You will get no blowback from us. Thanks for the call."

Chapter 19

Sterling was pretty sure that Jamal would blow through most of the remaining $1,000 on drugs in just a couple days. Then he would need more cash. Having represented many drug addicts, he knew their capacity for critical thinking was outweighed by their addiction. Sterling would be better prepared this time. No more reliance on Krav Maga. His reliance would be better placed with the fine Austrians at GLOCK.

Sterling's personal daily carry was a .45 caliber GLOCK 36 with hollow point rounds. Sterling liked the way hollow points mushroomed upon entering the body, creating a larger hole and more damage. The damage to the round itself made them harder to match in a ballistic test.

Some people preferred using high velocity 9mm rounds for their ability to create shockwave disruption inside the body cavity, damaging organs. Both schools of thought had merit, but Sterling's view is that there is no replacement for the stopping power of a .45.

Although he trusted his GLOCK for self-defense, there was no way Sterling was going to use own his daily carry pistol as a murder weapon. Thankfully he had an untraceable gun ready to use. Shortly after opening his humble law practice in a strip mall on the outskirts of town, Sterling took on a client who was facing a potential murder charge. His client gave Sterling the murder weapon and asked him to keep it in a safe place. Sterling reluctantly took the gun and kept it buried deep in the client file.

Upon further consideration, Sterling reviewed the RPC's (Rules of Professional Conduct) that he had largely forgotten and noted that attorneys cannot knowing accept murder weapons to be held in safekeeping. If the police found out, they could charge him with obstructing justice, or tampering with evidence. The bar association could sanction him again or even disbar him. Sterling didn't need that kind of trouble. Before Sterling could get the weapon back to his client, his client was killed in a drive by shooting. Sterling was stuck with the gun.

The gun would now find its way back to productive use, doing what it did best. The gun was a stainless-steel revolver known as "The Judge" and was capable of firing either .45 caliber rounds or 410 shotgun shells. It was a hand cannon meant to kill at short range. Sterling had all five cylinders loaded with .45 caliber hollow point bullets. For the best results, he would need to be right in front of Jamal while taking the shot. This was not a long-range weapon.

Sterling paused for a moment, trying to assess whether this was a good idea. Sterling's main concern was getting caught. From what he understood about prison, it would not be a good experience for him. He had no interest in forming an involuntary romantic relationship with a larger and stronger cell mate. He didn't worry about the morality of taking someone's life. Jamal had it coming.

Feeling fairly confident that he could complete the mission without getting caught, Sterling knew there was no other way to handle this problem. He had to do it himself or lose credibility with the Crips. Taking a quick look through his client files, he found Jamal's address.

Chapter 20

Jamal walked away from Sterling's office with $11,000. If it wasn't for that greedy prick Reggie keeping most of the money, Jamal would have made a pretty good haul. Jamal knew his time with the Crips was over. If he returned to their turf, he was likely to get shot. He needed to get out of town, and he needed some travel money.

Jamal's broken nose hurt even more than it did the day before. He wished he could have a do-over. If given a second chance, he would not let that punk ass attorney sucker punch him like that. And he surely would make sure his gun hit its target. He was upset with himself for not tearing up Sterling's entire office to find more money. If Sterling gave up $11,000 that easily, he must be stashing a lot more cash somewhere. Jamal was in a hurry last time but now Latisha was safe, and so was he. He needed more money. That asshole Sterling owed him, and he was going to collect. And this time, he wouldn't let Sterling just run away.

Jamal needed to get out of town after he killed his lawyer and stole his money. He hadn't prioritized travel as part of his daily needs, and consequently didn't own any luggage. But Latisha had a suitcase with roller wheels, and a sleeping bag. Maybe she would help him. Using the last of the monthly minutes on his cell phone, Jamal called Latisha and asked if she would bring over the suitcase and her sleeping bag. Latisha agreed, hoping that Jamal would get far away and get his life back on track. He had been a different person before getting in bed with the Crips. He was her older brother and always watched out for her. She tried her best to do the same for him.

Chapter 21

At his downtown law office, Sterling waited for darkness to fall across the sky. When he was satisfied that the time was right, he removed a dark gray hoodie from his gym bag. He slipped the hoodie on over his dark shirt. He shoved a pair of black leather gloves in the pocket. To further obscure his face, he put on his reading glasses and a non-descript baseball cap. He pulled the hood over his head, on top of the baseball cap.

He pulled the untraceable "Judge" handgun out of the client file and slipped it behind his back, tucking it firmly inside his belt. He gave himself a quick look in the mirror, satisfied that his face was mostly obscured. Sterling walked down the stairs of the Wells Fargo building, wanting to avoid running into anyone taking the elevator. Pushing the door of the ground floor exit, he walked along the sidewalk keeping his head down to avoid security cameras. Two blocks later, he hailed a cab to get him most of the way to Jamal's apartment. He paid in cash.

Sterling walked toward the entrance of Quinlan Gardens. The brick housing complex consisted of three-five story buildings arranged in a U shape. It was widely considered to be the most dangerous public housing complex in the Lower Portland Avenue area, and likely the most dangerous in Tacoma. Crime was rampant. The police avoided the area when possible.

Sterling avoided the place as well. He had never been here before, and hoped he would never need to go back.

The flames of open fires burned in steel barrels while a few residents used the heat to cook some kind of meat in the improvised BBQ. Sterling wasn't sure what they were cooking. The food smelled good, but he wasn't going to get close enough to trade recipes.

Overlapping stereos belted out competing sounds of rap and Latino music from open windows. A few feet from the entrance, a group of young men huddled together laughing and pointing as two females walked by. Sterling couldn't make out their words, although it seemed to be an effort to gain the affection of the women. The men were unsuccessful, but their focus allowed Sterling to go about his business unnoticed.

His appearance, obscured by darkness and his hoodie, helped him blend in with near anonymity. No one paid much attention as he made his way through the open glass doors that formed the entrance to Building #3. Sterling assumed the building had a security camera. Looking at the level of disrepair of the building, his best guess is that the camera hadn't been functional in years, but he wasn't going to risk looking up. He kept his head down, ensuring that the hoodie and the hat would block most of his face.

Jamal's apartment was on the third floor of Building #3. Trying to adjust his eyes upward while keeping his head down, Sterling found the entrance to the stairs. The aging elevator was closer, but he wanted to stay out of sight and assumed the stairs would be clear. He was right. Arriving on the third floor, Sterling put on the gloves he had stashed away in his hoodie. He grabbed his gun from behind his back and made sure it was ready. Spotting no one in the hallway, he cocked the hammer on the pistol. He followed the numbers posted above the doors until he reached apartment 315. Sterling knocked on the door. He moved away from the center of the door, just in case Jamal started shooting through it.

Jamal came to the door almost immediately. The knob turned and Jamal started to say, "Latisha, what took you so …" He paused when he realized it wasn't Latisha. Yet it took him a moment to recognize the man in a hoodie with the swollen black eye. The look of recognition in his eyes gave away his awareness. He started to shut the door but now it was Sterling's turn to push the door, much as Jamal had done in Sterling's law office. Sterling pushed hard with his shoulder, throwing his full weight into the door. The force sent Jamal bouncing backward off balance. He fell on the floor.

Sterling briskly followed Jamal inside, giving him a hard kick to the ribs. Jamal grunted and let out a gasp, making a wheezing sound. It was possible that the kick broke some of Jamal's ribs, but Sterling was not there to administer first aid. Jamal attempted to get up to his knees. Jamal inched his way to the coffee table to retrieve his .22, but Sterling moved quickly and had the "Judge" revolver up against the side of Jamal's head. Jamal froze in place, not afraid, but upset with himself that he again let that attorney get the drop on him.

Jamal knew enough about lawyers to feel he was in no danger of being harmed by this paper pusher. Jamal apologized to Sterling and started to explain that he was just trying to save Latisha. He said, "Nothing personal Sterling." Sterling calmly replied, "I agree Jamal. It's nothing personal." Sterling pulled the trigger.

The bullet entered the left side of Jamal's temple. His head exploded out the other side, leaving brain, blood and bone fragments decorating the old black and white TV along with part of the wall. Jamal fell to the floor and a pool of blood outlined his head spreading from his exploded skull. Jamal's brain matter offered a small amount of muffling of the gunshot, but the blast of the big handgun was still loud in the small apartment. Seeing no need to keep the murder weapon, Sterling wiped it down with his hoodie, then opened the window and tossed it out. The gun clanked on the asphalt below. With any luck, someone would pick up the weapon, use it in a crime, then draw away the attention of the police.

Trying to act casually, Sterling exited the apartment and made his way down the hall toward the stairs. A door across the hall opened and some woman yelled, but Sterling didn't turn around. He walked down the stairs arriving at the ground floor. He walked past a couple tenants who generally avoided eye contact with him, and he did the same. His heart was pounding but he focused on walking out of the building at a deliberate pace rather than drawing attention by running. Block after block he continued his walk, listening carefully for sirens. His eyes darted around trying to make out the lights of police cars. He focused on looking casual. He wanted to appear that he was in no hurry. Walking five blocks he never heard a single siren, nor did he see any police cars. No one was chasing him. In this part of town, a gunshot didn't get much attention.

Making his way to a slightly better part of town, he flagged down a taxi, paid cash, and got out of the cab two blocks from his office. He walked inside a chain restaurant famous for its endless refills of French fries. Giving the appearance that he was meeting someone already seated inside, he bypassed the greeter at the entrance. The noise of the patrons provided a welcome background. No one seemed interested in him. The restaurant was filled with families and hardworking people enjoying a night out.

Sterling walked straight to the bathroom in the back. He removed his hoodie, hat and gloves, depositing them into the trash, making sure to push them down deep. He repeatedly washed his hands, arms, and face as vigorously as possible without a scrubber. He dried himself with a dozen paper towels, which he piled on top of his discarded clothing.

Sterling exited the bathroom and approached the bar. He took a seat on an elevated chair with a low backrest. He ordered a light beer and took a look at his reflection in mirror. Except for the black eye, he looked good, especially for someone who just shot a man. The black shirt and tie he had worn under the hoodie was a solid choice. To anyone watching him would think he looked like any other guy grabbing a beer after work. He paid for his drink with his AmEx card so he could establish an alibi, and at least limit the timeline. It was all overkill. Everyone, including Latisha, and the police, would assume that Jamal was killed by the gang, or in some kind of a drug deal gone bad. No one would suspect that Jamal was killed by his own lawyer.

Chapter 22

The previous day had been productive for Sterling, but he had not yet filed his motion to dismiss LTC Carter's case. He would get his chance since Judge Anderson called an emergency hearing to address MAJ Rankin's comments to the media. The judge set the motion for 1:30 pm today. Military courts tend to assume that everyone is available at any time. Sterling assumed correctly that the judge didn't much care about any other cases or commitments Sterling might have made so he cleared his afternoon calendar. Sterling arrived on post early and filed his motion ahead of the hearing.

Sterling tracked down the court clerk and filed the original for the record. He gave the bailiff a copy for the judge to review and dropped off a copy at the prosecutor's office. His last stop took him to the Trial Defense Services office, where he spoke to the paralegal manning the desk. As he was leaving a copy for CPT Jane, she walked around the corner, escorting a client to the exit. She approached Sterling and her eyes lit up with concern. She approached Sterling and without hesitation, cupped her hand on his face near his badly swollen eye. She said, "Oh no! What happened?" Sterling enjoyed her touch. Her hand was soft and slightly chilled as if the heater in her office wasn't working.

Sterling responded, "I got mugged in my parking garage." She gave him a sympathetic look and pulled her hand away slowly. "Want to come back to my office? That was my last client scheduled for the morning. We can talk about our hearing set with Judge Anderson." Sterling nodded and followed her back to her office.

"Feel free to shut the door if you like," said CPT Jane. Sterling obliged, then took a seat across from her at the large desk in her cramped office space. He wasn't surprised she was stuck in the small office. Rank tended to dictate office assignments, and since she was a fairly new JAG, she got the least amount of private space.

Sterling scanned her office, finding a few family photos hanging on the wall. His attention next turned to a photo of CPT Jane standing next to her Jeep Wrangler covered in mud. The finish line flags seemed to suggest she competed in some kind of event, but Sterling was not familiar with that type of recreational activity. He found the photo amusing, especially seeing her covered with the dark sandy mud. It made her thin, feminine frame seem athletic and strangely attractive in a rugged outdoorsy sense.

CPT Jane couldn't take her eyes off the large black and blue area of Sterling's face. A trace of yellow outlined the darker colors. It looked like it hurt like hell. Something about his injury made him seem approachable, even vulnerable. She wanted to give him a hug and tell him it would be OK. Up until this point, she had only seen him strut around like a peacock trying to prove he was the smartest and most charismatic person in the room. She liked seeing this different side of him.

He noticed she was making eye contact with him. Or maybe she just couldn't stop looking at his injury. Sterling enjoyed having her attention for a moment. He had a tough week, and getting a chance to chat with the beautiful JAG lawyer seemed like a good use of his time.

Sterling went over his motion with CPT Jane. The basic premise was exactly what CPT Jane proposed when they met up at the Mexican restaurant the day prior. MAJ Rankin's statements could taint the jury pool. He also agreed with her previous opinion that Judge Anderson was unlikely to grant the motion. But it is the kind of motion that as defense attorneys they needed to make. Failure to address such an obvious violation of their client's rights would be malpractice.

Sterling asked if CPT Jane had been able to approach MAJ Rankin about a plea. She had not, but she noted that they could make a run at him before the afternoon hearing today. He might be most flexible right before the motion. Sterling was curious as to what MAJ Rankin would do. In terms of strategy, Sterling couldn't imagine MAJ Rankin being any more committed to his current path that he was already. That meant hitting him up for a plea offer now would just come across as desperate. "No, let's see where things are after the hearing then if you happen to run into him maybe you can get a sense of what he wants to do with this case." replied Sterling.

CPT Jane wanted to change the subject. "What time is our client going to meet up with us?" Sterling let her know that LTC Carter would meet them shortly before the afternoon motion. LTC Carter found it difficult to drop everything just because the judge decided to hold a random hearing. He could be there on time but wasn't able to fit in a strategy session with his lawyers.

"We have some time. You up for lunch?" asked CPT Jane. Looking at her thin frame, Sterling had assumed she didn't eat. "Let's do it!" Sterling had skipped breakfast and really needed something in his stomach. He also wanted to spend some time with CPT Jane. She was pleasant company and an attractive lunch companion.

They settled on a pizza joint off-post in Dupont not far from the JAG office. There was no sense in both of them driving since they both needed to come right back to the same building after lunch for the motion hearing. Sterling, feeling insecure about driving his Camry, asked if CPT Jane wanted to drive. She agreed, and they loaded up in her Jeep.

Entering the restaurant, they could either sit in the dining area or the bar area. Sterling offered to buy CPT Jane a drink at the bar. At first, she couldn't tell if he was joking, but as he awaited her response, she became convinced that he was serious. "Dang Sterling, it isn't even noon yet. Plus, I am on duty. And in uniform. And we have a motion set for 1330. You civilians live on the edge, don't you?!" Sterling smiled and said, "Another time then." CPT Jane found herself drawn to the crazy attorney, black eye and all. She didn't respond to his question, but then, he didn't really phrase it as a question. More like he was already penciling in a date with her.

The motion really required no preparation. Sterling knew his argument well. Instead, they spent the lunch hour just talking. CPT Jane described her life. She grew up in Chicago. Her father was a policeman before a fleeing suspect shot him. She was ten years old at the time. His death while serving his community influenced her career goals. She wanted to give back to the community. After college, she worked for a victim advocacy group supporting victims of domestic abuse. Getting some experience assisting victims in the courtroom, she decided to become a lawyer. Joining JAG gave her a chance to serve her country and be a lawyer. It was the best of both worlds.

"So why Trial Defense Services," asked Sterling. He figured her for more of a law-and-order prosecutor type. CPT Jane smiled, thinking to herself that Sterling didn't miss anything. She had to admit it was a bit incongruous to defend criminals given that her father was shot by a criminal.

CPT Jane responded, "Honestly, I wanted to move to the Seattle area and TDS had an opening at Ft. Lewis, so I jumped on the chance to come here. Defense work isn't my passion, but I enjoy the people I work with." Sterling replied, "Defense work gives you a chance to keep the system honest. Absolute power corrupts absolutely, or so they say."

"Do you really believe that?" asked CPT Jane. She was having a hard time getting a feel for the real Preston Sterling. He came across as self-absorbed, but maybe underneath it all he was a true believer. Sterling replied, "I'm a pragmatist more than anything. I like to

find the simplest solution to any given problem."
"Occam's razor" interjected CPT Jane. "Yes, exactly!"
Sterling was impressed. CPT Jane continued, "So why
are you committed to taking the hardest path possible
against MAJ Rankin? If you just treat him with respect
and play on his ego, he is a lot more flexible. That is
what I do, and I am able to settle all of my cases with
him."

"Your strategy is sound but he doesn't deserve to
have anyone play on his ego just so he will do what he
should be doing anyway. I don't know the guy the way
you do. I don't work with him. But I have seen people
like him many times. He has more power than
compassion. He hides safely behind a desk never taking
a risk, then sits in judgment over those who keep him
free. He is petty and values his own advancement over
everything else, including justice. Did you see how he
pounced on his opportunity for a few minutes of fame?
He is prosecuting LTC Carter not because LTC Carter
is a bad man, but because MAJ Rankin is a small man."
Sterling had climbed up on his soapbox, and it was time
to get down. This poor woman didn't need to hear his
fight against the oppressors speech. Yet she hadn't
taken her eyes off him the whole time.

CPT Jane almost never found herself captivated by
someone but yet she hung on to Sterling's every word.
Sterling was the opposite of most everyone she ever
met. The part of himself he shared most often came
across as smart but defiant. He seemed to intentionally
provoke adversaries without any visible advantage to
himself. Most people put on a front and act nicer than

they really are on the inside, always trying to hide their true selves for fear of being discovered. She suspected Sterling also put up a front to prevent others from discovering his true self, except at his heart Sterling was hiding a decent person.

"You are an interesting and articulate man Mr. Sterling. Are you ready to put that talented mouth to work in the courtroom?" She found herself wanting to take him up on the drink he offered earlier, but they needed to get back to post. She enjoyed their strategy session.

Sterling said, "Guess we do need to head back to court. Let's make the magic happen in defense of our client. Thanks for putting up with me during lunch." He wondered if she would have time to meet up again after the motion, but he decided not to push his luck.

Chapter 23

LTC Carter arrived early and took a seat at counsel table while waiting for his lawyers. Hearing some chatter behind him, he turned around and looked up as his attorneys entered the courtroom together. He couldn't help but notice Sterling's beat up face. At least his attorneys seemed to be getting along well, judging by their smiles and idle chit chat as they entered the courtroom. Apparently, he had missed out on a team building exercise during lunch. His busy schedule of saving the world didn't leave much time for lunch dates with his lawyers. But he was here now and ready for the judge's impromptu hearing. From what Sterling explained to him, this hearing would be to address MAJ Rankin's media statements, although the judge hadn't given either side notice of the exact subject of the hearing.

MAJ Rankin entered the courtroom just seconds later. He had Sterling's Motion to Dismiss in his hands and he didn't look happy. Passing by LTC Carter and his attorneys, MAJ Rankin took a seat at counsel table. This whole hearing was unnecessary, he thought. His comments to the media were taken out of context. This was just an opportunity for Sterling to slander him instead of trying to defend his client. MAJ Rankin's head drifted unconsciously in the direction of Sterling. Only then did he realize that Sterling was injured. The black and blue, swollen eye looked like it hurt. MAJ Rankin thought this would be a bad day. He was wrong. Someone did to Sterling what MAJ Rankin had wanted to do to Sterling.

The defense team took their seats, waiting for the judge. Sterling had no interest in discussing anything with MAJ Rankin. The feeling appeared to be mutual.

Judge Anderson entered the courtroom and the bailiff announced, "All rise." The judge then directed everyone to be seated. Judge Anderson started the record by welcoming the parties for an emergency hearing in the matter of US v. LTC Carter. Judge Anderson looked up at MAJ Rankin, then at Sterling. He held his gaze on Sterling for a moment as he made a mental note of Sterling's beat up face. Judge Anderson thought to himself that someone must have done to Sterling what the judge had wanted to do to Sterling.

The judge couldn't help but notice Sterling's purple suit. It seemed to be made of a decent fabric, but the color violated Judge Anderson's decorum rules. If not for Sterling's beaten face, the judge might have called him out for looking like a pimp.

Judge Anderson turned his attention to the defense table, and asked, "Mr. Sterling, I understand you have had a chance to review the article in the Seattle Times that came out yesterday." It was a statement, not a question, but Sterling answered, "Yes Your Honor, the defense filed a Motion to Dismiss based on MAJ Rankin's prejudicial comments to the media." Judge Anderson responded, "I see that Mr. Sterling but your motion was not filed timely." Sterling replied, "Not timely for the hearing the court set this morning? The defense would be happy to continue this matter until such time as the court is ready." Judge Anderson could already feel his face getting red. "Mr. Sterling, you seem to forget, you did not set this hearing. I set this hearing." CPT Jane had seen this pattern before and wondered if Sterling would ever stop being self-destructive.

MAJ Rankin smiled, enjoying seeing the judge put Sterling in his place. His smile dropped when the judge turned to him and said, "MAJ Rankin, we are here to address your statements to the media. What on earth would possess you to say such stupid things?" MAJ Rankin replied, "Your honor, my statements were taken out of context. I never said that LTC Carter illegally imported weapons of mass destruction. I just said the weapons were very dangerous."

For once it was Sterling's chance to sit back and enjoy the show. Judge Anderson tore into the prosecutor, "MAJ Rankin, if that is the best you can do then you have entirely missed the point. You said LTC Carter 'illegally' imported weapons. Did they ever teach you the word 'allegedly' when you were in law school? Or maybe you could say he is 'charged with' illegally importing weapons. Or better yet how about learning the phrase 'no comment'?" MAJ Rankin fell silent, a skill he now wished he had mastered two days earlier.

Judge Anderson continued, "For now, I am placing a gag order on this case. No more statements to the media. This order applies to both sides. Mr. Sterling, I will hear your Motion to Dismiss one week from today. At that time, we will address MAJ Rankin's comments such as 'As bad as ISIS' and determine if that irretrievably poisoned our jury pool. Any questions?"

Both sides responded, "No your honor."

Chapter 24

LTC Carter excused himself from the company of his attorneys. It seemed like they were enjoying this process much more than he was, and he had real work to do. What a waste of time he thought to himself. If we waited for lawyers to win wars, we would still be a collection of colonies answering to the British. He was curious about Sterling's swollen eye, but that could wait for another day. He let Sterling know he was heading back to work. Sterling gave him a thumbs up.

CPT Jane wanted to take Sterling up on his offer to buy her a drink, but it was too early for her to slip out without her boss noticing. Before returning to her office, she pulled Sterling aside and suggested that they meet up after work about 6pm for drinks. Sterling smiled approvingly and nodded his head. "Hand me your phone." CPT Jane said. He unlocked his phone and handed it to her. She dialed her own number then hung up. Now he had her number. And she had his number. They exchanged glances then parted ways.

Returning to his apartment he sent her a text suggesting that they again meet up at the pizza joint in Dupont. They had unfinished business there, and it was close to Ft. Lewis. CPT Jane agreed. Always one to seek the tactical advantage, he arrived early and took a seat at the bar. He ordered a light beer. He didn't want to be the first to lose his sobriety.

CPT Jane walked into the bar barely resembling the woman he saw in uniform earlier in the day. Her tight black jeans and white satin blouse caught his attention. Her dark hair was no longer restrained by a dozen metal clips, instead flowing freely past her shoulders. Her deep blue eyes were as striking as ever. He couldn't help but smile with anticipation. Her head turned toward him, and she spotted him at the bar. She smiled back at him and walked over to the bar. He began to pull out a barstool for her, but she stepped around it and gave him a big hug and a kiss on the cheek. "Hello Preston" she said with a smile. "Hello to you Taylor" he said, making sure to drop the rank and use her given name. The hug lasted longer than would be customary for mere colleagues. Their chemistry began to take on a life of its own.

He offered her the drink he had tried to buy her earlier. She accepted this time, and she ordered a large pour of a local Chardonnay. Sterling asked her for additional details about her life and she obliged. She was an open book, sharing her life and her views without the tendency to be guarded, which was typical of so many people, and even more so for lawyers. Sterling on the other hand was hesitant to tell her too much about himself, particularly on a first date. He didn't want to get into details about being recently divorced, or about having two kids. He didn't want to share details about week-on, week- off parenting duties. In the unlikely event they started dating, he would open up about his life, but for now he just wanted to enjoy her company.

As one drink became two, then three, Taylor relaxed and moved her barstool closer to Sterling. She leaned in and placed her hand on his thigh while they talked. He leaned in closer and gave her a kiss. She moved her hand higher up his leg, sparking a physical reaction from him which she couldn't help but notice. The large bulge in his pants grew larger and she couldn't help but giggle in amusement. She was attracted to him and he had trouble hiding his attraction for her. Taylor said to him, "Want to come to my place? I live close to here." Taylor rented a small home in Dupont. Although unknown to her, she did not live far from LTC Carter.

Sterling accepted her invitation without hesitation. He followed her Jeep Wrangler to her house, feeling slightly self-conscious about driving his trusty Camry. This would have been a good time to impress his date with his G-Wagon, but the Mercedes was finishing up getting some detailing work done in what he hoped would be the last of many body shops. Sterling assumed correctly that it didn't matter to Taylor.

Arriving at Taylor's house she invited him inside and shut the door. Sterling pulled her close and reached his arms around her waist, then grabbed her ass and lifted her up. Laughing, she wrapped her legs around him. He carried her to the wall, pressing her back against the flat surface. Her light frame made it easy to move her in any direction he pleased. Grinding his hips into her, her hands groped his body while he pressed his lips against her neck. Her hands grabbed toward his belt, and he set her down so she could focus on unzipping his pants.

Taylor pulled his pants down, exposing Sterling's boxers. She dropped to her knees and pulled again, this time taking his underwear down enough to expose the large bulge he had maintained since dinner. She couldn't help but notice that his jeans had only hinted at what remained underneath. She looked up at him and smiled. She paused as if to see if he was going to stop her. He smiled back and nodded, removing any doubt as to his approval. She guided his girth into her mouth, stroking gently as her saliva moistened his shaft. Sterling moaned, enjoying the moment. He feared he might enjoy it too much too soon. He didn't want to let loose just yet. He wanted to enjoy her and make her as excited as he was feeling. He pulled himself away from her mouth and lifted her up gently by the hand. He dropped his pants down the rest of the way, then reached for her white blouse. She was already unbuttoning it, so he focused on her pants.

Dropping her pants, Taylor kicked off the legs and stepped through. Preston admired her thin frame and her pink lace panties. He reached a hand between her legs, rubbing the front of her panties until a wet spot appeared. He kneeled down and slowly pulled on the edge of her panties until they slid off her hips. He pushed his face closer to her midsection. She pulled away and took a step toward her bedroom. Sterling followed, filling up with anticipation.

She slowly slid her back along the top of her white comforter and Sterling matched her speed, crawling along the bed on top of her. As he closed the distance, he dropped his head down and kissed her on the mouth.

She reached down and guided him inside her, letting out a gasp, followed by a smile. Sterling grabbed her wrists with his hands, stretching her arms upward as his chest inched downward on her body. Picking up the pace, he drove himself inside her. He teased her by pulling out, then slowly going back in for more.

She rolled on top of him, straddling his hips, controlling the pace, and keeping him just a half step away from losing control. She pulled her hair back teasingly, looking down at him as if he was her captive. Sterling preferred to be in control when in the courtroom, but in the bedroom, he had no problem letting Taylor take the lead.

He reached up and pressed her nipple between his thumb and forefinger. Placing his hand flat, he let himself enjoy her breast. Lifting his hand slightly, he made a soft circling motion which caught the tip of Taylor's erect nipple. Taylor's body began to shake, and Sterling worried for a moment that she was having a seizure, before realizing her body was not in danger. Her response was contagious, and he found himself fighting off his own orgasm. He gave up trying to stop it and let himself enjoy the moment. He found himself overcome with joy and almost started laughing. Wave after wave of pure pleasure ran through his body. He steadied himself as she rolled off his body. Her face looked the way he was feeling.

Chapter 25

Taylor had a hard time processing what happened the night before. She considered herself to be a modern woman who could take agency of her body. That was the mature way to reflect on her encounter with Sterling. She didn't regret sleeping with him. In fact, she really enjoyed the sex. Clearly, they had significant chemistry working in their favor. But she was also feeling awkward. Despite their engaging conversation spread out over the course of a few drinks, she really didn't know much about him.

As she pondered the merits of casual sex, her phone beeped, indicating an incoming text message. It was a message from Sterling. Her heart pounded, but she wasn't sure what she was hoping the message would say. At least he had the courtesy to send her a text instead of ghosting her. "You are wonderful Taylor! Hope to see you soon." Admittedly, that was what she was hoping to hear. She still had a serious case of first date jitters.

It would be less complicated dating him if they didn't have a client in common. Technically, it wasn't an ethical violation, but it could be a distraction. Also, would he really take her input seriously if they had a romantic relationship? Men never had these types of problems. No one would question Sterling's qualifications as an attorney, but if word got out that she was sleeping with Sterling, it would undermine her credibility as an advocate. She would simply be another notch on Sterling's belt. His solid performance in the LTC Carter case would merely be compounded by his successful seduction of his co-counsel.

She wanted to be taken seriously as an attorney. She wanted clients to respect her. She wanted Sterling to respect her. Most importantly, she had to respect herself. She enjoyed her date with Sterling, and maybe those concepts were not completely incompatible. The attraction was more than just physical. Sterling had lifted his protective veil. He was kind and vulnerable in her presence. She was able to get him to reveal a hidden, more gentle side of himself. Why would he do that unless he respected her and trusted her? "Grrrrr! Guys are so complicated," she said out loud to herself.

Taylor responded to Sterling's text, "Good morning sexy! Yes, I would like to see you too. Let's make it happen."

Chapter 26

Sterling had to admit that he was smitten with the young JAG lawyer. Maybe it was just the impact of the exchange of pheromones. Some kind of evolutionary holdover from ancient times when procreation ensured the survival of our species. Maybe he needed her affection to balance out the violence he had inflicted on Jamal. Either way, he had to admit to himself that he was already looking forward to their next date.

Attraction aside, this was not a good time in his life for romantic entanglements. When he wasn't tending to parenting duties, he was working hard to build his law practice. He didn't need the distraction of also satisfying someone's emotional needs. He had become a private person. He liked dating, but only casually, and mostly to satisfy his sexual needs. Relationships were a hassle he didn't think he could handle.

Why did he have to contact her so quickly after their night together? He hoped that he didn't seem desperate. Eventually he had to satisfy himself that he did what his gut told him to do. He didn't try to out-think himself. He resisted the urge to plot the worst-case scenario. Not everything needed an unhappy ending.

His iPhone dinged and he grabbed his phone to read Taylor's response to his text. He enjoyed her response. He was pleased to see that she would be up for a second date.

Chapter 27

An unknown caller rang his landline at his office. Sterling picked up the phone. It was Buster King. Buster asked to set up a meeting in person. "Sure, I have some time this afternoon. Want to come to my office?" Sterling would prefer to meet at his own office, where if something went wrong at least his dead body would be found in a reasonable amount of time. Buster agreed to Sterling's offer and promised to come right over.

Sterling didn't think Buster would be too upset about the disappearance of Jamal. It was Buster who more or less gave Sterling the green light to kill the man. Hopefully this would be a routine business meeting. Maybe Buster would bring an envelope full of cash and hire Sterling to represent a couple of low-level street dealers and they would carry on their professional relationship. Sterling knew he needed to be more careful in his dealings with gang members. He got sloppy. Or maybe he had always been sloppy. But now he had gang clients. He could no longer take it for granted that his clients wouldn't try to hurt him.

Since his unfortunate interaction with Jamal, Sterling made it a habit to keep his handgun nearby. Never again would he accidentally leave the gun in his car. In reality it was highly unlikely that Buster wanted to harm him, or if he did, he would not set an appointment to come do it.

Thirty minutes later, Kathleen at reception rang Sterling's phone announcing the arrival of his client. Sterling walked to the waiting area to find Buster King wearing a tailored suit, looking like he just stepped out of GQ magazine. Adding to the look, Buster carried a brown leather sport bag. Kathleen may have even assumed that Buster was opposing counsel wanting to discuss a case. Sterling smiled and congratulated his client on an excellent wardrobe choice.

Back in Sterling's office, Buster could sense that his lawyer was a bit uneasy about taking a meeting so soon after Jamal's unfortunate demise. Sterling's badly bruised eye acted as a flesh and blood testimonial that his concerns were warranted. Buster said, "Sterling, relax, this is not about Jamal. Well, in a way it is about Jamal but I'm not mad." Sterling breathed a sigh of relief. Buster clarified, "In my line of work, it is hard to trust anyone outside who I know. You impressed me, Sterling. You showed me respect by asking my permission to kill Jamal. By taking care of the problem yourself, you showed me you don't need a babysitter. And you showed me you are willing to personally take care of the hard work that needs to be done. You are a twisted lawyer, but you a damn good lawyer." Sterling thanked him for his kind words. He was getting used to people referring to him as "twisted." It just kind of fit.

Buster continued, "Sterling, we are looking to diversify our interests." Sterling was impressed. His client was really working hard to convey an impression of greater sophistication. "Smart move Buster, how can I help?" asked Sterling.

Buster went on to explain that they were looking to buy some real estate in Tacoma. They wanted to buy it cheap. The general idea was that they would terrorize a neighborhood through gang activity. Then when property values tanked, they would buy up the homes. As soon as they bought a bunch of homes, they would shift the gang activity to an adjacent neighborhood. Once property values bounced back up, they would sell the assets at a profit. Buster figured they could basically keep shifting neighborhoods forever.

Sterling liked the plan, but he knew the Crips couldn't exactly open a new real estate investment fund on Wall Street. Nor could they pay cash for homes without the IRS crawling up their ass. Buster then announced, "Sterling, we want you to be our corporate lawyer." Sterling could see this was a good opportunity for him, but he tried to diminish expectations. "You know, business law isn't exactly what I do." Buster gave an incredulous look, then replied, "You got a law license don't ya? Plus I know you been duckin' the IRS. You been taking the money I been paying you for client representation. I know you been switching that G-Wagon around to ten different body shops to get fixed up. I know you can be creative."

Ever since hiring Sterling nearly a year ago, Buster had kept track of his lawyer's spending habits. If Sterling played his cards right, he could earn a lot more money, but Buster wasn't about to give so much cash to anyone without checking to see where the money had gone in their past dealings. Sterling didn't have any obvious vices. He wasn't into drugs, gambling, or prostitutes. He enjoyed a few drinks now and again, but he wasn't a drunk. Buster was pleased when he found out that Sterling, despite his fancy law license, was just a crook who wanted a better life. Sterling wanted to be a baller and spent his cash money fixing up a G-Wagon. Can't get much more baller than that thought Buster. Attorneys who are motivated by rational self-interest were easier to understand and were far more predictable than the idealists who wanted to save the oceans or some bullshit.

Sterling grinned. Good thing the Crips had better investigators than the IRS. He thought he had been smart by rotating body shops to fix his G-Wagon, but Buster had a solid intelligence network. Buster was right. Sterling could be creative in ways to optimize his income and dodge the tax collectors.

The wheels in Sterling's head were already turning. Buster would need a way to launder drug money into legitimate money. He would need to finance the home purchases through a maze of hidden LLC's. Once he owned the homes legitimately, he could sell them and keep the profit. He might even turn legit enough to open an IRA and retire someday. The problem was how to launder drug money.

Sterling pointed out that the gang needed legitimate businesses in order to launder the cash. Sterling suggested the gang needed a literal laundromat to launder money. Maybe a used car lot. A coin operated car wash. A convenience store. Anything that took in cash would be useful. Buster looked at Sterling unimpressed. "We thought of all that on our own. We don't need no lawyer for that small stuff. Those ideas all work, but they don't clear enough clean cash to buy neighborhoods," said Buster.

Sterling took a moment and tried to think on a larger scale. He needed a way to launder large amounts of cash. He needed something that was hard to prove was a fraud. There had to be some kind of a business where people were known to throw away lots of money. His mind wandered to a conversation he had with his daughter Susie. She enjoyed art projects. She would splatter paint around on paper, smack it with her hands, smear it around, then let it dry. Sterling joked with her that people get paid millions of dollars for such paintings. Susie enjoyed her dad's praise. But what if it wasn't a joke? No, he couldn't literally have Susie create art, but why couldn't he get someone else to make art?

Art was something that Sterling always thought was a scam anyway. He remembered some artist years ago getting paid thousands of taxpayer dollars to place a crucifix in a jar of urine. As he thought about it some more, he realized that artists don't need a license, and anyone could lawfully pay cash for a painting. The buyer didn't need to be vetted by the art studio. A willing seller and a willing buyer could come to their own agreement as to price. And since the value of art is highly subjective, who would the IRS be to say that any given painting was overpriced.

Looking up at Buster, Sterling said, "How about art? Let's open an art gallery." Buster noticed that Sterling used the term "let's" as if he was Buster's partner or something. Ignoring his lawyer's overreach, Buster asked, "Oh so like sell fake art?" Sterling replied, "No, that would be illegal. I mean selling terrible art in exchange for lots of cash. Have you seen the work of Jackson Pollock? Let's outsource to anonymous artists in some third world shit hole to create that kind of crap, that way the art can't be traced back to a real person. We will say it was created by some visionary in the hood who is inspired by growing up in a dangerous part of town. Then we create fake invoices for fake people who buy worthless art produced at almost no cost. The cash will flow into the studio hand over fist from drug proceeds. The art studio will be in an affluent area downtown where rich people shop. Those fools will think to themselves that the art is so good that they are unable to comprehend its meaning, but then they will tell their friends that it speaks to them at a higher level. Hell, you might even get some actual customers. The proceeds are then deposited into an actual bank. Then we transfer the profits from the gallery into an LLC shell company to purchase real estate. The profits from the real estate then get transferred into yet another LLC offshore in which you are an officer of the company and draw a salary. You will be a pillar of society."

"What the fuck Sterling! You came up with that just sitting here on your ass? See, that is why I came to you. I knew you had it in you." Buster was genuinely impressed. "Buster, it won't be cheap setting this up," said Sterling. Buster would have been surprised if his attorney didn't shift to the subject of money. "I thought you would say that, Sterling." Buster opened up the leather bag, turned it over, and dumped out a pile of cash on top of Sterling's glass desk. "Here is $311,000. $300,000 to get you started, plus $11,000 that Jamal stole from you." Sterling had never seen that much cash. It wasn't excessive for what Buster wanted him to do, but it was a lot of money. It was a life-changing amount of money.

Sterling accepted the position of corporate counsel for the Crips. He and Buster shook hands. Sterling knew he didn't need to fill out a W-9 to submit to the IRS. He enjoyed doing business with the Crips, and decided, at least for now, that the rewards outweighed the risk.

Chapter 28

Taylor Jane couldn't seem to shake Sterling from her mind. She enjoyed their time together. She looked forward to the next time she could see him, even if it was in court. It wasn't like she didn't get lots of male attention. Men found her attractive, especially in the Army there were many men to choose from, but she generally rejected their advances. She had a hard time placing why Sterling was different than other men. Yes, he was good looking. And charming. And good in bed. In that context maybe it wasn't hard to figure out what she liked about him.

She worked out in the morning, making sure to get in a good run followed by a core workout. After a shower, she went to the JAG office. She assisted a few clients who were seeking advice on administrative discharges. That kind of routine matter was what she needed to take her mind off Sterling. A couple hours later, the lobby full of clients had all been assisted by the four defense attorneys available that day.

Now without the distraction of clients, she thought of him. She considered texting him, but in the etiquette of budding romances, she knew he was supposed to text her next since she had been the last one to text. If he wanted to go out with her, he would need to take the initiative. She wasn't going to beg. She walked down the hall to see if any of her fellow JAG's were available to chat. Some friendly, non-Sterling conversation is what she needed. Seeing no one available, she decided to see if MAJ Rankin was available to discuss LTC Carter.

She walked down the long hall to the office of the Trial Counsel. There was no one working at the reception desk, so she walked in and announced herself, "TDS on the floor!" That warning was supposed to give the prosecutors a chance to stop whatever super-secret prosecutor conversations they were having so that the defense attorney wouldn't learn their secrets. The prosecutors always thought whatever they were working on was the most important matter in the world.

She made her way to MAJ Rankin's office. The door was open. He was alone, staring at his computer screen, seemingly lost in thought. She knocked on the side of the door frame, and he turned his head. Without standing, he invited her to have a seat. "What can I do for you CPT Jane?" he asked. CPT Jane responded, "I wanted to chat with you about LTC Carter. Is there anything we can work out?" "Yes," responded MAJ Rankin, "If your client and Sterling will both agree to go to jail, I will let them share a cell." CPT Jane played the game and laughed politely. She said, "I know you don't like Sterling, but I have a client to represent. You no doubt have many important cases you could focus your energy on instead of this one. What are you hoping to get out of the case?"

MAJ Rankin liked CPT Jane. She had a job to do and he understood it was her duty to explore options. If she wasn't opposing counsel, he might even consider dating her. He didn't know how she could stand to represent people like LTC Carter, or how she could stand to be in the presence of that hack Sterling. He might as well just level with her. "CPT Jane, my only offer is to let LTC Carter plead guilty as charged to all offenses. I will agree to a five-year cap. If we go to trial, I am asking for ten years, and I will get it too."

MAJ Rankin knew that even if he was in trouble for making his comments to the media, no one could un-ring that bell. He managed to bring to light the heinous crimes that LTC Carter committed. This case had become the center of the nation's media focus, all because of MAJ Rankin's initiative. Judge Anderson would feel the pressure of the national news. He would feel the need to make an example of this rogue snake eater Special Forces type. The Army needed to prove to our allies around the world that we are a nation of laws.

CPT Jane was visibly disappointed. "I was hoping we could discuss options short of incarceration. Maybe let him submit a resignation in lieu of court-martial." MAJ Rankin knew they were too far apart to have a meaningful discussion about resolving the case. "CPT Jane, your client is a disgrace to the Army. You should prepare your client for trial. I'm going to place my boot on Sterling's throat and watch him squirm around in court while I smash him and his client like the cockroaches they are. This might be the best case I have ever had and I'm not going to let go of this opportunity. Don't worry, I won't forget the little people when I am famous." He thought he was funny. CPT Jane gave him an obligatory smile but inside her stomach churned just being in his presence.

Sterling was right about MAJ Rankin. He is a small and petty man. It wasn't about justice for him. He valued self-aggrandizement. He wanted to be one of those legal consultants who offered opinions on the news networks. More than that, MAJ Rankin wanted the world to know that he is a smart and powerful man. Plus, he really wanted to stick it to Sterling.

CPT Jane thanked him for his time. Leaving his office, she thought about Sterling. For all of his bluster he had a good heart. He believed in justice.

Getting back to her office she picked up her cell phone. Damn! She had missed a call from Sterling. She shut the door and called him back immediately. She was glad she called him back. He invited her out on a date. A "real date" as he phrased it. She accepted his offer and agreed to meet him for dinner.

Chapter 29

Flush with cash, Sterling called Taylor Jane and asked her out on a "real date." He enjoyed their time at the pizza joint, but he wanted to make a good impression. He reserved a table for two at The Fish Peddler downtown near the marina. She accepted and agreed to meet him at the restaurant.

True to form, Sterling arrived early for his date. He managed to charm his way into a table along the bank of windows facing the water. He ordered himself a beer but decided to deviate from his "go to" light beer and order an IPA. That was about as fancy a drink as Sterling would ever order, unless it was champagne, or unless he was going to share a bottle of wine with his date. Maybe he would get a chance to share a bottle of wine with Taylor.

Taylor arrived just minutes later. She nailed the dress code. Her blue jacket covered her pink blouse. The laced fringe of her blouse reminded Sterling of her laced panties that he had taken off her sleek body just the night before. Sterling stood and gave her a hug and a quick kiss. He pulled out her chair and she nodded at him, conveying her appreciation for treating her like a special person in his life.

Sterling thanked her for meeting him, especially so soon after their last date. "I don't want to make a nuisance of myself," he said. Taylor teased him and said, "Oh you are way beyond being a nuisance."

Hoping he understood that she was joking, she clarified in a more serious tone, "I am honored to be your date two nights in a row." She reached over and grabbed his hand. She had that soft, cool touch that he enjoyed so much.

The waiter arrived quickly. He took their food and drink orders and promised to be back soon. The view of the water was stunning. The sun glimmered off the water. A pink hue of the approaching sunset danced off the white sails of the boats in the marina. The setting was romantic. There was lots of smiling and eye contact between Sterling and his gorgeous young date. The electrical charge of new romance permeated the air.

Taylor smiled sheepishly and told Sterling that she really enjoyed their night together. She wanted to make it clear that she doesn't typically do that. She doesn't sleep with men on the first date. Sterling suggested that they count that as their second date since they were at the same pizza restaurant twice on the same day. That way her virtue would remain intact. Taylor joked, "Well that is different. Second date is fair game." Sterling assured her that he has nothing but respect for her and wouldn't have asked her out again so soon if he was just looking for a one-night stand. Satisfied for the moment that her reputation had been salvaged, she moved on to a different subject.

She told Sterling about her conversation with MAJ Rankin. She told him it didn't go well and it looked like the LTC Carter case was going to trial. Taylor thought Sterling seemed oddly unconcerned about the prospect of going to trial. She wondered if he was so distracted by their date that he put LTC Carter's case on the back burner. Maybe she should stop talking about work. If he was so clearly more interested in her than in their case, maybe that was a good sign.

He had taken the initiative and asked her out twice in two days. Against her better judgment, she asked about his plans for the weekend, hoping maybe they could meet up. Sterling explained that he had plans for the weekend and the following weekdays but would be available the week after that. Curious about his plans, she asked what he had going for the next week. Sterling knew they were getting into dangerous territory but knew if they were going to date each other then she would need to know more about him.

"I have my kids for the next week. It's part of the divorce agreement. I managed to get joint custody of my kids. My ex-wife and I share them, week-on, week-off." Taylor's face registered the gravity of what he had just told her. She had never dated a man with kids, or anyone divorced, so she kind of assumed he didn't have kids. Sterling could read her face and see that a million thoughts were running through her head. Sterling assumed that everyone knew his history. Last year he was the most infamous JAG lawyer in the country thanks to his adultery scandal. But Taylor was new to the JAG Corps, and clearly not in the loop.

Taylor tried hard to appear unconcerned about Sterling's revelation, but it wasn't working. She couldn't be mad at him for having children, or for being divorced. That was just part of his life. She wished he had been more forthcoming with her before she slept with him. She also blamed herself for not pressing him last night for details about his life. She had a good time last night, but last night might have never happened if she had a more complete understanding of his circumstances.

She had said yes to a second date and was on the verge of proposing a third date. Clearly, she liked him. Less clear to her was whether she wanted to be part of that kind of mess. Suddenly she had way more questions about what she wanted in life, and it seemed that she had to figure it all out right now. If she and Sterling became serious, would he want her to be a stepmom to his kids? If she and Sterling were together, would he want to have children with her? She wasn't entirely sure she wanted to have kids, and until this moment she thought she had plenty of time to decide.

Too many thoughts at once crowded her head and her stomach started to twist in knots. She tried to make light conversation, but her efforts seemed to fall flat. Large periods of silence slipped into their limited conversation. She focused on eating her meal. She stuffed her mouth quickly, using her claimed appreciation of the food's delicious taste as cover for clearing her plate without saying much. She declined Sterling's offer to buy her another drink. She also declined dessert. She just wanted to leave. She considered getting up and leaving before the end of dinner. It wouldn't be a lie to say she had an upset stomach. She had never walked out on a date, and decided this wouldn't be her first time.

Time stood still but finally they wrapped up dinner. She pulled back her chair and stood. Sterling did the same. She thanked him for dinner. He gave her a hug. She gave the hug a second but couldn't maintain an embrace. She pulled away and made her way for the door. Outside of the restaurant, Sterling moved in to give her a kiss. She leaned in the opposite direction and gave him a quick hug. A single pat on his back signaled the hug was over again quickly. He offered to walk her to her car, but she pointed to her nearby Jeep, explaining that she got a great parking spot in front of the restaurant and assured him she would be safe. He watched as she walked away.

Sterling stood there stunned. His hope had been to celebrate a profitable day with Taylor. She even seemed to be asking him about his plans for the weekend so they could have another date together. He had whiplash from her sudden change in demeanor. Sterling watched until Taylor made it to her car. His recent encounter with violence made him hypervigilant. When he was satisfied that she was safe, Sterling made his way to his own car.

Getting to her car, Taylor found herself confused. "Guys should come with a fucking warning label" she said to herself. Was she being a bitch? Sterling was nothing but a gentleman to her and she kind of freaked out on him. Still, it seemed like she had fallen for a bait and switch con job. He presented himself as interested in her, but he never mentioned having kids, or being divorced. He wasn't even available as a dating partner half of the time due to his parenting duties.

She enjoyed his company, and he gave her butterflies like no one had in a long time. She liked that feeling, but maybe this was too much for her to handle. More accurately, this wasn't a matter where she was at fault, nor was he at fault. Maybe they were just not the right people for each other right now. And that is fine.

Chapter 30

A week with his kids was just what Sterling needed to take his focus off the disastrous dinner with Taylor. He knew he was wrong to stray from his preference for casual sex and disposable women. As far as Taylor went, the outcome was the same either way, so no harm done. She was gone nearly as quickly as his one-night stands. Except in this case, he let himself have feelings for her. The one time he let himself embrace the possibility of a relationship it turned to shit quickly. It seemed that the universe was trying to tell him something. His lifestyle was simply incompatible with forming and maintaining a relationship. There was nothing he could do except categorize this as a learning experience and move on.

The rest of the week, every minute Sterling wasn't with his kids, or sleeping, he was working. The Crips were not known for their patience, and they wanted to get moving on with the real estate investment company ASAP. Sterling focused on securing office space for the new art gallery, contracting with talentless Chinese "artists" and setting up LLC's. He found himself amazed by the large number of real licenses he needed to set up his fake businesses.

Sterling's other clients also needed his attention, including LTC Carter. On the day set for the Motion to Dismiss due to Prosecutorial Misconduct, Sterling arrived at Ft. Lewis ready to make his argument. Sterling chatted briefly with LTC Carter. He commented on Sterling's bruised eye, which had healed significantly since their last meeting. Sterling again used the story of getting mugged in his parking garage. LTC Carter was skeptical for a second. Sterling seemed like he was in good shape, but then again lawyers aren't known for their combat skills. LTC Carter didn't question the cause of his attorney's black eye.

Taylor entered the courtroom. She looked at Sterling and approached, not knowing how she should address the elephant in the room. She wanted to apologize for dashing out so quicky after dinner, and for ghosting him. That would need to be a conversation for another time.

"Good afternoon CPT Jane. Good to see you. Are you ready to get started?" Sterling addressed her by her rank. Was she no longer 'Taylor' in his eyes? Maybe he was just being formal in the courtroom, but his blank face conveyed no sense of affection. She was prepared for him to be irritated with her, or for him to feel the awkwardness that she was feeling. He instead conveyed a chilling indifference. They had shared the most intimate of experiences together yet his reaction to her was of the type reserved for strangers. "It's all you boss," replied CPT Jane.

LTC Carter noticed that the mood between his attorneys had changed since he last saw them. Last week they were smiling and giving each other lots of flirtatious eye contact. Now it was all business. It took LTC Carter all of a millisecond to figure out that they fucked, and it had already turned to shit. Given

Sterling's history, he was pretty sure that CPT Jane was not the one to blame.

MAJ Rankin made his way directly to counsel table. Two days ago, he filed a response brief opposing the Motion to Dismiss. His position was that the comments he made to the media were within the bounds of his ethical duties and were unlikely to create undue prejudice. He went a step beyond those arguments and claimed that the media has a 1st Amendment Right to know the status of the case and so, as the government's representative, he had a duty to support the Constitution. MAJ Rankin's response was generally predictable although Sterling viewed it as annoyingly over the top. MAJ Rankin positioned himself as a champion of free speech who found himself unfairly criticized by the defense team. He suggested that the defense motion to dismiss was nothing but a pathetic attempt to distract the court from the real issue in this case which was LTC Carter's guilt. He couldn't exactly respond that he was showboating in front of the media to satisfy his own ego. From Sterling's perspective, the response was untenable, but it would probably be a winning argument. Judges seldom granted suppression motions based solely on the prosecutor's bad behavior. They preferred to let the evidence determine the outcome.

Judge Anderson took the bench and heard the arguments of the parties. He reserved his ruling on the dismissal motion, promising to have his written opinion filed by the close of business the next day. He made clear that the gag order would remain in place. Outside the courtroom, Sterling again advised his client not to pin his hopes on a dismissal.

Sterling couldn't help but cast a gaze in the direction of Taylor. She looked great. Dinner at the marina was one of the worst dates he had ever endured, but he also thought about their night at her house. He knew they had a mutual attraction. It didn't take a lot of imagination to figure out what triggered Taylor at the restaurant. Sterling loved his kids and had fought hard for equal time with them. He understood that having his kids around his home would be a deal breaker for some women. There was nothing he could do about that, and it didn't make him love his kids any less.

Taylor caught him catching a glance at her. She didn't turn away, instead meeting his eyes. Maybe they should talk about their dinner date. Sterling left the courtroom without saying a word.

Chapter 31

After months of waiting, Sterling's 2007 Mercedes G-Wagon was ready to pick up at the last of many shops. He could hardly contain his excitement. What seemed like a great idea months ago had become a much bigger hassle than he had imagined. By the time he got done fixing the flood salvaged luxury SUV, he had spent nearly as much money as it would cost to buy a similar vehicle that had never been flooded. But he needed to spend down the cash he earned from representing the Crips without tipping off the IRS, so rotating through a series of body shops was not a terrible plan.

He gave the Indium Grey Metallic G-Wagon a full inspection before signing the final invoice and handing over yet another stack of cash to a body shop. Hitting the road, he barely had the patience to let the engine warm up before he put his foot down hard on the accelerator. Merging on to I-5, he let the supercharged eight-cylinder engine spool up. He was happy with his decision to have paid extra money to get the G 55 AMG version of the heavy SUV. It was fun and fast, and no one does comfort like the Germans. The heated leather seats were firm and supportive, although there was no way to ignore that this was a top-heavy vehicle which tipped the scales at nearly 6,000 pounds. It wasn't a sports car, but it conveyed a sense of rugged luxury. It was the SUV version of Sterling himself, or at least the version of himself he was trying to cultivate.

Sterling picked up the kids from school and gave them big hugs. They were excited to ride in dad's new car. He took them around town. They stopped by the grocery store to get some food for rest of the week. He did his best to cook meals for them, but sometimes dinner consisted of cereal or Lunchables. Preparing nutritious meals was a skill he was still working on.

Driving around town, he gunned the engine a couple times just to hear kids scream their delight and try to get him to go even faster. He knew they would tell their mom about dad's new car, if she didn't see it when he dropped off the kids at her place. He could picture their conversation. The first words out of her mouth would be "Looks like you can afford to pay more child support."

Two days later he got the answer, and he was off by a little bit. He parked his new car in her driveway while he unloaded the kids and collected their gear for the exchange. His ex-wife saw his vehicle. Her first words were actually, "Well hello." Then the next words were, "Looks like I can expect a bigger child support check." He wasn't off by much, so he gave himself credit for being right. He considered saying something confrontational, or challenge her to go to court, but he decided not to poke the bear.

Having secured his dream car and owning it free and clear, he would next need to focus on upgrading his living situation. His current two-bedroom apartment was fairly new and in a good part of town, but as the kids were getting older, he needed more space. Finding money for a down payment on a house wouldn't be hard but getting a bank loan based on his claimed income, rather than his actual income, would be a challenge.

Thankfully he was in the process of organizing a series of semi-legitimate businesses for the Crips. If he could get Buster a job title with an actual salary, he could probably work a similar deal for himself. Although he would pay more in income taxes, it would be easier to spend the money. But then again, he also enjoyed the benefits of tax-free income. He would need to weigh his options.

Driving home in his G-Wagon, thinking about his growing wealth made him almost forget about Taylor. Despite his convincing display of indifference at the motion hearing, a part of him missed her. Deep down he knew he was better off without her. He really needed to focus on meaningless relationships.

Chapter 32

Taylor hadn't heard from Sterling since the motion hearing. He didn't even comment on Judge Anderson's ruling. Although Judge Anderson denied the Motion to Dismiss, his findings regarding MAJ Rankin were the harshest she had seen in her short time in the JAG Corps. Findings like "unquestionably bad judgment" and "potentially prejudicial impact" and "conduct unbecoming an officer" should have at least merited some kind of comment from Sterling. Her co-counsel's motion was well received by the judge, and he should be taking a victory lap.

Having had a week to consider their disastrous dinner date, she had given a lot of thought to what she wanted in a relationship. Most of her friends complain that they have a hard time finding a true connection. She had experienced a true connection with Sterling, but her lawyer mind focused on all the reasons why it couldn't work rather than recognizing why it did work.

Thinking back on their discussion regarding his kids, she remembered him saying he has his kids every other week. That would mean that he was starting his week away from parenting. He would be available unless he had made other plans. She couldn't believe she was doing this but figured, "What the hell. Why not?"

She sent him a text, "Hey, wanted to give you uninterrupted time with your kids last week. Hope you had a good time. Can I buy you a drink to celebrate

Judge Anderson's ruling?" It was, in her mind, the perfect text. She wanted to convey interest, and cover up her ghosting him, by presenting the impression that she was respecting his time with his children. It would not excuse her failure to text him after dinner, but maybe Sterling would be gracious enough to let it go.

It was not like he was any better. Treating her like a stranger after what they shared was nothing short of rude. He couldn't exactly claim the moral high ground.

Her feelings for him were still complicated. She hadn't resolved her apprehension about dating a man with kids. She didn't know if he was on good terms with his ex-wife, and she wasn't seeking to get caught up in a shitstorm of post-divorce acrimony. Or worse, maybe he was pining away for his ex-wife, hoping for reconciliation. And the issue of kids was still a big unknown. She wasn't ready to be a stepmom. Did that mean she would only date him every other week? Ultimately those were problems for another day.

Sterling was surprised when he read the text from Taylor. He assumed he would never trade messages with her again. He convinced himself that there was no room in his life for an actual relationship. His life was too chaotic right now, and his needs were superficial, or so he thought. In this context, it came as a surprise to him that his heart skipped a beat when he read her text. He was happy to hear from her, and he wanted to see her. She seemed pleased with the judge's ruling and wanted to celebrate. He had been so busy that he hadn't checked to read his decision. For a second, he even wondered if the judge had dismissed the case. That would be good but also bad. He needed to buy his client some time.

Taking a quick moment, he logged into his computer, pulled up the email with the attached file from the judge, and read the ruling. Predictably, Judge Anderson did not dismiss the case, at least not now. He left open the possibility that future lapses in judgement by the prosecutor could change the "totality of the circumstances" analysis in favor of the defense motion. His rebuke of MAJ Rankin was more forceful than Sterling was expecting. It brought a smile to his face as he imagined MAJ Rankin's reaction to the ruling. MAJ Rankin was probably complaining to his JAG friends about how unfair the judge had been. Sterling wondered if MAJ Rankin's boss knew about any of this. Surely, they must have some adults in charge of the place but so far no one has put a stop to MAJ Rankin's nonsense.

Switching his attention to Taylor, he was ready to respond to her text. He resisted the urge to overthink his attraction to Taylor. He responded, "Good to hear from you! I hereby accept your offer. How about I pick you up in an hour?" Admittedly, he wanted to show off his new G-Wagon. It was a source of pride for him, and maybe she would find him more attractive if he conveyed a certain level of success. It was his impression that women found that type of thing sexy. Taylor liked him just fine when he was driving the Camry, so perhaps he was engaging in some kind of emotional transference. At least that seems like something his therapist would tell him, if he wasn't too arrogant to believe in the value of therapy.

"I have a bottle of Chardonnay at my place. Maybe pick up some takeout for us and meet me here?" Sterling again registered the thrill and anticipation of meeting up with her. He responded, "You like Thai food?"

Chapter 33

Sterling arrived at Taylor's house almost two hours later. The Thai place kept him waiting longer than he had hoped. The fragrant aromas escaping from his selection of curries and cashew chicken threatened to embed themselves in the leather of his new SUV, and for a moment he regretted not opting for delivery. Many years ago, back in high school, he delivered pizza for nearly two years. The part-time job put cash in his pocket, but his beloved Scirocco never shook the smell of pizza.

Approaching Taylor's house, he slowly pulled into her driveway, reaching his hand across the Thai food to keep it from tipping over. He saw Taylor taking a quick peek out the window, looking between the shades. A look of confusion crossed her face as the glare from the windows of Sterling's new car prevented her from identifying the driver. As he opened the driver's door, her face lit up with excitement. She met him in the driveway as he circled around to the passenger side of the vehicle to grab the food. Blocking his path, she wrapped her arms around him and gave him a long, hard kiss on his lips. Sterling could feel his body relax as Taylor managed to set the tone for their dinner date. It promised to be a much better date than last time.

Taylor commented on his beautiful new vehicle. He appreciated her efforts to admire his favorite new possession. She played on his ego by telling him it suits him and makes him look successful. In truth, she didn't care that much about his G-Wagon. It was an objectively beautiful car, but it wasn't the car that made him attractive to her.

He followed Taylor into her house, carrying the big bag of Thai food. Taylor had some dishes on the counter ready to load up some food. As Sterling opened the containers of curry, Taylor poured him a glass of wine. Taylor had a nice table in her dining room but they both decided to take the food to her coffee table.

Sitting on her couch, they enjoyed the dinner and wine. Sterling let himself take pleasure in recounting Judge Anderson's findings against MAJ Rankin. Enjoying the small talk, it was Taylor who made the effort to clear the air between them. She was honest in her feelings for him as well as her concerns. Sterling wished he could be as thoughtful as Taylor, but he was much more prone to interpreting discussion as conflict, and in turn he tended to act defensively. But not tonight. Maybe the wine eased his tension, or maybe Taylor's ability to disarm his insecurities by leading with a discussion of what she liked about him helped to set the mood. He was able to resist his need to feel defensive.

Sterling was honest with her as well. He was not in a perfect place in his life. His relationship with his ex-wife was not good, in large part to her efforts to get him court-martialed last year. He also admitted that his kids took a large amount of his emotional bandwidth. They filled his heart with love, and he would do anything for them. He described his dating life as fairly shallow. Abandoning the pledge he made to himself to avoid romantic entanglements, he told her that he had developed feelings for her, but understood if she needed a simpler relationship. Looking up at her he said, "Want me to leave?"

"You know what I want?" She grabbed his hand, and he followed her into her bedroom. Sterling smiled and nodded approvingly. Taylor had a good way of making him feel secure enough to be open with her. He set down his glass of wine on her dresser. He stood watching as she held up a hand for him to wait. She slowly undressed herself, and he watched longingly as she teased him by seductively throwing each discarded item of clothing at him. She stood before him entirely naked, exposed both physically and emotionally. She said, "I give myself to you Preston Sterling."

He stood there for a moment admiring her body and mind, trying to digest the meaning of her gift. A part of him wanted to resist. If he moved forward, he feared it would mean more than casual sex. He had worked hard to keep relationships at arm's length, especially dating relationships. It was easier that way. No one could alter the course he had set for himself. He sensed the change that would come if he reciprocated and gave himself fully to her.

But he was drawn to her. He undressed and stood before her. He accepted her gift and vowed to give of himself fully in exchange. He walked toward her, and she matched his pace, backing away toward the bed. He followed her as she pulled back the comforter. She gave herself to him completely. Nothing was off limits. No judgements were allowed to penetrate their intimacy, and they both left their doubts behind. For Sterling, dropping his protective shield was almost impossible. But Taylor's uninhibited playfulness and inviting eyes allowed him the level of trust he needed to let her into his inner self, the self he hides from everyone including himself.

Sterling tried to remember a time when he had felt so free and so loved. He admitted to himself that he had never before been able to let himself feel this way. Somehow Taylor was able to see beyond what he tried to show the world. She recognized the wall he had erected, and she found a way to crack the façade.

Sterling suspected it was easier for her to let go of her concerns. She hadn't been a lawyer as long as him and hadn't fully developed the level of cynicism he had. She likely had not been betrayed the way he had, or for that matter she probably hadn't betrayed others the way he had. He was willing to scorch the earth to suit his needs. He couldn't place why she was different.

For Taylor it wasn't that she had lived a sheltered life. True, she hadn't developed the level of cynicism that seemed to plague Sterling, but for the last week she thought of little else except all the reasons why Sterling was not right for her. She looked deep inside herself to contemplate the conflict in her attraction for him despite her doubts. If they were ever to explore a relationship, she would need to take charge. He clearly wasn't going to humble himself after being rejected by her last week. She was better emotionally equipped to initiate a connection with Sterling than he was able to initiate with her. If she had left it to him, they would not have been able to move forward. She knew that he needed her to help them find a sincere bond.

Sex with Sterling was different that night than it had been last week. The first time was pleasurable. So much so that she had given serious thought to accepting a purely physical relationship. But this time he was more focused on her. He was slower and more deliberate. While he hadn't lacked confidence last time, he was freer in his touch this time. His excitement aroused her and encouraged her to push the boundaries as well.

Chapter 34

Sterling spent most of the weekend with Taylor, interrupted only to give each of them some personal time to work out and change clothes. She brought him along for one of her favorite pastimes. She enjoyed taking her Jeep off-road through some muddy trails near Puyallup. She offered to let him follow behind in his G-Wagon, but Sterling declined. Although his Mercedes SUV was a capable off-roader, he didn't want to get it dirty, and after spending months in various shops, he didn't want it to get damaged. Sterling opted instead to ride shotgun in Taylor's Jeep Rubicon. He had more fun than he expected. Taylor enjoyed taking control. She knew the limits of her Jeep and pushed it hard. At one point Sterling could feel his chest pressing against the tensioners in the seatbelts as she pointed the Jeep down a steep decline. She was in her element and enjoyed showing Sterling something she excelled at more than him. Something just seemed to click with them. Sterling couldn't remember having such a good time.

Getting back to work on Monday, Sterling continued setting up the corporate shells for the Crips. They were impatient and wanted to begin operations immediately. They had little interest in Sterling's excuses about needing time for contractors to renovate a retail storefront for the art gallery.

He found a recently vacated photography studio on 'A' Street. It's owner, Doc Simmons, had a passion for taking iconic photos of the Puget Sound including the San Juan Islands and the Olympic Mountains. As the proliferation of powerful digital cameras gave way to powerful camera phones, many people became their own favorite photographer. Doc found himself with unsold photos, and eventually closed his studio. It had been a good run.

Sterling formed an LLC, Pacific Art Limited, and signed a 12-month lease for the studio. Sterling didn't know much about art, so he toured local galleries in Tacoma and Seattle to get an understanding of what he would need for a basic layout. He often brought Taylor along as his date, figuring he was killing two birds with one stone. The Crips were basically paying him to date his girlfriend and to take her to art galleries. Yikes, he was starting to think of her as his girlfriend.

He hired a remodeling company to transform the former studio into the kind of gallery where rich people would expect to find high quality art. Buster kept tabs on Sterling's progress but generally gave him a free hand to concoct a convincing front for laundering drug money.

Sterling arranged for expedited air shipping for "art" to be imported from China. He learned that because the cheap art, likely produced by child laborers, had almost no value, it was generally exempt from many of the taxes and inspections that were becoming commonplace. He had stumbled upon a nearly perfect scam.

The Crips had already begun terrorizing the neighborhoods adjacent to Hilltop. It takes time to depress housing values in an otherwise hot real estate market, but so far, they were ahead of schedule. The police response was prompt and robust. This created even more clients for Sterling since the gang was now retaining him to handle most of their criminal defense needs. He was a major beneficiary of the Crips and their new business ventures.

Buster was sitting on piles of cash that needed to be laundered for the Crips. Sterling was under pressure to open the gallery quickly. Sterling had a full-time job and couldn't work in the gallery. Plus, he didn't know much about art. Buster pointed out that it didn't matter how much actual art knowledge the gallery manager would need to have since all of the paintings were going to be sold to fake clients in exchange for bags of drug cash.

Sterling conceded the point in terms of the mechanics of the laundering operation. For that purpose, which was admittedly the reason for having an art gallery, no real knowledge of art would be necessary. But, to maintain appearances, he preferred the illusion of having an actual, functional art gallery complete with at least one employee. Inevitably, the bank would notify the IRS about all the cash coming in from the gallery. Sterling didn't want the IRS arriving to find a store front which looked like a money laundering operation.

Recognizing that there was no way to get around staffing the art gallery, Buster agreed. However, Buster insisted on hiring the manager. He promised to find someone with a background in art, and who would pass muster with all but the most discerning eye. Buster barely trusted Sterling and wanted someone trusted by the Crips to handle the money and make the deposits. For Sterling, this arrangement solved a lot of problems. He didn't want to be the one depositing cash into the bank. He didn't want that kind of direct involvement, and he sure didn't want to be on the hook if money went missing. He wanted to be their corporate lawyer. Staying out of prison had long been high on his list of priorities.

Chapter 35

Two weeks later, the contractors completed renovations on the art studio. Buster hired someone to be the gallery manager. He was anxious for the gallery to officially open. He invited Sterling to come meet with the two of them at the gallery. It wasn't so much an invitation as an order.

Sterling arrived at the gallery to find the front door unlocked. He was surprised to find a well-lit and welcoming environment that looked very much like an art gallery, complete with a tasteful selection of the "art" Sterling purchased from China.

Sterling made his way to the back office and found Buster dressed in a dark suit along with an attractive woman who was probably slightly older than Sterling, although it was hard to know for sure. Except for tiny crow's feet outside her eyes, he would have guessed she was his age or younger.

Susan Maddox stood and introduced herself. She explained that she had accepted Buster's offer to become Pacific Art Limited's very first Gallery Manager. She wore high heels and a black pencil skirt with a purple blouse. She looked sophisticated and professional. She looked nothing like what he was expecting. He feared that Buster would hire some down-and-out cousin or put some dew rag wearing banger in the studio to scare away real customers.

Mrs. Maddox offered Sterling a seat. She and Buster had opened a bottle of champagne. She offered him a glass and he accepted. "Tell me what you think of the champagne. We are doing a little quality control ahead of the grand opening. We would be honored if you would join us. Buster tells me that you are our corporate attorney." She smiled knowingly as if Buster shared more details than Sterling would have preferred. Also, he couldn't help but notice she said "our" corporate attorney.

Buster explained that Mrs. Maddox is the wife of Tricky and will be handling Sterling's payments from this point forward. Buster would be moving to the operations side of the business. Sterling enjoyed watching Buster transform into some kind of business tycoon, but what really got his attention was that he mentioned "Tricky." Sterling didn't dive too deeply into the hierarchy of the Crips, but he had heard the name Tricky. Sterling was pretty sure that Tricky was some kind of regional boss for the Crips. If his memory served him right, Tricky caught a RICO conviction a few years ago and was still serving time in prison.

Susan Maddox explained that she is a fan of art. Not this fake shit that Sterling purchased from China, but actual art. She and Tricky own a collection of paintings by real artists such as Van Gough, Picasso and Rembrandt. For obvious reasons, most of the paintings were hidden away in storage. The Feds confiscated everything in sight following Tricky's RICO conviction. She then circled back, clarifying that she found Sterling's idea to set up a laundering operation in an art gallery to be nothing short of brilliant. She even thought the selections of terrible art from China were "so bad they are good." It is the type of art that idiots with money, but no taste, might actually buy. It was exactly the impression Sterling had in mind, so he was pleased to receive some validation. Sterling couldn't help but look at Mrs. Maddox and appreciate her position as Gallery Manager.

Buster smiled at Sterling, reading his thoughts all the way. "She is perfect, isn't she?" Sterling replied, "Buster, you did well." Turning his head he said, "Mrs. Maddox, you are indeed the perfect person to run this gallery. Welcome aboard!" They raised their glasses, clinking them gently.

Chapter 36

Taylor accepted Sterling's invitation to attend the opening of Pacific Art Limited, although he had been vague about his interest in that particular gallery. She got the feeling there were parts of his life that Sterling kept secret, even from her. Nonetheless, an opportunity to dress up and attend a fancy event with her boyfriend (Yikes! She was calling him her boyfriend), meant a lot to her. They were good in bed, and she loved their time together, but there was something meaningful about being the one on his arm for events in the community. It just seemed more official, or more important, knowing they shared these moments together.

Sterling picked her up in his G-Wagon. He was obviously in love with that vehicle and truthfully it did seem to be a suitable ride for the opening of an art gallery. It all seemed so fancy. Plus, it gave her a chance to bust out her formal wear, in this case a sleeveless black dress with high heels. The knee length dress gave her a chance to show off her calves, which she had been working on at the gym. Sterling was sporting a very dapper black tuxedo. He considered wearing his trademark purple tuxedo, but decided he needed to break in Taylor slowly. Tonight, he would just do his best to look appropriate rather than showboating.

Sterling parked on the street, close to the gallery. As they reached the gallery door, Taylor asked him to take a picture of the two of them with his iPhone. She had recently signed up for a new social media service called Facebook and she wanted to post their "selfie" on her wall. Sterling didn't keep up with social media, and he didn't have a Facebook account, although Taylor encouraged him to get one. She said it could help him boost his reach and get more clients.

Sterling didn't need more clients. He was up to his ass in Crips getting arrested. That along with his legitimate law practice kept him working until midnight on a consistent basis. To appease his enthusiastic date, he took the selfie she requested. The two were all smiles when the camera took their picture. Stumbling through the icons, he found the photo section. With Taylor's help, he sent it to her phone. He still wasn't getting along with his overly complicated iPhone.

Walking into the gallery, Sterling was shocked to find a lot of rich looking white people milling about. The opening had somehow managed to create a buzz. Ms. Maddox had really done a great job of creating the impression that this is an actual art gallery.

Taylor turned her attention to a large piece of art hanging prominently on the wall. The multi-colored speckles on a white background punctuated by random streaks seemed to have no discernable pattern. She said, "What a beautiful painting." Most likely she was trying to be polite, but maybe she liked it. Sterling was basically color blind when it came to art. Even though he purchased the cheap paintings in bulk, and was familiar with each of them, he didn't understand art enough to know if this piece was good or bad.

Sterling grabbed a couple glasses of champagne off a black service tray held by an employee of a catering company. If Sterling didn't know better, he would think he was at the real opening of a real gallery. He handed Taylor a glass of champagne and placed a hand behind her back, guiding her through the crowd. They slowly made their way to the back of the gallery. Rounding the corner, Susan Maddox spotted Sterling and approached him smiling as if they were old friends. "Mr. Sterling, I am so glad you could make it! Always a pleasure to be in the presence of our corporate attorney." Sterling replied, "Mrs. Maddox, you have done a wonderful job with the opening. I am truly impressed. I would like you to meet my girlfriend, Taylor Jane."

Taylor was pleased that Sterling referred to her as his girlfriend. She also caught the part about him being corporate counsel. She didn't know that art galleries needed a corporate counsel, but it seemed like this Maddox woman was complimenting her man, so that must be a good thing.

"Nice to meet you, Taylor," replied Mrs. Maddox. "Sterling, she is beautiful! You will have to bring her by more often," she added. "Yes Ma'am, I will do that," said Sterling. Susan Maddox spread her arms, placing a hand on the forearm of both Sterling and Taylor and said, "Well, I should mingle. I will be seeing you soon Mr. Sterling."

As Susan Maddox walked away, blending into the crowded gallery, Taylor said, "Corporate counsel? Is there anything you can't do?" Brushing off the compliment, and not wanting to get into too many details he replied, "She is being generous. I helped the gallery with some legal paperwork to get them going. Incorporation applications, customs forms, that sort of thing. No big deal."

Looking to change the subject he said, "Hey, I hope I wasn't overstating my status by referring to you as my girlfriend." Taylor looked up at him and said, "So far that has been my favorite part of the night, boyfriend."

Chapter 37

Sterling spent so much time handling business for the Crips that his other clients struggled to get his attention. Somehow the LTC Carter trial was sneaking up on him. Eventually, LTC Carter took the initiative and requested a meeting with his lawyers. He was working during the week, but hoped they could meet him on Saturday. They agreed to meet at the pizza joint in Dupont.

LTC Carter left his home not far from the restaurant, driving his black Range Rover. On his way, a white Jeep Wrangler coming from the side street on the left pulled in front of him, causing him to slam on his brakes to avoid broadsiding the vehicle. Coming from the same side street, a dark gray G-Wagon pulled in behind LTC Marcus. A mile down the road, the three vehicles each turned into the parking lot of the pizza place. LTC Carter turned to CPT Jane as she exited her white Jeep. He said, "Do you live in Dupont?" She said, "Yes Sir, I sure do." As Sterling got out of the G-Wagon, LTC Carter asked him, "Wait, you live in Dupont too?" Sterling sheepishly responded, "Um, no, just visiting someone here." Sterling's eyes darted to CPT Jane, who turned away quickly. An embarrassed smile crossed her face.

LTC Carter was pleased that his attorneys were getting along again. Apparently, Sterling didn't manage to completely fuck it up. At least not yet. "OK, if you two can keep your hands off each other for an hour or so I just want to make sure my defense team is on track and that I won't be going to Leavenworth."

CPT Jane took notice of LTC Carter's confidence in the ability of his defense team to keep him out of prison. In fact, he treated it like they were just there to nail down some final details. Sterling did nothing to correct their client's rosy outlook. She found that odd as well. Usually, lawyers try to diminish their client's expectations. Most attorneys lived by the mantra, "Under promise and over deliver."

Inside the restaurant, CPT Jane updated LTC Carter on the possibility of a plea bargain, or more accurately, the lack of such a possibility. LTC Carter didn't seem bothered by his limited options. Just to make sure he understood, she said, "Sir, that means if you lose at trial, the prosecutor will ask for 10 years in prison. If you plead guilty, he will cut his recommendation to just five years." LTC Carter gave her a curious look as if she was speaking a foreign language.

CPT Jane's intuition told her something was off. From what she had seen, Sterling is an excellent lawyer. And LTC Carter seems convinced that he isn't going to prison. But MAJ Rankin won't cut a deal, and the evidence that she reviewed as part of discovery is damning. Then it hit her. She clearly did not know all the facts. She was part of this defense team, but she clearly wasn't sitting at the grownups table. "Sterling, cut the bullshit. What are you not telling me." She was clearly upset but not nearly as upset as she was going to be once Sterling told her the truth.

As requested, Sterling cut the bullshit and let her know that the case was a sham. Pretending to fight it was simply a tactic to protect their client. CPT Jane could live with that. At least Sterling had a plan to protect his client, but then her mind figured out her role in the defense. "Wait, so you used me to keep MAJ Rankin off balance? You valued my ability so little that you used me as bait?" It was totally true and there wasn't much Sterling could do to defend himself. Even worse, this revelation occurred in front of the client.

LTC Carter was impressed. Sterling was obviously fucking this woman but yet didn't betray his trust. He kept her out of the loop so that she would unwittingly assist in his defense. Sterling was worth every penny he paid him. He was twisted but reliable.

Sterling couldn't help but feel like he betrayed Taylor's trust. He could see the hurt look on her face. She looked at Sterling, then LTC Carter, and said, "Good luck to both of you. You deserve each other." She grabbed her keys and left.

Chapter 38

Sterling called Taylor but she didn't answer. He sent her texts, apologizing and asking to meet up to discuss the situation. Taylor did not answer. The next day, he got word that CPT Jane filed a motion to withdraw as co-counsel, citing an "Irreconcilable conflict with co-counsel." LTC Carter did not object to her motion, and the judge signed it ex-parte. CPT Jane was no longer part of the defense team. It was quickly appearing that she was not going to be part of Sterling's personal team either. She might as well have submitted an order withdrawing as his girlfriend.

MAJ Rankin interpreted CPT Jane's motion to withdraw as proof that Sterling is an asshole and LTC Carter is guilty. Most likely they had asked CPT Jane to do something unethical and she declined and had to withdraw as co-counsel. He knew she was better than them. He considered asking her out on a date. He would have loved to get the inside details about Sterling and his client but decided to hold off until after the trial. He wouldn't need to wait long since the trial was just days away.

Sterling was mad at himself for messing up his relationship with Taylor. She had been good to him. She forgave many of his faults and shortcomings. She made him want to be a better person. If he had known that he would fall in love with her, he would have made other choices early on in the case. He was the one who set the wheels in motion that he could not stop, and now he was paying the price for those bad decisions.

The timing was bad. Sterling wanted to share the glory of the victory with her. He would tell her the outcome, but that is nothing like being there to see the trial unravel for MAJ Rankin. Then again, Taylor didn't revel in the misery of others the way that Sterling did. She is a good person, and probably would have regretted making this case personal rather than professional. Being off the defense team would likely preserve her working relationship with MAJ Rankin. As opposing counsel, Taylor needed to think about her future clients and their best interests. Humiliating MAJ Rankin would severely compromise her ability to work with the prosecutors. Now she was safe and so were her future clients. Plus, she genuinely believed that Sterling embarrassed her. She could not work with him.

Chapter 39

MAJ Rankin remained oblivious to the shortcomings of his case until the day before the trial. He ordered CID to have the RPG launchers and grenades available as exhibits. MAJ Rankin would be ready to admit the evidence during trial and show the jury beyond a reasonable doubt that LTC Carter was guilty of his crimes.

When MAJ Rankin examined the evidence, he noticed something that the photocopied photos did not capture. The launchers had massive holes in the sides. He was not a metallurgist, but it looked like someone took a welder and cut out sections of the launchers. He next examined the grenades. He picked up one of them and saw a hole that had been drilled in the bottom. He shook the grenade. It was light. It was empty. There was no explosive material in the grenade whatsoever.

His face went white. He had been played. He had already contacted MSNBC, CNN and even FOX letting them know about the justice he was going to mete out during the trial. The promotion he once thought inevitable had evaporated in front of his eyes. He was ruined. With his back against the wall, he saw no other option than to cover up the evidence. If the actual evidence made it to the jury, he was done. Not only would he lose the trial, but he might be in trouble for negligently prosecuting baseless charges.

The next day MAJ Rankin asked for time to address the court prior to selecting the jury. He looked behind him and noticed at least half a dozen journalists taking notes, sitting in the back rows of the small courtroom. Sterling also looked in the back of the courtroom, but he was looking to see if CPT Jane was present to watch the proceedings. She was conspicuously absent.

Judge Anderson took the bench and agreed to take up whatever issue kept him from getting a jury selected. MAJ Rankin thanked the judge and said he just wanted to address a simple bookkeeping matter regarding the evidence. "Clearly since the RPG's are dangerous weapons, we cannot have them admitted as evidence in the trial. Instead, the government moves to admit photographs of the deadly weapons."

Judge Anderson asked, "Mr. Sterling, do you have any objection to substituting the photographs of the items in lieu of the actual weapons?" Sterling was going to have some fun with this. "Your honor, I would first like to see the photographs that MAJ Rankin is proposing to admit." Judge Anderson responded, "Fair enough, MAJ Rankin please provide counsel with copies of the photos you are moving to admit."

MAJ Rankin had a shovel and continued to dig his own grave. "Well, your honor, actually I have photocopies of the photographs. I am handing them to Mr. Sterling now." Sterling knew the photocopies were low resolution black and white images and almost impossible to use as identification. Pretending to review the photocopies, Sterling responded, "Your honor, these are of such low quality that I cannot determine if they fairly and accurately depict the status of the launchers and grenades."

Judge Anderson assumed that Sterling was just being difficult but decided to go through the motions and ordered MAJ Rankin to provide the court with the photocopies. Examining the photocopies, Judge Anderson squinted at them, then put on his reading glasses, and yet could not make out the details of the weapons. "MAJ Rankin, these are the worst photocopies I have ever seen. Your motion to substitute them for the actual evidence is denied."

MAJ Rankin thought he saw an opening. There might still be a way to save himself from embarrassment. If not, then he was heading for trouble. "Your honor, these are dangerous weapons, and I can't in good conscious allow them to be admitted as evidence in a courtroom. And what if the jurors wanted to examine them? They could injury themselves," responded a panicky MAJ Rankin. Judge Anderson turned his attention to Sterling. "Mr. Sterling, what is your response?" Sterling replied, "Your honor, I would like an offer of proof. If after an examination of the physical evidence the court rules that the weapons are too dangerous, then I will defer to the court."

Judge Anderson got the impression that he was being played. Sterling was not known to be flexible or deferential to judicial authority. Unknown to most people, including Sterling, Judge Anderson had at one time served in the Army as an enlisted man: 11 Bravo (infantry) back in the day. He completed his enlistment, went to college then went to law school. He was not a stranger to danger, and he didn't fear the thought of touching actual weapons of war.

"MAJ Rankin, you will produce the physical evidence for my inspection, then I will make a ruling," said the judge. MAJ Rankin knew he was in a very bad place, and it could get much worse. "Your honor, I can't in good conscious allow such dangerous weapons to be present in the courtroom. With great reservations, I would be forced to dismiss this important case, but protecting lives is my top concern."

"Let me get this straight. You are moving to dismiss this case just so you can avoid admitting the actual weapons as evidence?" Judge Anderson could smell a rat. His bullshit detector was pegged to the limits. "Your honor, I would have no other choice, ethically I mean," replied MAJ Rankin.

"Mr. Sterling, what is your response?" Sterling surprised the judge by objecting to the dismissal. Sterling proposed that the parties, including the court, examine the evidence outside the courtroom, in a safe setting. Judge Anderson had never seen such a display of stupidity from both sides in one trial. "Mr. Sterling, are you telling me that you are objecting to the dismissal? Let's be clear on the record that your client understands he can have a dismissal of all charges right now." Sterling looked over at LTC Carter and they nodded to each other. LTC Carter needed to have his name cleared. He wanted exoneration, not some plausible claim that the prosecutor dismissed the case out of some benevolent concern for safety.

Judge Anderson was in a position he had never been in before. The prosecutor moved to dismiss, and the defendant objected to the dismissal. What kind of upside-down world was this? His bullshit detector was now pegged past its limit. He needed to see this through. "MAJ Rankin, I am ordering you to produce the evidence. I am not ruling on your dismissal motion at this time." MAJ Rankin responded, "Yes your honor, I understand the court's ruling." Judge Anderson adjourned for one hour.

MAJ Rankin needed to stall for time. His brain needed to come up with a better plan. He had none. He called the CID office hoping they could permanently misplace the evidence, but they didn't pick up the phone.

Judge Anderson called the post commander, General Dunn. He explained the situation to the general and requested assistance with securing evidence from the evidence room. General Dunn was a good sport, but questioned if this wasn't a bit below his pay grade. Judge Anderson apologized for involving the general, but assured General Dunn that he had no other avenue to achieve justice.

Judge Anderson called an end to the recess and ordered the parties to return to the courtroom. MAJ Rankin tried to stall for time, that is until Judge Anderson sent the MP's to escort him to the courtroom. On the record, MAJ Rankin explained that he was unable to reach CID to arrange for an examination of the weapons, and that he needed to adjourn for the day to make such arrangements. Judge Anderson advised

MAJ Rankin that a delay would not be necessary, and that General Dunn had personally helped to secure an examination of the weapons. MAJ Rankin's face again lost all color.

The doors of the courtroom opened wide as a cart carrying RPG launchers and grenades being pushed by two CID agents rolled through the aisle and stopped next to the court clerk. "MAJ Rankin, the clerk will now mark your exhibits as evidence," said Judge Anderson. He then continued, "MAJ Rankin, I can't help but notice that the launchers have large holes cut in the sides, and if I am not mistaken, the grenades look like they have holes in the bottom. Is that also what you are seeing?" MAJ Rankin answered, "Yes your honor, that is correct." Judge Anderson pressed the issue, "MAJ Rankin, do any of these grenades contain any explosive material?" MAJ Rankin could feel the walls of the courtroom closing in on him. Judge Anderson was nearly out of patience. His face was now even redder than when he was mad at Sterling. The scowl on his face deepened. MAJ Rankin finally responded, "No your honor, there is not any explosive material in the grenades."

Judge Anderson continued, "And were you already aware of the condition of these items?" MAJ Rankin responded, "No your honor." Not letting MAJ Rankin escape the consequences of his lies, Judge Anderson asked, "So you did not know the status when you and Agent Smith checked out the evidence for examination yesterday?" MAJ Rankin had not planned on the judge pulling evidence log.

He answered, "Yes, I mean no, I didn't know before yesterday." Judge Anderson pressed the issue, "So you knew the launchers and grenades had both been rendered inert by LTC Carter and his team prior to being loaded into the Conex in Iraq?" MAJ Rankin offered a feeble last Hail Mary. "Your honor, these are still dangerous weapons despite whatever alterations LTC Carter's men performed. Sterling stood up. He was ready to drop the hammer. He said, "Your honor, at this time defense moves to admit proposed exhibit D-4. It is a legal opinion from an Assistant US Attorney who determined that under Federal Law these items no longer meet the definition of weapons." Judge Anderson didn't need Sterling to tell him what he already knew, and he didn't need an opinion from some Assistant US Attorney.

Red in the face, with spittle flying through his gritted teeth, Judge Anderson responded, "Mr. Sterling, that won't be necessary. Any idiot can see that this pile of junk doesn't meet any definition of dangerous weapon." He turned to MAJ Rankin, and said, "MAJ Rankin, you personally examined this pile of scrap metal yesterday and yet you are still in my court trying to convict a Special Forces officer of serious crimes. What would you like to say for yourself?" MAJ Rankin knew his goose was cooked. Way too late he answered, "Your honor, I am invoking my rights under the 5th Amendment."

Judge Anderson looked over at Sterling and said, "Mr. Sterling, do you and your client now accept a dismissal of this case, based on the court's own motion to dismiss?" Simultaneously, Sterling and LTC Carter responded, "Yes your honor."

Although a generally unpleasant man, Judge Anderson held justice in high regard. He was mad that his courtroom was nearly used to convict and innocent man. Not just an innocent man, but a decorated officer who defended our country. Judge Anderson offered an apology to LTC Carter and assured him that this matter would be fully investigated. LTC Carter nodded and thanked the judge.

Judge Anderson formally entered the dismissal on the record and adjourned. The bailiff announced, "All rise" as the judge got out of his chair and walked to his chambers. MAJ Rankin wasted no time and headed for the exit. On his way out, the journalists he had coveted to cover this trial blocked his path and asked for his comments on the dramatic conclusion of the trial. He pushed passed them and managed to mumble, "No comment."

Sterling also headed for the exit with his client not far behind. The same journalists who tried to get a comment from MAJ Rankin seemed anxious to get Sterling's comments. Sterling had a lot to say. The trial having ended in a dismissal, he was no longer subject to the judge's gag order. He was filled with righteous indignation. His plan to crush the prosecutor turned out even better than he had predicted. Given a chance to talk, he would take advantage of the moment. He earned it.

Sterling told the reporters, "I had the toughest job a defense attorney can ever have. I defended an innocent client. It was clear from the beginning that the prosecutor had no interest in justice. I am pleased that Judge Anderson fully and carefully considered the evidence in this case and dismissed the charges."

The attractive blond reporter from MSNBC wanted to know what would happen to the prosecutor. Responded Sterling, "That is not for me to decide. My entire focus has been on defending my client. Despite what happened in this case, I have confidence in the ability of the JAG Corps to deal with MAJ Rankin in a fair and just manner." It was a good statement, but also the truth. Despite his own negative experience with the military justice system, he was still a believer. He also believed that he played a part in keeping the system honest.

The reporters next wanted comments from LTC Carter. He told the reporters that he is grateful for the hard work of his attorney. He assured the viewers that despite his unjust prosecution, he remained committed to protecting American interests. His chest seemed to fill a bit more. He was a confident man, and on this day even more so. His innocence had been proven. His reputation was restored. It was a good day.

A couple of the reporters asked for Sterling's contact information so that they could conduct follow-up interviews. Sterling gladly shared his information. This was his time to shine, and he wasn't going to miss the opportunity.

The next day, Sterling watched all the TV networks to see their coverage. It was unusually fair and accurate. They focused on LTC Carter and his innocence. They also gave Sterling heavy praise for his advocacy. It was a strange experience for Sterling, who had been on the receiving end of so much negative publicity the year before.

Sterling then read through the local newspapers. The Seattle Times covered the story. They described his defense of an innocent client as representative of the cornerstone of our democratic republic, but questioned whether similarly situated defendants in the civilian world would receive the same level of zealous advocacy from public defenders. The tendency to balance any positive story with an examination of something negative seemed on brand for the paper. Still, Sterling enjoyed the article.

The Tacoma Gazette was his favorite. They called him for an interview over the phone after he returned to his office the day of the trial. The limited distribution newspaper was grateful to get the attention of Sterling, and their coverage reflected their gratitude. The headline read, "Sterling is Gold." They described his defense as inspired, zealous, and noteworthy. "I couldn't have said it better myself," said Sterling to himself.

Chapter 40

"Congratulations Sterling," was the brief text he received from Taylor the day after the dismissal. Sterling thanked her and apologized again for his deception. For what seemed like the 100th time, he asked if they could meet up. This time, she agreed.

They met at her place. She did not wait at the window hoping to catch sight of him when he pulled in her driveway. She did not run outside to greet Sterling with a hug. She wasn't sure what she wanted to get out of meeting with Sterling, but it seemed like she needed to share with him what she was feeling.

Sterling's deception played on her worst insecurities. As a young lawyer, she wanted to build credibility. In a male dominated profession, sometimes she had to work extra hard just so that others would take her seriously. She previously worried that dating Sterling would undermine her position as a more or less equal partner in their representation of LTC Carter. She had no idea that it would be Sterling himself who would undermine her standing. That was the part that hurt the most.

Sterling knocked on the door and she opened it, standing aside so he could enter. He put his arms out for a hug, but she instead straightened her arm, sweeping it to the side, gesturing in the direction of the couch. "Come on in and have a seat, Sterling." She didn't offer him a drink, and he quickly got the idea that this wasn't a romantic visit.

"You humiliated me, Sterling. I trusted you. I slept with you. I opened up to you in ways that I have never done before. You had me going. I believed you cared for me. I totally fell for your game of calling me your 'girlfriend' and worse, I thought you were my boyfriend." She was near tears, but she wasn't going to give him the satisfaction of losing her composure. He had already taken too much from her.

Sterling could feel himself falling into old patterns. He was feeling defensive, and his mind raced to find ways in which she was to blame. Instead, he said, "You are right. You deserved better. I went into the LTC Carter case with a plan, even before I met you. That isn't an excuse because I should have told you about our plan to have you keep MAJ Rankin feeling good about his case. At the very least, I should have been honest with you when I developed feelings for you, and especially when we started dating. I had many chances to be honest with you but I somehow rationalized keeping secrets from you. I regret that choice but most of all I regret the hurt that I have caused you. I hope you know that I have developed serious feelings for you. I want to be a better person. I want to be someone more deserving of you."

Taylor's efforts to maintain her composure were fading, and a tear fell from her eye. Looking at Sterling, he seemed so sincere. Part of her wanted to believe him. Part of her wanted to feel his embrace, not in a sexual manner, but a simple hug for support.

"Why go through so much trouble to drag out the case? You had to know the case was a loser for MAJ Rankin. Why not file a motion to dismiss at the very beginning? You could have won this case long ago." Taylor hoped there was some good reason other than Sterling's massive ego.

"Part of it is my ego," said Sterling. Taylor cringed when he uttered those words. It was like he was trying to insult her. His ego was worth more than her feelings, worth more than her reputation. Sterling continued, "I admit that I have an axe to grind against the Army. I want them to feel the humiliation they put me through last year when they court-martialed me. But there is another reason." Taylor hoped the next reason was better.

Sterling paused and looked at Taylor. "You are no longer co-counsel. If I tell you my client's reason, I will be violating my duty of confidentiality. If you want to know, I will tell you." At this point, she wondered if Sterling was hoping she would say no. That way he could pretend there was some really good reason, even though there is not, and he could conveniently hide beyond his ethical duties. She called his bluff, "Tell me the other reason."

Without hesitation, Sterling said, "LTC Carter made some mistakes. He didn't want the Army snooping around his finances too closely. He needed time to cover his tracks. We needed MAJ Rankin so satisfied with the strength of his case that he didn't need to look for more. If he did look for more, my plan would be to claim a failure to properly join the charges. I hoped to discredit MAJ Rankin so that any charges he might later file would be seen as retaliatory. I had no idea that MAJ Rankin would destroy himself so thoroughly, but that was a bonus. LTC Carter is now safe."

Taylor couldn't help but be confused by Sterling. On the one hand, he put a lot of trust in her by alluding to LTC Carter's other crimes that Sterling was trying to help his client cover up. On the other hand, she wasn't sure that anything he said took into consideration what the impact would be on her. She found herself about equally sure she could forgive him and equally sure she should never see him again. Her mind could not reconcile her competing thoughts.

"Look, you are a mess of a human being. You just need to leave," Taylor told him. Sterling looked disappointed, maybe even sad. He said, "So, where do we stand? Is this something we can overcome?" Taylor responded, "Honestly Sterling, I don't know. There is a lot that I need to process. Until I can sort this out, I want you to give me some space. Do not contact me. This is something I need to figure out on my own." Sterling now looked shocked. "Taylor, are you serious?" She nodded. He got up and made his way to the door. Before walking out the door he said, "I want you to know that I really care for you. I hope we have a future. If not, then I want to thank you for being so good to me." He walked out and Taylor shut the door.

Inside her house, Taylor stood frozen at the door and burst into tears. Part of her wanted to run outside, forgive him, and figure out what kind of a relationship they could build together. She believed that he had feelings for her. And she had feelings for him which were stronger than she had ever felt for anyone else. But she was not sure that Sterling could be the man she needed. He harbored so much hostility that it clouded his judgment. His insecurities caused him to overcompensate by creating some kind of alter ego. To the world, he projected confidence to a level nothing short of arrogance. He was a damn good lawyer, but she needed him to be a good partner. She knew he had shown her a crack in his wall. He seemed to be on the verge of becoming a decent human being, at least in her presence. She admitted to herself that she loved him, faults and all. Was love enough? Could he be open and honest with her? She needed him to consider her needs.

Chapter 41

Sterling drove back to his apartment. Even driving his G-Wagon did not boost his spirits. He walked up the stairs to his apartment and crumpled on the couch. His first instinct was to send Taylor a text to see if she had a chance to process her concerns. Thankfully he resisted that urge. She seemed serious when she told him not to contact her until she had a chance to process her thoughts. Sending a text now would convey that he didn't respect her. He needed her to give him a chance to rebuild her trust. He would respect her wishes to leave her alone.

As so often happens when he faced adversity, his mind began the process of constructing a new narrative. Being a worst-case scenario planner, a trait only useful in the legal profession, he began to plan a life without Taylor. He figured she would most likely decide that he was too broken as a person and that she needed someone more balanced and stable. He tried to convince himself he was better off without her. This was a familiar pattern for him.

Sterling pulled a lowball glass out of the cabinet, threw in a couple of ice cubes, and poured himself a generous serving of Maker's Mark. His time in Kentucky had given him a taste for Bourbon. He missed Taylor already.

On the upside, he had resolved the LTC Carter case, and it didn't look like he would be spending time with Taylor, so he had time to focus on setting up the Crips' shell companies. He would also have time to resume his training for the Coeur d'Alene Ironman triathlon. With all of his competing interests, he had neglected his training.

Last June he completed his first Ironman, and it was not pretty. He had 17 hours to complete the event, and he managed to take 12 hours 20 minutes, which was no better than average. By the time he completed the event it was nearly dark outside. Although just finishing is an amazing accomplishment, he wanted to do better. He convinced himself that his equipment was inadequate and so he upgraded his road bike to a pure triathlon bike. There wasn't much difference except for being able to remain in a tuck position while riding. The added aerodynamics should help him but mostly he just needed to be in better shape.

He committed himself to working out more. From a relationship standpoint, the more he worked out, the better he looked, and the better his dating prospects. Yet the more he dated, the more he neglected his training. It was a vicious cycle. The obvious conclusion is that dating in a traditional sense is a waste of time. He needed companionship but maybe sex was enough.

Taylor made him think that he was capable of maintaining something more than a casual relationship. He was drawn to her. He was in love with her. If she wanted to, she could convince him to focus on an actual relationship and all that entails. But she was gone. This line of reasoning brought him back to his center. He didn't need Taylor. He needed to resume his pursuit of, well, everything. She would only hinder his efforts to get to the top at all costs. It was best that he put her out of his mind.

Taylor considered calling him. At least she could send him a text. Processing their last conversation at her house, she believed that he cared for her. He didn't always do a good job of communicating his feelings for her, but she was convinced he was sincere in his affections. She put off contacting him.

Day after day she delayed making any decision. She appreciated that Sterling had not attempted to reach out to her. He respected her enough to give her space. Most likely she would follow her heart and give him another chance. But she didn't want to seem like a pushover. She would give it a little more time.

Chapter 42

Susan Maddox sent Sterling a text. She needed to meet up with him. They had business to review. She invited him to meet her at the gallery. Sterling knew the invitation was an order. The gallery was not far from his office, so he agreed to meet her at the gallery during his lunch break. She agreed and requested that he bring some food. She suggested sandwiches. Sterling didn't want to seem like an errand boy, but considering she would likely be handing him an envelope full of cash when he arrived, he didn't argue.

Arriving at Pacific Art Limited, he secured a parking spot in front of the gallery. Grabbing the bag of sandwiches off the passenger seat, he again regretted using his new G-Wagon as a food delivery vehicle. He feared the smell of sandwiches would permeate the headliner and leather seats.

Walking to the back office of the gallery he saw Susan sitting at the desk. She looked good. "Hello Mr. Sterling, how are you?" She smiled and stood up from her desk. Grabbing the food from his hands she set them down on a small table in the office. He returned her greeting. She gave him a hug, which he considered to be a bit overly familiar, but he didn't complain. "And how is that lovely girlfriend of yours?" asked Susan.

Sterling considered telling her that everything was just fine but decided instead to tell her the truth. "We are in something of a no man's land. She is mad at me and we stopped talking. I really don't know what the future holds for us, but it doesn't look good." Lowering his head for a moment, he continued, "She deserves someone better." Sterling's honesty surprised Susan, but she wasn't surprised about the status of their relationship.

"Sterling, I wouldn't say she deserves someone better than you, just different than you. Buster told me about how you handled Jamal. There are very few people who could kill a man on one day then go out on a date the next day, but all of those people are known as sociopaths." She could see that Sterling's face registered a sense of disappointment, maybe even failure. "Please don't misinterpret what I am telling you. You have a gift. Bad things happen and you are able to move past them. You adapt and move on. You watch out for yourself, and that is good."

Sterling found Susan's comments to be consistent with what he had suspected about himself. He was a mental case. Even so, he kind of liked himself that way. Likely he was a narcissist in addition to his other diagnosable conditions. He had once heard that asking someone if he is a narcissist is just as accurate as having him take a one hundred question test. The reason is that a true narcissist doesn't view this status to be an insult and will therefore readily admit to it.

"And what about you Mrs. Maddox? You seem to have figured me out, but I know so little about you," said Sterling. He was growing weary of being the focus of her psychobabble and hoped to change the subject. She went on to explain that she grew up in the same neighborhood as her husband Tricky. Unlike Tricky, she studied hard and set a goal of making it out of the neighborhood. She wanted to live the American dream she had heard so much about but seen so little of in real life. She was able to secure a scholarship to the University of Washington. She graduated cum laude in the Social Sciences program. She wanted to figure out people and make the world a better place.

"I had heard that Tricky is in prison. Is that true?" asked Sterling. "Yes, that is right. He is eligible for early parole in three years. In his absence he asked me to be his eyes and ears on the ground. Especially now that things are changing so quickly, he doesn't want to get left behind. Dealing drugs is a fairly straight forward business, but all of this real estate investment trust business is outside his area of expertise," explained Mrs. Maddox.

"If your goal is to save the world, how does that fit in with the drug trade?" asked Sterling, hoping he was not pushing her too far. She laughed at the question and replied, "I still hope to save the world, or at least our community. Tricky handles a business that doesn't interest me, but I would be lying if I said I don't enjoy our lifestyle. Tricky makes money, and I help him spend it. He thinks I make him a more cultured man, and he is right. As for saving the world, it takes money to do good things. Honest labor will never get me where I need to be."

Sterling began to see her as something of a kindred spirit. She recognized something in him that he didn't think was an attractive quality. The expression "A fisherman can spot a fisherman from afar" crossed his mind. He might be a sociopath, but she found that quality to be a gift. Mrs. Maddox had her own flaws, or attributes, depending on the viewpoint of the observer. She saw no moral conflict between helping to run a drug empire and simultaneously wanting to save the world. Similarly, Sterling saw no conflict between fighting for justice on one day, then killing a former client the next. It wasn't that he was flawed, it was just that he didn't see things the same way as most people.

Sterling knew he didn't start out this way. For most of his life he had been a fairly compassionate person. He cared about others. He saw great hope for his fellow man. He noticed he had drifted in the last year or so and had lost much of what made him a good person, at least in the traditional sense. Taylor had been something of an aberration. She anchored him and helped him regain a piece of his eroding humanity. Now she was gone. Untethered from any need to ground himself, he was adrift, and being pulled into the vortex of satisfying only his own needs.

His time in the Army contributed to his current personality disorders. He only held two jobs during his decade or so in the Army. First, he enlisted as a psychological operations specialist (PSYOPS). The Army trained him to develop and distribute propaganda. He learned to identify a target audience. The main skills he learned were persuasion, deception, and manipulation. As an attorney with the JAG corps, the main takeaways were persuasion, deception, and manipulation. Like overlapping waves creating a tsunami, these skills, which were the same but applied in different ways, enhanced each other into a cognitive blast of destruction.

Sterling talked more with Mrs. Maddox over the course of their lunch. Each gained a deeper understanding of the other. Eventually the conversation turned to business. Sterling updated her on the status of the shell companies. He made sure she had copies of the business licenses and bank accounts. The less personal involvement he had in the operations, the better, and the feeling was mutual. She had no desire to share control with Sterling. She was very much in charge. With lunch now concluded, Mrs. Maddox produced two white envelopes full of cash. It was payment for the two clients she would be sending over to his office later today. They were foot soldiers caught up in the battle for control of neighborhoods.

Sterling thanked her for the referrals. He slid the envelopes into the inner pocket of this Armani jacket. She gave him a hug on his way out, along with a kiss on the cheek. The hug was longer this time, and the addition of a kiss on the cheek was kind, or perhaps meant as a romantic gesture. He wasn't sure. For just a moment, he gave her a look as he allowed dangerous thoughts to enter his mind. She could see his thoughts. She smiled and said, "Be careful. That kind of look can get you in trouble." He winked at her and said, "I have no doubt." He walked out of the gallery, admiring the terrible art.

Chapter 43

The positive fallout of LTC Carter's case gained a head of steam. Sterling found himself the darling of the legal community, and the community in general. The public seemed fascinated as to how their own government could prosecute a war hero. It never occurred to them that many people are motivated by their own desire for attention and power. Prosecutors are not immune from these agendas.

Sterling found himself making the rounds on the news shows. Fox, MSNBC and CNN all asked for interviews, and he obliged. NBC's Today Show gave him a few minutes as well. Sterling was thankful that these newsrooms all had New York offices so that he could cover the events without taking time away from his kids. The highest compliment he received was an invitation to appear on the Bill Maher show. Sterling was a fan of the show and promised to make himself available, but the show ended up booking some political candidate instead.

Soon, Sterling had the best of all problems that a lawyer can have. He was too busy. He found himself turning down potential clients. Some of them had good cases, but he avoided taking any cases which involved excessive travel. His week on week off parenting plan limited his ability to be gone overnight, which meant he couldn't take on trials outside of the Seattle-Tacoma area. Trading weeks with his ex-wife wasn't an option because she hated him and didn't want to be helpful.

She outright refused to trade watch the kids if she perceived he would benefit from her actions. Strangely, she had no problem asking him to help. Sterling never said no. He genuinely loved being with his kids.

The biggest growth was in the legitimate side of Sterling's business. In terms of income, that side was still dwarfed by his gang business, but at least now he also had significant legal income which he could declare to the IRS. His kids had been begging him to ditch the two-bedroom apartment. They each wanted, and needed, their own room. He now had enough income on paper to qualify for a moderate sized loan.

He managed to find a dilapidated home at the crest of a hill in the North End area of Tacoma. The home had a sweeping 180-degree view of Commencement Bay. Normally, a home like this would be out of his price range, but it had suffered from decades of neglect. The aging widow who previously owned the home had little interest in the upkeep of the property and lacked the physical strength to take on any serious repairs. Her family didn't help much, instead waiting for her to die so they could inherit the home. They got their wish and eventually the old widow succumbed to old age.

When the family realized that the property needed a renovation budget roughly equal to the present value of the home, they gave up and listed it on the market. Sterling looked at the property not just as a home, but as an opportunity to launder money. He now had enough legitimate income to secure a bank loan to buy the home. He could easily fund the renovations with cash from the less legitimate side of his business.

Sterling made an offer on the home. It was less than the asking price by a large amount. The sellers accepted his low-ball offer. While it seemed like he secured the home for a song, in truth there was little competition. Other potential buyers found the long list of fixes daunting. Sterling's bank required an inspection before they would even fund the loan. It was a close call. The inspection revealed a long list of necessary repairs. The sellers had no interest in putting any money into fixing the home. Sterling waived any recommended repairs that he could, then even went so far as to pay for some of the most troublesome repairs himself prior to closing.

Even with some much-needed basic repairs, the home struggled to merit a certificate of habitability, but eventually he secured a bank loan for its purchase. Now he needed an army of people to fix the old home. Finding contractors to work under the table wasn't hard. Like him, many of them preferred to get paid in cash. The first order of business was to fix the pool. Sterling wanted his kids to be able to enjoy the pool starting on the first day of Tacoma's short summer.

Working with architects and designers, Sterling found the right mix of bachelor pad, and kid-friendly home. The most major constraint was complying with the city's extensive building codes. His original intent was to expand the home. His general contractor had to break the news to Sterling that changing the existing footprint would create costly permitting delays. He trusted his contractor and ultimately approved a design featuring exposed wood, metal trim, and a dark grey palette. The overall theme borrowed heavily from designs by Frank Lloyd Wright. Sterling admired the architect's incorporation of striking angles and generous use of glass. The latter helped him take advantage of the flowing views of the water.

There would be a lot of work needed to make this house his dream home, but he understood that the sooner he started the sooner he would finish. With plans in place, he prepared himself for a long wait.

Chapter 44

Back at work, Sterling needed to make some upgrades as well. The other tenants on the 7th floor were registering concerns. The volume of calls coming into the receptionist, which were in some way associated with Sterling, consumed a disproportionate amount of her time. The new shift toward meeting Sterling's phone needs resulted in the other tenants half-jokingly referring to the 7th floor as Sterling and Associates.

Similarly, the number of his clients taking up chairs in the small lobby exceeded any other business on his floor. Although not said in so many words, Sterling got the impression that his gang clients frightened off the mostly white clientele of the other tenants. The two psychologists on the floor catered to an already fragile demographic, and their clients demanded that the lobby qualify as a "safe space."

The landlord of the Wells Fargo building approached Sterling about moving his office space. He presented the potential move as a great opportunity for Sterling's growing business. A tenant recently vacated a large office space on the 6th floor. If Sterling agreed to rent the space, he would get five times the space at just double the cost. He could have his own reception area, a small conference room, a larger office, a second office, and a dedicated copier. As a further incentive, the landlord would throw in free parking for one year.

Sterling had some reservations about growing his practice. His taxes would become more complicated if he hired a receptionist. That complication would increase his chance of an IRS audit. Plus, he would need to provide sick days, vacation days, health insurance, dental insurance, 401K and pay into the employment insurance fund for his receptionist. He wondered if maybe he should shrink his practice instead. He would suffer far fewer frustrations, and if he wasn't working 100 hours per week, he might be able to have a social life.

His ego knew only one direction and that was forward. More was always better. In the last year or so his life had turned a corner and the material possessions he coveted were falling into place quickly. Thanks to Taylor's absence, he didn't need to devote time to a girlfriend, so work was his greatest passion.

Chapter 45

Sterling moved his practice to the 6th floor. His new office even had a partial view of the Puget Sound off to the west. He upgraded his office furniture. His new desk was made of dark mahogany and featured hand cut engravings. It took a six-man crew to wedge the three pieces of the desk into the service elevator, then assemble it in Sterling's office.

He moved the glass desk into the smaller second office. He wasn't sure if he wanted to rent out the other office or not. Although he valued privacy, he also liked the idea of collecting rent for the space he wasn't using. He would figure that out later.

Just for kicks, Sterling purchased two pieces of art from Pacific Art Limited. More accurately, he ordered a couple extra paintings from the supplier and diverted them to his law office. Hanging in his lobby they made a statement, suggesting that Sterling's practice was doing well. The terrible art was gaining a favorable reputation among critics, reinforcing Sterling's perception that art is a scam.

Never one to miss a marketing opportunity, Sterling held an office warming party. He invited a cross section of community members. Sterling didn't claim to have many friends, but there were a few attorneys he liked, a couple he respected, and a couple dozen who could help advance his career in some way. They all got invitations. He invited some of his new fans from the

ACLU who appreciated his work defending low-income minorities. He invited the lawyers and psychologists from the 7th floor, a smattering of local officials, and a couple reports. He invited his favorite clients including LTC Carter, who declined the invitation, as well as Buster and Susan Maddox. They both accepted his invitation.

Sterling hired a catering company to serve hors d'oeuvres and champagne. He wanted this to be the type of event that would stand out in the minds of the attendees. The event reminded him of the grand opening of the gallery and the night he shared with Taylor when they briefly established themselves as boyfriend and girlfriend. He wished she was here to share this moment with him.

As the guests arrived, Sterling made the rounds, thanking each of them for attending his office opening event. His smiling attendees patted Sterling on the back congratulating him on the new office, and for his recent success in court. Almost without exception, they would then scan the room looking to see who else was present at the event. It was a time to see and be seen.

Standing out from the crowd, Buster and Susan Maddox arrived at the same time. Sterling assumed they had carpooled to the event. Buster had fully embraced the corporate CEO look. He did his best to mingle with the other guests.

Mrs. Maddox's entrance caught Sterling's attention. Her blue dress sparkled in the lights of his office. Sterling grabbed a couple glasses of champagne and brought one to her, keeping the other for himself. He thanked her for coming to his event. "Beautiful office you have here Mr. Sterling." Their eyes made contact. Exchanging smiles, Sterling asked, "May I give you the tour?" Susan Maddox followed Sterling as he guided her through the office. There wasn't all that much to see, but he enjoyed walking with her. He hadn't had much female company lately. Dating didn't interest him right now. Part of him was holding out hope that Taylor would reach out to him. She hadn't, so he filled his time with work.

Susan's perfume lingered in the air, filtering up to Sterling's nose. He knew he needed to make the rounds and visit with other guests, but he was finding her company irresistible. He thought about their previous conversation and understood her warning about thinking dangerous thoughts. Even he wasn't stupid enough to sleep with Tricky's wife. One of the things he enjoyed most about his life was being alive.

Politely excusing himself, he grabbed another glass of champagne and made the rounds. The office warming party was a resounding success. Sterling's status as a near celebrity resulted in nearly all of his invitees attending, and he even had a couple of party crashers. They were lawyers who heard about the event, and their presence didn't bother Sterling. There was plenty of food and drink to go around.

Eventually, the crowd began to thinn, and the caterers packed up. They had three bottles of champagne remaining. Sterling kept one and gave the other two to the caterers along with a generous tip. He asked them to leave two champagne flutes, and they obliged. They would probably bill him for the missing glasses and that was fine with him.

The last of his guests took their leave, with one exception. Waiting in his office was a straggler. Her sparkling blue dress gave away her identity before Sterling could even see her face. She was sitting on his new mahogany desk, legs crossed, with her arms behind her back supporting her as she leaned back. He had hoped she would stay, and she did not disappoint him. He offered her a glass of champagne. She looked up at him and smiled, "Sterling, I might have had too much to drink already. I fear my inhibitions have largely abandoned me." Sterling began to set down the bottle. She looked up at him and said, "You may have misinterpreted what I said. That wasn't a no. Please be so kind as to hand me a glass. I intend to chase away my remaining inhibitions."

Sterling laughed at her flirty invitation and poured her another glass. She raised the glass as if to say cheers, but Sterling didn't have a glass in his hand. He took a step toward her and wrapped his arm around her back pulling her close. He gently lifted the glass out of her hand and set it down on the filing cabinet. She leaned her head toward his and he met her in the middle. Their lips touched and Sterling's pulse surged. They maintained their embrace as Sterling worked his hands over her body, while enjoying the feeling of her soft lips.

Even after a few drinks, Sterling knew this was a bad idea. It was a really bad idea. But that added to the excitement of the moment. Knowing that surrendering to his kind of passion could provoke a deadly response from Tricky if he found out, added to the thrill he was already feeling. He pulled Susan off the desk and rotated her body so her back side was facing him. He reached down and pulled up her dress. He reached down again to drop her panties but discovered she wasn't wearing any. He pressed gently on her back, and she leaned forward, spreading her hands on the desk to support her torso.

Sterling dropped his pants. She moaned and said, "Looks like we both chased away some inhibitions." Sterling thrust himself closer to her and slid slowly inside her. Susan grunted for a second, her back arching as she tried to relax. It had been a long time for her. "Easy soldier. Take your time." Like Sterling, she was very aware that they had crossed a line, and the consequences could be deadly. Maybe deadly for her, but certainly deadly for Sterling if Tricky found out. She wanted to make sure she enjoyed their tryst.

Chapter 46

Construction on Sterling's new house progressed quickly, or at least quickly in terms of home construction projects in Tacoma. His crew, which he paid exclusively in cash, had an incentive to get the job done and move on to the next project. They prioritized his renovation over every other job they had pending. They were paid well and all of it was tax free.

The permitting process was frustrating. He avoided the need for a variance by keeping the same footprint. He wanted a bigger house, but then he would need time for public hearings to consider the variance, then the neighborhood planning commission would weigh in, then the city permitting office had final say. He was pleased that he didn't need to wait for that excruciatingly long and unpredictable process to play out.

Despite his efforts to game the system by keeping the same footprint for his house, even seemingly routine matters like a new deck required a permit. Any major remodeling required a permit and his whole house was pretty much a gut job. Unlike the contractors he hired, the city inspectors don't accept cash in exchange for services. They tend to consider such incentives to be bribes, and then it would become a criminal matter. Sterling had to rely on his less refined skill of simply being nice and asking politely if they could fit an inspection into their busy schedule. When that didn't work well, he relied on his almost non-exist skill of patience.

Sterling's decision to prioritize repairing the pool paid off. The crew finished the pool slightly ahead of schedule. The long-term weather forecast predicted a warming trend with highs in the mid-80's. That gave him time to fire up the pool heater and burn enough natural gas to make the pool generally comfortable.

Sterling's kids were excited about the pending move. He had driven them by the property a couple times, and even let them walk through the house on a day when the contractors were waiting for the permits to clear. While they liked the house, they loved the pool. Soon they would get to spend the weekend splashing away, and sunning themselves on the deck.

During the weeks they spent with their mom, they excitedly updated her on the progress of dad's house. She encouraged them to continue telling her about dad's lifestyle. It became clear to her that Sterling had improved his financial status significantly after their divorce, and she wanted a piece of his success. She seemed to have little else of interest in her own life and obsessed compulsively about all aspects of his life.

Her offhanded comments about his G-Wagon and expecting an increase in child support became a constant drumbeat with no end in sight. With his purchase of his dream home, and its expensive remodel, she grew weary of waiting for Sterling to voluntarily pay her more child support. She threatened litigation if he didn't double the support payments. Sterling could easily afford the increase, and he may have considered paying her if he had any confidence that his kids would benefit. He feared, with good reason, that any increase would benefit her exclusively.

She already ran her budget like a drunk teenager with a credit card. Her efforts to mirror Sterling's improved status had left her heavily in debt. Payments on her new BMW left her with very little money to spend on the kids. She blamed Sterling for his failure to properly support her, seeming to forget that the two were divorced.

She hired a lawyer and took him to court, suing for more child support. Since more than a year had passed since their divorce, she could legally file for a modification. Sterling took the opportunity to learn about family law and represented himself. Even with Sterling's talent for cooking the books, his legitimate business had grown significantly. Deducting expenses from his earnings, he was still left with a sizable amount of money. Thankfully his ex-wife had also earned more money last year. The net outcome involved Sterling paying 50% more in child support than the year before. His ex-wife considered it to be a victory, despite paying her own attorney thousands of dollars.

For Sterling it was a clear win. If he had he been too willing to agree to her demand to double the child support payments, he could count on fighting the same battle every year. This way, he created a disincentive for her to make repeated trips to court. Her gains were modest, and she had to pay a lawyer. She wouldn't be too anxious to repeat this process soon.

Chapter 47

Sterling found himself making regular trips to the art gallery. Sometimes he would pick up envelopes full of cash to represent clients, sometimes he would just go there to see Susan Maddox. Most of the time he would steal a kiss, sometimes more. She started to become an occasional visitor at his law office. He even brought her by his apartment a couple times. The house was not yet ready for guests.

He enjoyed her company. The sex was amazing, and she lacked any kind of concern about his morals. She didn't worry about whether he was respecting her as a professional. It was a transactional relationship. She was using him for sex as much as he was using her. The attraction was real, but both of them lacked the ability to form a strong emotional connection. Sterling had abandoned that endeavor as part of his drift away from any attachment which could slow his progress. It was better this way.

Susan admired Sterling's ability to find his true self. She worried about him when he dated Taylor. Although she was a beautiful young woman, she had the capacity to deprive Sterling of what made him great. Sterling had a gift in the same way that she had a gift. They were both able to rise to the top of their fields, but to do so they each needed to be free from the responsibility of caring for the emotional needs of a partner. By her way of thinking, Taylor did Sterling a huge favor by breaking up with him. Taylor also did Susan a huge favor. Susan needed him to focus on work, plus she enjoyed his availability to satisfy her other more primal needs.

Like Sterling, Susan Maddox at one time had feelings. Years ago, her heart would ache for her husband and his role in the decline of society. His drug trade ruined lives and destroyed families. She loved him and for a long time she hoped he would invest his ill-gotten gains and get out of the drug business before he died or ended up in prison. Tricky never seemed to find the right time to get out of the business, and Susan lost hope that he ever would. Over the years, they drifted apart emotionally, but Tricky trusted her and relied on her to help him run his drug empire.

When Tricky went to prison, Susan took the reins of the drug trade, but under the supervision of Tricky. She found it was easy to run messages back and forth to him in prison. Anything sensitive just needed the cover of a lawyer. The lawyer would secure a private booth in the prison visiting room and update Tricky on the status of the Crips. Tricky would then relay instructions to Susan. As time went by, Susan became so adept at running the operation that Tricky didn't have much advice he needed her to follow.

Susan missed her husband, but they no longer had a romantic relationship. He didn't request, nor did she offer to participate in, conjugal visits even though the prison offered this service. She couldn't put her finger on what had changed, other than he just wasn't that interested.

On her most recent trip to visit him in prison, Tricky was pleased to hear that the gallery was doing so well. He asked her to thank Sterling for helping to set up the money laundering operation. They had never successfully laundered so much money in the history of the gang. Now they were using the proceeds from the gallery to gobble up homes in Tacoma with semi-legitimate funds. They were on the verge of making a staggering amount of money. Tricky feared that the next three years behind bars would go by slowly. He wanted to be out of prison when the avalanche of money showered on top of him and his beloved Crips.

Chapter 48

The new receptionist, Wendy, came to the Law
Office of Preston Sterling from a temp agency. Sterling
didn't really need his receptionist to do much.
Basically, she just needed to answer phones and take
messages. Sterling resisted the idea of paying someone
a salary and benefits to babysit his clients. If he wasn't
afraid his clients would steal from him while waiting in
the lobby, he probably wouldn't even bother to have a
receptionist.

At least by hiring a temp he could avoid paying her
benefits and he didn't need to give her any vacation
time. When it became apparent to her that he wasn't
going to offer her a permanent position, she would
likely quit, but then he would just get another temp. He
liked the idea of seeing a new face every few months.

Sterling still hadn't decided what to do about his
extra office. It would be a great office for a newer
attorney looking for experience. He had so many clients
that he could pawn off some of them on the new guy.
He again put off making any decision.

The phone rang at the reception desk and Wendy
dutifully answered, "Law Office of Preston Sterling,
how may I direct your call?" A moment later Sterling's
phone rang, having been transferred by Wendy. She
knew how to operate the forward feature, so that was a
good start, thought Sterling. On the other line was a
potential client. Colonel Drake is a board licensed

physician working at Madigan Army Hospital. He explained that he was facing a medical review board for some questionable medical practices. The board had the authority to make findings, and potentially recommend that Dr. Drake's medical license be suspended or revoked.

COL Drake came to visit Sterling for a consultation two days later. Dr. Drake had been accused of using his patients as a research project. He theorized that many of his patients suffering from nasal blockage didn't need surgery. He believed that more often than not the blockage was the result of the proliferation of drug resistant bacteria. In order to clear the infection, he prescribed next generation antibiotics. His clients didn't complain, and many showed improvement of their symptoms. Dr. Drake documented his findings, hoping to publish in the JAMA (Journal of the American Medical Association).

Some clients, especially those with polyps, didn't respond well to the antibiotics. Dr. Drake referred those patients to a surgeon. Even those clients appreciated Dr. Drake's willingness to explore a non-surgical option before sending them in for painful procedures. In all, Dr. Drake received zero complaints from patients.

His actions would have gone unnoticed except that the medications were expensive, costing over $5,000 for the two-week treatment. His patients, who were either active-duty military or their dependents, didn't pay for the medication. Instead, Madigan Army Hospital paid for the medications. An audit discovered that Dr. Drake cost the hospital more than any other Ear Nose and Throat doctor in the history of the hospital.

As was his usual practice with potential military clients, Sterling asked his client if he had consulted with Trial Defense Services on post. Their representation would cost him nothing because it is a benefit of military service. COL Drake explained that he had consulted with a JAG defense attorney, and her supervisor. The attorneys offered to help him, and they seemed competent. He then asked them a simple question. "If money was no object, and your ass was on the line, who would you hire?" He explained that the young dark-haired attorney, CPT Jane, advised him that she would hire Preston Sterling. Her supervisor agreed.

Chapter 49

Sterling was pleased to know that CPT Jane thought of him highly enough to recommend him to a client. Hell, he was pleased that she thought of him at all. He still missed her, although in his heart he knew he was drifting farther and farther away from the man she needed him to be. The thought of them somehow being a normal couple holding hands in a mall and shopping at Williams Sonoma for a fancy coffee maker seemed like a pipe dream. He was not cut out for that, at least not anymore. Susan had helped him to understand his gift.

COL Drake's case was the type that Sterling loved. This was a client who was a decent person. He was a doctor just trying to make the world a better place. Sure, he used his clients as part of a research project but that didn't bother Sterling. At least the doctor was trying to help people. If somehow along the way Dr. Drake's research earned him a Nobel prize for medicine, that would be an added bonus.

Sterling devoted countless hours of research to medicine and all of its generally accepted boundaries. Like most professions, medicine and law have a significant overlap. There are also areas of conflict. Sometimes what is legal isn't ethical, and sometimes good medicine isn't legal. Given Sterling's many hours researching this case, he should, at least in his view, have earned an honorary doctorate.

Medicine is one of the few professions that Sterling genuinely respected. It was part science and part intuition. The goal of the entire medical profession was to save lives. Sterling's ability to safeguard liberty struggled to measure up to the ability of medicine to literally prevent death. Now he had an opportunity to help a doctor. In an ideal world, this is what the practice of law meant to him. So many of his clients were not good people. Some of his clients even wanted to harm his community by spreading death and violence. But COL Drake was a good man and Sterling vowed to save this man's career.

Unfortunately, the same office of JAG attorneys who attempted to destroy LTC Carter oversaw prosecuting this case. Thankfully, MAJ Rankin had other issues he was dealing with, including a potential court-martial, but Sterling was not confident in the system's ability to police itself. COL Drake made a good choice by hiring Sterling.

This time, Sterling attempted to take the high road when negotiating the case. He asked the prosecutor to take into consideration COL Drake's contribution to the Army, and to medicine. He pointed out that the field of medicine thrives on the research of doctors. Patients don't need to be advised that their outcomes may become the subject of published studies. Ultimately, Sterling argued, there were no victims in this case. The Army and its bloated budget suffered an impact, but it was medically justified. No patients ever complained.

Sterling often fell victim to a kind of trial psychosis in which he got so wrapped up in his own argument that he tended to believe what he was saying despite all evidence to the contrary. This case was different. COL Drake was innocent in an objective sense.

JAG had reason to be cautious when dealing with Sterling. The prosecutors villainized him and his most recent victory against MAJ Rankin. Most of the prosecutors believed that Sterling somehow tricked MAJ Rankin into committing legal and ethical violations. They would not be fooled again.

LTC French was the highest-ranking JAG prosecutor at Ft. Lewis. He had more trial experience than any JAG on post. He knew about Sterling's reputation and was immediately on the defensive. When Sterling made an appointment to discuss COL Drake's case, LTC French was mentally prepared to disregard anything Sterling said as just being the desperate tricks of an arrogant windbag. But LTC French knew something else. He read in the newspaper about Sterling's masterful manipulation of MAJ Rankin. LTC French approached the meeting with Sterling in equal measures skepticism and caution. He had to consider the possibility that Sterling had a defense prepared for his client. He could not let himself get caught up in the trap that destroyed MAJ Rankin.

Sterling laid it all out. He told LTC French exactly what he would present in the defense of his client. He gave LTC French time to research what Sterling knew about medically accepted practices. Sterling even threw a bone to the prosecutor and agreed that COL Drake didn't always secure the proper authorization for disbursing expensive medical treatments. His client probably deserved a written reprimand for his disregard of hospital policy. Sterling assured LTC French that he would recommend his client stipulate to violating hospital billing policy in exchange for an agreed finding that COL Drake did not violate medical ethics, nor did he engage in malpractice. LTC French digested Sterling's offer with a heavy measure of skepticism but promised to consider the offer.

LTC French did his own research. Unlike MAJ Rankin, LTC French wasn't seeking personal gratification. He truly believed in justice. He believed in the goodness of people, despite so many opportunities to find only the worst in the soldiers he prosecuted. He couldn't help but wonder what Sterling had up his sleeve, but promised himself that he would weigh the evidence fairly.

Taking most of a week to find ways around Sterling's argument, he failed. He knew that meant one of two things. First, it was possible that Sterling had outsmarted him and found a way to defeat a righteous prosecution. Second, it was possible that Sterling was right, and COL Drake committed only minor administrative errors in his excessive use of next gen antibiotics. Prosecutors seldom consider deficiencies in their cases to be evidence of the weakness of the case. Rather they get caught up in the belief that the case has merit and just needs to be prosecuted properly to overcome the perceived weakness.

LTC French came to the conclusion that Sterling was right. COL Drake had a legally and medically defensible position. He didn't have any complaints from patients. He cost the Army a lot of money by breaching protocol and authorizing the release of controlled medications without approval from the bean counters in the finance department. LTC French advised Sterling that he would sign stipulated findings and COL Drake would receive a written reprimand for violating hospital policy but there would be no request to suspend or revoke Dr. Drake's medical license.

Sterling notched another victory. This time the media did not cover the event and that was fine with Sterling. Sometimes a good outcome doesn't need to be broadcast for the world to hear.

Chapter 50

Although the media did not cover the outcome, someone had been tracking the COL Drake case. CPT Jane logged on to the JAG database and printed a copy of the COL Drake findings. Sure enough, Sterling secured an amazing outcome for his client. CPT Jane knew she was right to recommend Sterling to COL Drake.

CPT Jane wondered what had kept her from reaching out to Sterling. She had forgiven him months ago. A couple times she even resolved to call him up, or at least to send him a text. Whenever she had more than a drink or two, she considered drunk texting hm to see how he was doing, and to see if he might consider coming over to her place. Yet she never did. Worse yet, she had ordered him not to contact her until she had processed her thoughts. So even if he wanted to work it out with her, she foreclosed that option.

Maybe it was too late for them. She hadn't moved on emotionally, but after five months she figured that Sterling had. She wouldn't know if he had any interest in her unless she reached out to him.

"Congratulations on saving COL Drake's career. I knew you could help him. You are the best!" It was the third glass of chardonnay that gave her the courage to send the text, and she immediately regretted her decision. With any luck, he would ignore her text.

Chapter 51

Sterling was enjoying his third deviant sex act of the evening with Susan Maddox when his phone buzzed. Thankfully the phone was on vibrate so as not to take attention away from this night of debauchery. He ignored the text message and continued to grind on the woman who had become his frequent companion.

Waking up the next morning alone in his apartment, he needed a cup of coffee to shake away the cobwebs in his brain. The previous night he enjoyed a purely physical connection. It was perfect. The emotional connection wasn't important to him. He loved the freedom to come and go as he pleased without judgment.

It wasn't until he nearly drained his first cup of coffee that he even thought to reach for his phone. Turning over his iPhone the screen notified him of a missed text from Taylor Jane. As was always the case when he got messages from her, his heart skipped a beat. He didn't think he would ever hear from her again. He was thrilled to hear from her even after so long. He didn't understand why it should mean so much to him, but it did.

"Hey beautiful, good to hear from you. How have you been?" Was the text Sterling sent to Taylor. She heard the "ding" sound from her phone and hesitated before checking the screen. The text was from Sterling. She spent the previous night second guessing her decision to text him. When he didn't respond right away, she convinced herself it had been a mistake to reach out. Why couldn't she just ignore him and let their time together fade away into a mostly pleasant memory?

Reading the text message from Sterling a smile spread across her face like an autonomic reflex. She had no control over her reaction. Her brain simply sent impulses to the nerves which told her face muscles to contract into the form of a smile. She hadn't even thought about what she would do if he texted her back, and now she needed to confront the fact that they had re-established contact.

She was committed now, and texted, "I'm well! Want to catch up? I'd like to see you." Sterling's immediate response was, "Absolutely! When?" Taylor texted back, "I got roped into some field training for a few days, but how about next Friday? Drinks at the pizza place in Dupont, 6pm?" Sterling responded, "It's a date!" Taylor leaned her head back on the couch wondering if she had made the right decision. She would find out next week.

Chapter 52

Sterling looked forward to his date with Taylor. He didn't mention anything to Susan Maddox. There was no need to clear it with her. They didn't have a relationship in a traditional sense. It was business and it was sex. They met each other's needs. Taylor was different. At one point, he really thought they had a future. He had fallen in love with her, and he really didn't understand why she broke it off so abruptly. When he didn't hear from her in nearly five months, he assumed they were done.

It was just a matter of coincidence that Sterling's name again crossed her radar, bringing up memories in her head and the recognition of unfinished business. They never really had closure. Maybe that is all they needed. They could meet up at the pizza joint, talk about old times, and wish each other well. Then they would each move on knowing that their chapter was over. But she wouldn't have a chance to find out for nearly a week. Before their scheduled date, she had to complete a four-day FTX (Field Training Exercise).

Taylor attended her field training at the "beautiful" YTC (Yakima Training Center) in central Washington. This is an area reserved for war fighting in a simulated desert environment. Stryker brigades from Ft. Lewis rotated in and out of the area learning to attack opposing forces. The goal was to provide a realistic training environment for our troops scheduled to deploy to Iraq and Afghanistan.

The 150-mile drive from Ft. Lewis to YTC would take about two and a half hours in a car. Maybe less if the driver pushed the speed limit and was driving a normal car. The HUMVEE she shared with the medical team was hot, loud and slow. The engine overheated once, necessitating a short stop on the side of I-90. Four hours after the start, the vehicle rumbled to a halt at its destination.

Time in Yakima was great training for the combat troops. Less clear was the value of sending a defense attorney into the simulated combat environment. Occasionally defense attorneys visited active combat zones to investigate crime scenes or conduct witness interviews, but they were usually escorted by combat troops. CPT Jane got the feeling that the Army didn't understand that attorneys specialize in narrow fields of law. CPT Jane was a good defense attorney but that didn't mean that she knew much about Rules of Engagement or the Geneva Conventions.

CPT Jane found herself assigned to a Tactical Operations Center (TOC) under camouflage netting. She had a field portable desk and a Toshiba Toughbook laptop. Thankfully the computer hard drive contained reference material including the Geneva Conventions and the UCMJ, along with various digital forms she may need in the field. The Army determined that the officers assigned to the TOC would embrace a true field environment, so she would be sleeping under the stars on top of a thin pad she packed in her rucksack along with her OD (Olive Drab) green sleeping bag.

In terms of defending soldiers, CPT Jane literally had nothing to do. The Army instead described her duties as an opportunity for "cross-training in various disciplines." It was the kind of duty description which would look good in her annual evaluation but didn't make particularly good use of her time and didn't really assist the Army.

CPT Jane did her best to appear busy, and even offered her assistance to anyone who seemed to have actual work to do. Her willingness to assist others ingratiated her with the leadership but also drew attention to the fact that she had nothing of value to contribute. The Army is a large organization and sometimes it loses track of its pieces. CPT Jane was a missing piece from a different puzzle.

Her lack of value for the mission would be forgivable in her mind if she at least had a place to sleep. A tent and a cot, or even a cot with no tent, would be an upgrade compared to sleeping on the ground. She was too hot during the day, then too cold at night. She tried to sleep but the ants followed her every movement, managing to dig into her ears until she wrapped a clean t-shirt around the side of her head. Then the ants only attacked her eyes.

Saying she woke up the next morning wouldn't be accurate. She never fully fell asleep. She now would start the whole process again and again until she was done.

Cracking open her MRE (Meal Ready to Eat), she grabbed the coffee packet and poured water into her canteen. She activated the heating pack with a splash of water and a chemical reaction caused the wrapping around her canteen to bring the coffee to a near boil. She added the sugar and creamer packets hoping that the coffee could clear her brain. It was better than nothing. She forced herself to stare at the computer screen, grateful the Army had seen fit to include solitaire as part of the basic software.

She chatted with the other officers and enlisted soldiers in the TOC and generally paid attention when the mock offensive began. Simulated battle reports streamed in and each officer with an actual job took turns playing their part in the pretend war.

To her surprise, someone actually needed a legal opinion. Intelligence reported that rebels were using the simulated mosque as a hideout. The mobile artillery brigade asked permission to level the building. CPT Jane correctly advised them that if the rebels were not actively using the mosque as a base for offensive operations, then the artillery unit could not destroy a building of religious significance without violating ROE. That was the highlight of her experience at the YTC.

Somehow, she made it to day four and found herself exhausted and cranky. The slow transport back to Ft. Lewis gave her a chance to catch a nap. Making her way back to her parked car on post, all she could do was think about sleep. If her house in Dupont wasn't so close to the JAG office, she wouldn't trust herself to stay awake long enough to get home. She considered cancelling her date with Sterling, but she figured she

still had a couple days to rest before they were
scheduled to meet.

Chapter 53

Sterling's house was nearing completion. Eventually the city inspectors issued their stamp of approval for the new electrical, plumbing, and HVAC systems. His crews quickly installed drywall, flooring, floor molding, and crown molding. The high-end fixtures and appliances soon followed. Sterling's new bed, mattress, dressers and nightstands completed the master bedroom.

He looked forward to spending his first night in his new home. The kids' bedrooms needed a little more work to complete the closets, but they would be done soon too. He knew his kids were ready to be done with the two-bedroom apartment. They had been patient with their dad, and they loved him, but they preferred the setup at their mom's house where they each had their own room.

Sterling parked in the driveway of his new home. The remote for the garage door was somewhere on his newly installed marble counter in the kitchen. Sterling did not yet have the remote in his vehicle. In fact, this would be his first time opening the garage door since its installation three days ago. He entered the code for the garage door on the dark keypad which was partially hidden in a section of the wood trim.

The recent progress on the home came as a welcome surprise to Sterling. At times, he had three sets of contractors working on the home at the same time. The home's status went from "no estimated completion date" to being nearly complete just in the last month.

Walking through the home he marveled at the skill of his highly paid contractors. They were worth every penny. By eliminating the attic, the home now showcased vaulted ceilings with twin skylights. Walking through the living room he admired the new ¾ inch hickory flooring. Without much furniture or carpeting to absorb sound, his steps echoed through the house as he made his way to the accordion style sliding glass doors leading to the back deck. The black trim of the glass doors provided a contrast from the otherwise white, almost sterile look of the main area.

Sterling preferred clean lines and light colors, especially in the kitchen. He initially balked at the quoted price of the cabinets but then relented when his designer argued passionately for their inclusion. Looking at the finished product, he had to admit she was right.

Sterling opened the glass doors and admired his view of Commencement Bay. It was this view that drew him to his property in the beginning. He saw the value in the land, even if the original home was an ugly gut job. His one concern had been the neighbors below. His home was high enough above their home so as not to obstruct his view. But he feared the neighbors might at some point in the future want to build a second story. In a visionary move, he purchased the sky rights of the property in front of his home. He was specific in the details of the restrictive covenant. His rights prevented the home in front of him from building above its current height above sea level. If he had simply restricted them from building a second story, he feared they might tear down the home, bring in fill dirt, and thus raise the height of their lot. If they then rebuild their home on top of the fill material, they could potentially block his view. By defining the height restriction as a measurement above sea level he foreclosed any problems.

The pool was the first of the major renovations to be completed. His kids had already enjoyed the pool a few times. They were even more anxious than Sterling to move in to the new home.

Having completed the walk through of his nearly completed home, Sterling's attention focused on his date with Taylor. He had been looking forward to seeing her and now it was almost time. With an extra spring in his step, he walked to his G-Wagon ready for the short drive to Dupont.

Chapter 54

Taylor arrived at the pizza joint and parked next to Sterling's familiar G-Wagon. Doubts again crept into the back of her head, and she wondered if she should send him a text message claiming to be sick. She didn't like the idea of backing out at the last minute, so she pressed ahead.

Walking into the restaurant she turned her head to the right, looking at the bar. She spotted Sterling sitting at a barstool looking in her direction. His face lit up when he saw her. She smiled back reflexively and walked toward him. He didn't wait for her to reach the bar before stepping toward her, wrapping his arms around her in an enthusiastic embrace.

Taylor let out a sigh as her body and mind relaxed. She had missed being in his arms. The doubt she harbored now dissipated slightly and her tension eased a bit. She knew there would still be an awkwardness. He would no doubt ask her why she hadn't contacted him for five months, and she didn't have a particularly good reason. She had played out their reunion in her head at least 100 times. The reasons, or excuses, for her extended silence were not compelling even in her mind.

Sterling surprised her by making her feel at ease. He wasn't judgmental and didn't press her for answers about her motivations for cutting him out of her life. The gap between her expectations and the reality of their interaction caught her off guard. He just seemed happy to see her. As they spoke, he maintained consistent eye contact. His face displayed a nearly constant smile. Taylor could feel herself getting caught up in Sterling's gravity, slowly pulling her in and challenging her resolve to maintain an emotional separation. She now questioned why she had stopped talking to him. She even questioned why she had been so hard on him to begin with.

They each ordered a drink, then another. Drinks turned into dinner. Sterling enjoyed her story of the FTX in Yakima. He could hardly imagine a more terrible experience as a JAG. Her experience made him happy he was no longer in the Army. Sterling updated her on his growing law practice. Trying not to appear like he was bragging, he also told her about his new home which was nearing completion. He told her he was happy with the new place, but did not mention the pool, the view, or the modern architecture. Sterling was trying to understand that even though he personally coveted material possessions, it was not polite to dwell on such things while on a date.

Leading up to their date, he wondered what their meeting would be like. Would it be like friends catching up on old times, or would they rekindle a romantic relationship? His own visceral reaction to seeing her ran in stark contrast to the new and improved Sterling he thought he had become. He thought he no longer needed love. His business was doing so well that developing feelings could only slow him down. He considered himself to be better than other people. He embraced the part of himself that Susan convinced him was a gift. His focus on his own self-interest replaced any need for emotional intimacy. Yet he was more attracted to Taylor now than he had ever been.

As their date came to an end, Taylor remained surprised that Sterling had not pushed her for an explanation for ghosting him. The whole evening, he did nothing but put her at ease. He was different than any man she had ever known. For that matter, he even seemed different than the Sterling she knew from five months ago. His arrogance now came across as confidence. He was more at peace with himself than she remembered. She could not deny that she found him even more attractive than she had five months ago when he was briefly her boyfriend.

Sterling slowly walked her to her car. His arm brushed against her arm, and she felt a shiver run up her side. Before the date started, she convinced herself that she was not going to sleep with him, at least not that night. Given Sterling's confidence, she knew he would invite himself to come back to her place. She had prepared for the moment and told herself she would say no. As she looked in his eyes, she no longer had the same commitment to rejecting his advances.

It was like the last five months had never happened. She had the same strong feelings for him that she had when he was her boyfriend. She was ready to say yes, and she knew he would make a move. There was a pause. At first, he didn't say anything. Maybe he was waiting for her invite him over. Going back on her previous plan she couldn't imagine the date ending here in the parking lot and she was ready to make a new plan. She decided she would invite him back to her place.

Before she could get the words out of her mouth, he said, "Taylor, it was good seeing you. Thanks for agreeing to meet up." He gave her a hug, then started to turn away. Everything about the moment was so off-script that she didn't know what to do. She wanted to invite him over, but she didn't. Instead, she got in her car, and she watched him get in his car. "What in the hell just happened?" She said to herself. She watched as Sterling drove away.

Chapter 55

Sterling had every intention of sleeping with Taylor that night. The date went far better than he had expected. Taylor was charming, fun and beautiful. He was attracted to her in a way which defied any rational explanation. For the last five months he tried to convince himself that he was better off without her. He started to believe he wasn't like other people. He didn't need love. During his date with Taylor, he questioned himself, thinking maybe he was wrong about love. Maybe he needed Taylor. Away from her he could convince himself he didn't need her but being in her presence again it was like he was possessed. His brain quit functioning.

If it was just a matter of sex, he would not have hesitated to invite himself over to her place. As it was, it took all of his remaining resolve to avoid throwing himself at her and hope she would take him back. Getting in his car and driving away was the hardest thing he had ever done. And yet, he could not stop thinking about her.

There was something about Taylor he couldn't shake, and he knew he couldn't just sleep with her without suffering the consequences. She had the potential to redirect his life. She had the power to change his mind about what he thought he had become.

Arriving at his apartment, he opened the refrigerator and grabbed a beer. He plopped himself down on his couch and reached for the remote. He seldom watched TV anymore, but he needed a distraction. Turning the channel to ESPN, he hoped that catching up on the latest sports news would take his mind off Taylor.

Twenty minutes later he picked up his phone and typed out a text. "Hi Taylor! Great seeing today. Are you free tomorrow? Oh, and do you have a swimsuit?"

Chapter 56

Early the next day, Sterling rushed to stock his new kitchen with a few essentials such as beer, wine, and snacks. He didn't have a BBQ set up yet, otherwise he would have picked up a couple steaks. Instead, he stopped by the store and loaded up on sandwich fixings. Not sure if she preferred roast beef or turkey, he got both. In a sign of his enduring optimism, he made sure to have eggs and bacon on hand just in case he would have a chance to cook breakfast for Taylor. That necessitated packing a frying pan and some dishes. Thankfully he had a new table and chairs already at the house, but otherwise he was pretty lacking in the furniture department.

He threw some clothes and toiletries in a suitcase and packed some beach towels for poolside. He wasn't entirely ready to move into his new house yet, but he could at least have enough supplies on hand for an overnight. Maybe even a weekend if he was lucky. He considered asking Taylor to bring a change of clothes, but he wasn't sure how well that would go over.

Sterling picked up Taylor at her place. Sporting a light green sleeveless summer dress and sandals, she looked amazing. Her dark hair flowed freely across her shoulders. He promised to take her sightseeing. What he meant was his place, and in fairness the view from his backyard was impressive. To his surprise, she did pack a small backpack. He wasn't sure if she had a change of clothes in there, but it seemed like a bigger bag than was necessary for just a swimsuit.

Weekend traffic was light, and they made good time. Sterling was excited to spend the day with Taylor. He wondered if she would find his house to be ostentatious. She never seemed caught up in material possessions. She didn't care for him more when he purchased the G-Wagon than when he drove his Camry.

Pulling up to the driveway of his new home, Taylor was most certainly impressed. "Damn! Is this your new house? It is beautiful!" Sterling pushed the garage door remote, removing any doubt as to ownership. "Welcome to my humble abode," replied Sterling. He offered to give her a tour and she accepted his invitation.

Taylor walked through the home admiring the obviously expensive fixtures and design. She scanned the home trying to discern any signs of a feminine influence. Her best guess was that Sterling hired a female designer, but the overall result shouted Sterling. Thankfully he had good taste and the home, while tilting toward the masculine, was neutral enough not to be offensive.

He walked her through the home, including the master bedroom. Taylor again glanced around, but did not find any sign that Sterling had a woman in his life. She nodded approvingly at the home. In the five months since she had seen him, he managed to up his game. The home suited him well.

Saving the best for last, Sterling brought her outside through folding glass doors. The doors opened up to the deck. Taylor stepped out and took in the view of the bay. Her jaw dropped as her head rotated from 90 degrees left, back to center, then 90 degrees right. "Oh my God! This view is stunning!" The sun danced off the water. Sterling could not have picked a better day to showcase his new home. Looking far across the water, Taylor could see the Olympic mountains off in the distance, obscured slightly by a faint haze.

Sterling did his best to feign humility and explained that the original house was a dump, and he was able to get a good deal. He told her about all the hard work that went into fixing it up. Not that he did the work, but he paid for it.

Taking note of the pool, she took off a sandal and dipped in her foot in the water. The water was warmer than she expected, and that was no accident. Sterling fired up the heater when he came by the place earlier in the day, ensuring the water maintained a perfect 80 degrees.

Taylor said, "I need to put on my swimsuit. Where should I change?" Sterling couldn't help but picture Taylor in her swimsuit. He replied, "Go ahead and use the master bedroom." Taylor went out to the car and retrieved her backpack. She smiled as she passed Sterling on her way to the bedroom. Inside, she closed the door. She took a moment and snooped inside the master bathroom. Again, finding no trace of a woman's presence, she let herself relax enough to be bold. "Sterling, would you please help me with something?"

Sterling opened the bedroom door to find Taylor standing next to the bed, totally naked. She placed her hands behind her back and cocked her head to the side. "Did you miss me?" Taylor wondered what his reaction would be. She was still a little confused about their date the night before. She suspected he might have misread the signs last night, so she was going to make her interest as obvious as possible. Sterling did not hesitate, wrapping his arms around her body, giving her a long kiss on the lips. She couldn't help but giggle with joy as his warm body pressed against her. She reached down and pulled down his shorts. In moments Sterling was completely naked and showing his obvious interest in bedding the beautiful attorney. Taylor took it as something of a compliment that he was so quickly aroused by her.

Sterling knew when he saw Taylor naked in the bedroom, it was all over for him. There was no doubt he would take her into his bed. Accepting the changes in his life that a serious relationship with Taylor would bring failed to dominate his thoughts. He just wanted her next to him. He wanted to sleep with her. He had never experienced a complete connection with a woman the way he had with her, and when she was gone for five months, he assumed he would never feel it again. But here she was with him now.

They explored each other's bodies, each remembering the nuances and trigger points that excited the other. The passion was still there. The attraction was undeniable. The tension of getting reacquainted added to the release that eventually came when the buildup of ecstasy exceeded their ability to hold back. Mirroring orgasms flooded through their bodies in waves, quickly finding unison in their execution.

Sterling looked over at his exhausted lover. Sweat glistened on her chest. He smiled and gave her a kiss. They held hands. He never wanted to be with another woman. This was it. He had found his true love.

Chapter 57

Sterling had guessed right. Taylor managed to bring a change of clothes with her. When she packed her backpack, she wasn't sure she would be needing the extra clothes, but when Sterling asked her to stay the night, she wasn't going to say no. They had reconnected in a way she had not thought possible. There were many questions that remained about what a long-term relationship with Sterling would look like, but now she was confident that they could find a way forward.

Taylor leaned back in the lounge chair letting the sun soak into her body. She let her lawyer mind shut down and just enjoy the moment. Sterling brought her a glass of Chardonnay and gave her a kiss. She could get used to this kind of treatment. As much as she told herself that material possessions don't matter, she found it easier to be happy at a gorgeous house with a gorgeous view and a pool. She assured herself that Sterling would still be her man without all the trappings of success. She wasn't shallow enough to fall for him just because he could provide her with a comfortable lifestyle.

Taylor stayed the night and tested the limits of Sterling's stamina. He exceeded her expectations. She wasn't used to a man letting her finish, but then she wasn't used to being with a man who could last long enough for her to get there.

Sterling liked that Taylor was there to share his first night in his new house. He knew they had obstacles to work through. Eventually she would need to meet his children. He hoped they would get along. Taylor might want to have children. Was he prepared to start another family with her? There were so many questions to answer, but Sterling believed they could figure it out. He wanted to be with her.

Chapter 58

The weekend ended too soon for Sterling, and he found himself at work on Monday. Susan called Sterling and asked him to come to the gallery to chat about a couple clients. Sterling obliged and met her at noon. He brought her a sandwich and a coffee, which had become their ritual.

Like many of their other visits, they enjoyed lunch, then she handed him a couple envelopes full of cash. She let him know a couple clients would come to his office in the next day or two. They had been arrested for a drive by shooting but were currently out on bail.

The gang was doing well to lower property values in their newest rotation of neighborhoods, and the property values where they originally purchased homes were rebounding. So far, the plan was exceeding expectations. Money coming into the gallery funded the real estate fraud. Sterling worried about so much money flowing to a single offshore bank. He suggested that they open a second account in a Panamanian bank. Susan gave him approval to work out the details.

Business concluded, Susan shut the office door and moved in to give Sterling a kiss. This time he backed away. "What's wrong baby? You don't like me anymore?" Said Susan as she gave him a pouty face. Sterling explained that he was back together with his girlfriend Taylor. Susan gave him an understanding nod. "Follow your heart, but remember, she isn't like you. You have a gift." Sterling no longer thought that he wanted such a gift. He had true feelings for Taylor. He wasn't going to mess it up.

Chapter 59

The contractors completed the remaining work on Sterling's home. His kids were excited to move out of the apartment. Their patience wore thin months ago. They enjoyed playing in the pool, but it tended to focus their attention on the fact the house looked way nicer than the apartment. They each looked forward to having their own room.

Sterling rushed to furnish his new house. The furniture at his apartment would look out of place at his new upscale home. He purchased the apartment's furniture shortly after he lost his job at the prosecutor's office. His law practice was in its infancy and did not yet generate much cash. Consequently, the furniture he purchased came from big box discount stores. Sterling spent countless hours putting together the beds, chairs and tables that adorned his apartment. Little by little he managed to provide a livable space for him and his kids. His slow pace made for something of a game for the kids. Each time they began their week with their father, they would look around the apartment to see what was new. Consistently, at least one additional item of furniture would arrive, until he finally completed the apartment. His budget was much different now.

Sterling failed to identify a single piece of furniture that would properly set the tone for his swank new home. A steady stream of delivery trucks stocked the new house. Sterling paid extra for the "white glove" service in which the crew would literally wear white gloves and fully assemble his new furniture. They then packed away the boxes and even swept the floor before leaving.

The kids didn't care much about the new furniture. They didn't know that the new items cost their dad twenty times that of their old furniture. It just didn't matter to them, but it mattered to Sterling. He wanted them to benefit from his increased wealth. He donated the old furniture to charity. Selling it wasn't worth the hassle.

Sterling filed his 30-day notice with the landlord. He could afford to keep paying for the apartment but there was just no reason to keep it. He didn't bother hiring movers since there wasn't a lot that he was taking with him. A few trips in his G-Wagon were all he needed to move the clothes, dishes and miscellaneous items which made the cut.

He picked up his kids from school so that they could start their week with dad. They did not know that today was their first day in their new home. Sterling pointed the car in the direction of the North End neighborhood of Tacoma, and the kids knew something was up. It didn't take them long to figure out they weren't going to the apartment. Pulling up to the driveway he pressed the garage door opener and waited. He turned around and saw the kids in the back seat, their faces beaming with anticipation. Sterling laughed, and said, "Welcome home kids!"

They bolted out of the back seat and raced to their rooms. Having toured the home a few times, they knew which room belonged to each. Sterling made sure they each had their favorite items in their rooms. Susie loved her stuffed bears, and Patrick had a chest filled with Legos. They each had soccer gear in the closet ready for the weekend's games. Sterling loved seeing the joy on their faces. They gave him a big hug and thanked him for their new house.

Chapter 60

Taylor knew that Sterling wanted her to meet his kids. She had been dragging her feet. She knew how much Sterling adored his kids. If she met them, and they didn't like her, would he give them veto power over their relationship? She knew that meeting the kids was a necessary step if they were going to advance their relationship. She had already come to terms with the fact that if she and Sterling married, she would automatically become their stepmom. She wasn't sure what that entailed. They hadn't talked about Sterling's hopes, or expectations.

Sterling invited Taylor to join him and the kids at his place to celebrate the Fourth of July. He suggested a pool party and BBQ. It was the kind of low stress, fun environment which would lend itself to forming a bond with the kids.

Taylor wanted to make a good impression. Sterling suggested bribery. "Bring ice cream," was his suggestion.

The weather cooperated with their plans. By early-afternoon, the temperature climbed to 90 degrees. Taylor arrived and as promised and came equipped with chocolate ice cream. The kids knew that dad had a friend coming over. They didn't think much about it, and probably didn't understand that this was a romantic interest. Sterling had not previously seen fit to invite anyone to meet his kids. He knew that was a big step.

Sterling introduced Taylor to his kids, and they were all smiles, although in fairness their focus was on the ice cream. As predicted, Taylor's offering helped to ingratiate her with his kids. They quickly devoured the ice cream. Without prompting, they thanked Taylor. That kind of courtesy meant a lot to Sterling. He tried to instill in them a basic sense of manners. Taylor smiled, told them "You are welcome," then looked over at Sterling. Sterling couldn't help but give her an approving smile.

He made sure the kids washed up before getting ready for pool time. Their mouths and hands were covered in sticky chocolate. The kids questioned why they needed to wash up when they were just going to get in the pool. The pool water would rinse off the ice cream. Sterling told them that the stickiness from the chocolate would clog the pool filter, but really he just didn't them messing up his perfectly clear water.

Sterling applied liberal amounts of sunscreen on his kids, and for that matter on himself. His 80-hour work weeks didn't leave much time for soaking up the sun. Taylor somehow managed to generate a tan. Maybe it was the product of a tanning booth. Sterling didn't know if she tanned, but he knew she looked amazing in her red two-piece swimsuit.

Taylor joined Sterling and the kids in the pool. They tossed around a beach ball. The kids took turns climbing on dad's shoulders waiting for him to jump up and throw them across the pool. Susie, Sterling's daughter, seemed to instantly bond with Taylor. She liked having another girl around so that the boys wouldn't outnumber her. Sterling's son, Patrick, was a tougher nut to crack. He and his dad were very close, and he tended to jealously guard his time with his father. He still clearly remembered the year his father was away on Army duty. It was a tough year for him. But even he seemed to warm up to Taylor.

Sterling took a break to get the BBQ fired up. Taylor assisted, mostly by keeping him company at the grill. She brought him a beer to make the BBQ process flow smoothly. Like most men, Sterling associated grilling with drinking a beer. Taylor wondered if it was proper to drink in front of kids. She didn't want to be offensive. Sterling assured her it would be OK and that they are well acclimated to dad enjoying a beer.

He drew the line at getting drunk in front of the kids. One time the kids watched a movie and observed a character getting drunk and behaving foolishly. His son observed that they had never seen their father drunk and asked him why. Sterling told his kids that they are the most important people in his world, and he needs to make sure he is able to think properly in their presence. He loves them and needs everyone to be safe. They seemed satisfied with that answer. There was never a day when his kids wondered if their dad loved them.

After gobbling down their hotdogs, the kids jumped back in the pool. The kids continued to play in the pool, demonstrating the kind of superhuman energy Sterling had come to expect from them. He and Taylor ate their hotdogs at a more leisurely pace.

Sterling and Taylor retreated to chairs under the pergola. Taylor considered the event to be a success, but the frenetic energy of the kids was a bit unnerving. It was just a lot to digest, and Taylor quickly accepted Sterling's offer of a drink. He poured her a large "house pour" of Chardonnay. She cruised through half the glass in a little over five minutes.

Taylor soon decided to declare victory and head out. She said goodbye to the kids and Sterling walked her to her car in the driveway. Away from the view of his kids, he gave Taylor a long kiss and thanked her for coming over. She headed home knowing that they had hit a major milestone in their relationship. She had met the kids and survived.

Chapter 61

Sterling knew he was leading something of a double life. Maybe a quadruple life. He worked hard as corporate counsel for the Crips. His legitimate business continued to grow both in terms of clients and profit. Plus, he was a devoted father and supportive boyfriend. And yet somehow, he made time for training. The Ironman Coeur d'Alene was quickly approaching.

In the months leading up to the event, Sterling's training started with an early morning swim at the YMCA. He had considered switching his membership from the YMCA to the Tacoma Athletic Club, a private, semi-exclusive gym. The YMCA had a bigger pool, and at 0530 the pools wasn't crowded so he stuck with his Y membership.

At noon, Sterling managed to get in a run. At night, he rode his bicycle attached to an indoor resistance trainer. If anything, that was his Achilles heel. Even with a better bike, he knew he would struggle to complete the cycling event. In all, Ironman presented the ultimate challenge. A 2.1 mile swim, then a 112 mile bike ride, then he would finish with a 26.2 mile marathon. It would be his second Ironman, and he hoped to best his previous performance, which was unimpressive when measured against the best competitors, but yet a feat which only small number of people ever accomplish.

Taylor accepted Sterling's invitation to join him for Ironman. She was not going to compete but she was happy to be his cheerleader. It would have been faster to fly, but the logistics of packing Sterling's bike and his gear gave the advantage to driving six hours each way. Taylor could feel Sterling's excitement and she wanted to support him. She stopped by the craft store and constructed a picket sign, which she covered in aluminum foil and decorated with colorful glitter stuck to glue. The sign read, "Go Ironman! I love you!" Hearts and stars completed the border.

Sterling set them up in a nice hotel. The Coeur d'Alene Resort boasted a great location just steps away from the starting line of the swim event. Their hotel room on the eighth-floor showcased glass windows from ceiling to floor. The elevated bed allowed for a view of the water and marina below while lounging under the covers. Taylor found herself transfixed by the view of the steep mountains surrounding the massive lake. She had never been to Austria but found the landscape to be reminiscent of scenes from "The Sound of Music."

The next morning, approaching the 6:00 am start time, Sterling made his way through the sandy beach to the water line. His black wetsuit and yellow swim cap made him impossible to differentiate himself from the other competitors, but Taylor cheered anyway.

The water was exceptionally cold this year, owing to late spring runoff from the mountain snow. The organizers authorized headcaps and booties to protect the swimmers, but Sterling had neither of those items so committed himself to powering through. He found the wetsuit provided him with so much warmth that he was relieved when it was time to hit the cold water.

Sterling mentally pictured the swim. He was going to approach this even differently than last time. The previous year, Sterling was too polite during the swim. He followed the generally recognized courtesy of letting swimmers pass him if they tapped his feet. This was considered good form when lap swimming in a pool, but given the mass start entering the lake, it simply ensured that he got passed by slower swimmers. This time Sterling was prepared to hold his own when all 1200 swimmers hit the water at the same time. He would push hard early and only yield to swimmers capable of passing him. Even so, he was prepared for the elbows smacking his head, and feet kicking his side.

Sterling's strategy paid off. His early burst of energy left him with a mostly clear path as he completed the first mile. He held his ground for the second mile and finished in the top 25% of swimmers, well ahead of most of the field. Unfortunately, Sterling knew his best event was the swim, so the rest of the competition would see him lose position at a steady clip.

Sterling's new bike didn't make him much faster than his old bike. He wanted to blame the Dura-Ace components for their lack of a granny gear for the hills, but Sterling knew he just wasn't an amazing cyclist. Half-way through the 112-mile bike event, Sterling's legs were screaming in protest. Only the sight of Taylor alongside the route waiving her sign at him saved him from hailing the rescue truck and accepting a "DNF" or

"Did not finish." She blew him a kiss. He smiled and waved.

By the end of the cycling event his legs were shot but he still had a marathon to complete. He pushed forward and did his best, but he wasn't able to maintain a run for the whole 26.2 miles. He managed to run most of the marathon but allowed himself to walk uphill saving some energy. This strategy helped him rest slightly different muscles in his legs.

Ironman started at 6:00 am and the competitors had to meet cut-off limits for each event. Sterling easily made the cut-offs, and it became clear that he would complete Ironman well ahead of the 17 hour limit, and well ahead of his previous time. Nearing the finish, Taylor again cheered him on waiving her sign and shouting encouragement.

Crossing the finish line in 10 hours, 40 minutes, Sterling marked a major improvement from his previous time. No one would confuse him for an elite athlete, but he was reasonably proud of his accomplishment. Sterling waiting for his turn on the stage to collect his medal and get a photo. His hat and shirt each were streaked by lines of salty white waves caused by the constant process of sweat soaking him then drying, but he had a smile on his face.

Taylor helped him grab his gear and they retreated to the hotel room where she gave him one last test of his endurance for the day.

Chapter 62

As the summer drew to a close, Taylor joined Sterling poolside for what seemed like it might be one of the last good pool days of the year. By this time, Taylor had become a frequent houseguest during the weeks when Sterling's kids were with their mom. A couple times she even stayed a night while the kids were there.

Taylor advanced her footprint at Sterling's house from maintaining just a toothbrush in his bathroom, to claiming two drawers in bedroom dresser, and even some closet space. Sterling's home was beginning to feel a lot more like "their" home.

She enjoyed their growing bond. Their relationship grew closer, and they had managed to overcome significant challenges to find themselves where they were. They had even talked about marriage. She liked the idea of marrying the man she loved, but they had yet to address an important issue. Taylor needed Sterling to weigh in on the issue of kids. She understood that she would become a stepmom if she married Sterling, and that was fine. She liked his kids. But she also needed something. She came to realize there was a very real possibility that she would want a child. She could feel the pull of her biological clock telling her she needed to be a mom. She wanted to have a child with Sterling.

Taylor knew that Sterling was in a different place in his life. He already had kids. She wasn't 100% sure she wanted to have kids, but she could feel herself moving in that direction. She needed to know that it would at least be something Sterling would consider in an open and honest way. She knew he had a vasectomy after the birth of his daughter. That made it convenient for Taylor in terms of birth control, and she liked that, but it might also signal that Sterling had made a final decision from which he would not turn back. She needed to feel like she had some control over their future, and this could be a deal breaker. She would rather know now than get married to him and find out later that he would not let her experience giving birth to their child.

Sterling knew something was up with her before she uttered a word. Normally they would be outside brushing up against each other, admiring the view of the bay, or looking longingly into each other's eyes. "What's wrong lover?" asked a concerned Sterling.

Taylor expressed her concerns and told him that she might want to have children. She would like him to be the father, but she really needed to know if that was off the table. She didn't present her concerns as an ultimatum, but Sterling was pretty sure she would need to rethink their future if he gave the wrong answer. He turned his head and locked eyes with her. He could see sadness coming forth. He said, "Taylor, I have two kids. I got a vasectomy knowing that I didn't want more kids." Taylor's sadness deepened, and she said, "So that's it then. You are done." Again, Sterling looked deeply into her eyes and said, "When I got a vasectomy, I knew I would never find someone who I loved so much that I would want to have another child with. I was wrong. I didn't know I would ever find someone like you. I love you. You will be a great mother. If that is something that is important to you, then it is important to me."

Taylor's eye released a tear, and it went streaking down her cheek. Sterling took his thumb and wiped it away. He gave her a big kiss. She had never loved anyone as much as she loved Sterling at that moment.

Chapter 63

Susan Maddox called Sterling on his cell phone. She didn't want to go through his receptionist. She feared her name would end up on a call log kept by the front desk. She had little to fear. Sterling was on his third receptionist from the temp agency. This one was by far the laziest to occupy a chair in his office. She could barely be inconvenienced enough to do the bare minimum, much less take the initiative to keep a call log.

Sterling didn't mind Mrs. Maddox calling him directly. For what she was paying him he was willing to be her 24/7 on-call lawyer. "Sterling, something is up. We need to talk. Can I come over?" It was nearing noon, and his receptionist usually left the office for a long lunch break. It was the perfect time. "Come on over. I'll see you soon." Sterling didn't like to talk on the phone, and he sure wasn't going to use her name on an open line just in case someone had tapped his phone.

Like clockwork, Mrs. Maddox arrived at his suite just after the receptionist had gone. Sterling opened the outer door and escorted her to his office. He invited her to have a seat. He had never seen her this nervous. She was visibly shaking.

She explained the situation. Their banker in the Bahamas, Felix, gave Susan a call. Felix said an agent from Homeland Security had questions about a bank account Sterling set up. Sterling was now grateful that

Susan handled the money. Felix reported that the US Agents wanted the bank to share their records with the agent. Felix refused the request, unless of course the agents had a search warrant issued by a Bahamian judge. The agents asked for a more informal level of cooperation and Felix declined.

Sterling was familiar with Felix. It was Sterling who opened the account in the Bahamas and made sure to pay Felix an extra allowance for "premium service." Apparently premium service pays for a phone call when US agents ask uncomfortable questions. "Sterling, you gotta fix this!" said a panicked Susan Maddox.

Sterling thought for a moment then gave her his analysis. "First let's close that account. It doesn't have much money in it at any given time. It is more of a pass-through account used to funnel money to the real estate investment trust. The origin of the account is well hidden behind levels of fake trusts. I will make sure the trust reports the deposit as a bookkeeping error then I will burn the trail by closing out the underlying LLC. Let's re-route the proceeds from the gallery to the new account in Panama."

Susan Maddox gave a loud sigh and smiled at her lawyer, "Sterling, you are a goddamn criminal mastermind! We are lucky to have you on our side." Sterling replied, "Happy to be of service Mrs. Maddox." Susan grinned slyly and said, "Speaking of service, I have been lonely since you got back together with your girlfriend. How about a little kiss to get me through tough times?" Sterling laughed and pretended that she was joking. He was in love with Taylor, and at least that part of his life needed to remain legitimate.

Chapter 64

Less than a week later, Susan Maddox called Sterling again. She was having a problem with Felix, the banker in the Bahamas. Felix was having a meltdown. The agents from Homeland Security again contacted Felix asking for details about the account, which by now had been closed out and rerouted. The agent still didn't have a warrant and Susan was tired of reminding him that the Bahamas is an independent nation not under the jurisdiction of America.

Mrs. Maddox lacked the reach to simply have the banker killed, so she asked Sterling to take care of the matter through legal means. By legal, she meant Sterling should bribe the banker rather than kill him. She offered to pay his travel costs, and even suggested that he could take his girlfriend. There was one catch: Buster would be joining them. Susan Maddox trusted Sterling more than any other lawyer, but that wasn't saying much. She wanted Buster to keep an eye on things, and if necessary, he could be the muscle.

From Sterling's point of view, he would get to take a vacation to the Bahamas with his girlfriend at his client's expense. Handing Felix an envelope full of cash to ease his nerves couldn't take more than a few minutes. The rest of the time he would have his feet up on a lounge chair admiring Taylor's tight ass as she strutted in the water wearing a string bikini. He still had not figured out what he would say about Buster, but that could wait.

Sterling told Taylor that he needed to fly to the Bahamas to resolve a paperwork snafu for a client. He invited her to come with him. She jumped at the chance to get out of town with Sterling for a couple days. She had never been to the Bahamas, and she wanted to scope out potential honeymoon locations, in the event Sterling asked her to marry him. She knew she wanted to marry him and given their closeness it seemed inevitable at this point.

Leaving Sterling's house together, they drove to the airport the next morning. They checked in at the United Airlines desk and made their way to the gate. Sterling didn't see Buster, but figured he was running out of time to tell Taylor that he would be joining them on their trip. Trying not to convey any sense of concern, he casually dropped the news that Buster would be joining them to assist with paperwork. Taylor didn't seem too worried about the inclusion of Sterling's business associate, although she wondered why he didn't mention it earlier.

Minutes later Buster arrived and approached Sterling. The men shook hands and Sterling introduced him to Taylor. Buster created an almost convincing facsimile of a businessman heading out of town on vacation. His floral Tommy Bahama shirt and khaki shorts would be perfect attire for his arrival in Nassau but made him stand out on a dreary day in the Seattle area.

The flight had a layover at Chicago O'Hare. Taylor thought about her family and her childhood in the suburbs of Chicago. She missed her dad, who lost his life at the hands of a fleeing criminal. She wished they had time for her to see her mom, and to introduce her to Sterling. Rushing to catch the connecting flight to Miami, they barely had time to stop at the restrooms.

On the plane to Miami, Taylor found herself wedged between Buster and Sterling. It turned out to be a fun flight. Buster and Taylor hit it off. She enjoyed his stories of growing up poor and working his way up in the art world. Buster fabricated many of the details, including his claim to have painted many of the originals hanging up at the Pacific Arts Limited gallery. Taylor accepted his lies as truth, assuming that Sterling would not let her get taken in by a conman. Buster sold the lie so well that if Sterling didn't know any better, he would have believed it too.

After a long day of travel, they arrived at the Lynden Pinding International Airport in Nassau. The trio exited the aircraft and were immediately hit with a blast of moist humid air. Navigating through a light rain, they took cover inside the airport and called for a cab to the hotel.

The hotel, the Royal Davenport on Soppadilla Boulevard looked like an old plantation home. The white pillars in front supported flags depicting the national flag of the Bahamas, as well as a flag bearing the hotel's royal crest. Noting that the weather was due to clear soon, Sterling prioritized taking care of business so he could spend time with Taylor. They checked into their room and Sterling politely excused himself. He met Buster in the lobby.

Sterling's plan was to meet Felix down the street at a local bar. He proposed taking the meeting himself, but Buster insisted on coming along. Mrs. Maddox was very clear that Buster needed to be the Crips' eyes and ears for all business meetings. Sterling wondered why he was even there at all since Buster could have just as easily handed over an envelope.

Sterling called Felix on his cell phone. Sterling asked the banker to meet him at the Bearded Clam Bar down the street. The banker excused himself from the bank, explaining that he needed a smoke break and would be back shortly. Sterling ordered three Bush Crack beers, hoping to convey to the banker that this was a friendly meeting.

The banker arrived minutes later and took a seat across from Sterling at the small table in the back. Felix looked like every guilty client Sterling had ever known, with the exception of his gang clients. Those guys knew how to keep their cool. In contrast, the banker completely lacked composure. His face convulsed with a nervous tik, and his eyes darted around the room seeming to find invisible agents packing the small bar.

Sterling handed him one of the three beers on the table, and the banker downed it in one long chug. "Hi Felix, I'm Sterling. We spoke on the phone months ago when I set up the account," said Sterling. The men shook hands and Sterling introduced Buster. Felix had trouble looking Buster in the eye and offered a simple "hello" spoken in almost a whisper.

Sterling tried to address the banker's concerns about the US agents, but he didn't make much progress. Felix continued to prattle on about agents and the threats they made if he didn't cooperate. The agents threatened a long prison sentence if Felix made them go through all of the trouble of getting a warrant instead of just cooperating like a gentleman. The agents said it makes Felix look guilty if he tries to hide behind Bahamian banking privacy laws. Sterling assured him that the agents were just trying to intimidate him. If they had a real case, they would get a warrant in a Bahamian court. These were all problems that Sterling thought they had already covered.

Sterling gave the man his business card and offered to represent the banker in any legal proceeding. "Just make sure to tell them that you have an attorney, and your attorney will do the talking. Any questions about that?" Felix offered a nervous, "No, I will tell them." Felix gave Buster a quick look. Buster nodded, as if to assure Felix that he was doing the right thing. Sterling then handed the man an envelope full of cash and explained that money was just a way to say thank you for the courtesy of a call regarding the agents. Sterling told Felix that everything was going be alright, unintentionally quoting Bob Marley. Felix left quickly, mumbling something about needing to get back to the bank.

Buster barely waited for the banker to reach the exit when he looked at Sterling and said, "Do you believe that asshole can keep his mouth shut?" Sterling replied, "I really don't know. Thankfully we have about five layers of protection between us and that dipshit. Hell, even the NSA couldn't crack the shell companies and false accounts that I set up to keep us out of trouble." Buster's nod retained a sense of doubt, not in Sterling, but in the banker.

Business having been concluded Sterling figured he had the rest of the day to hit the beach with his beautiful girlfriend. He rose from the table and excused himself. Buster stayed at the bar. Walking back to the hotel, Sterling spotted a jewelry store. He crossed the street, stopping for a moment, taking an opportunity to window shop.

A couple of diamond engagement rings sparkled in the sun, catching Sterling's attention, prompting him to daydream about proposing to Taylor. For a moment, he considered buying the nicer of the two rings on display and popping the question before they left the Bahamas. But he wanted to pick a time and place which were in no way connected with the Crips. For his peace of mind, he wanted the moment to be completely untarnished. The purity of his love for Taylor deserved the perfect venue. He would wait until a better time and place, but he knew he and Taylor were heading in the direction of marriage.

Chapter 65

Sterling didn't see Buster the rest of their stay in the Bahamas, and that was fine. He and Taylor directed their attention to making the most of their short vacation in the Caribbean. Taylor asked Sterling about his business meeting, observing that it didn't take him long to finish. Sterling gave her a vague answer about thinking the situation was under control.

For the rest of the day, Taylor and Sterling focused on enjoying Nassau. They lounged in the hotel pool and they hit the beach. Sterling marveled at how Taylor seemed to maintain a tan. In contrast, Sterling applied liberal amounts of sunscreen to his white body. Taylor teased him, joking that her new nickname for him is Casper. Sterling took her comments in stride, knowing that she was just having fun with him.

Sterling watched as Taylor set down her bottle of water and raced for the beach. She waived her arm trying to get him to follow. Unable to resist, he joined her in the warm water. Sterling wrapped his arms around her and lifted her up, lowering her slowly as her lips locked with his lips. Taylor's energy lifted his spirit. She had a way of making him forget about all of the stress he carried with him. She disarmed his doubts about relationships. He looked forward to their future together.

Late in the afternoon, they abandoned the water and walked around town. Sterling made sure to walk by the jewelry store. Pausing to look through the window, Sterling asked Taylor if she saw anything she liked. She liked one of the rings but preferred a princess cut rather than the round cut diamond. Sterling made a mental note.

After dinner, they grabbed a couple drinks from the hotel bar and took seats in the restaurant. Sunset was coming soon. They took seats at a table with a view of the water and enjoyed an amazing seafood dinner. It had been a good weekend. A lot of travel for a short vacation, but neither of them could complain about getting away for a couple days of sun and surf.

Walking back to the hotel room Sterling placed an arm behind Taylors back. He turned to look at her. He found himself caught up in her beauty. He knew he always wanted her by his side. She turned and caught him looking at her. She smiled, seeming to read his thoughts. Sterling said, "Taylor Jane, I love you!"

Taylor had been waiting to hear that from him. They had danced around their feelings, running out of words which properly conveyed their mutual affection. Sterling once told her that he has feelings for her. She told him that she enjoys their closeness. Neither of them wanted to be the first to say, "I love you." It is a big step. Although it was obvious that they were in love, they hadn't crossed the threshold of saying it. Sterling could no longer hold out. He felt like his heart was going to over-fill if he didn't let his words act as an escape valve. He hoped he hadn't made a mistake. Taylor held his gaze, and responded, "Preston Sterling,

I love you too!" Looking out into the sea, the sun made its last showing before disappearing into the waves.

The next day, the lovebirds were ready to return home after the weekend in the Bahamas. Arriving at the airport in Nassau, the couple boarded the plane. Buster was nowhere in sight. Sterling figured that Buster must be enjoying himself so much that he decided to stay another couple of days. Sterling didn't mind having Taylor to himself without Buster as a third wheel.

The plane touched down in Miami, and the couple made their way through customs. Taylor scanned her passport through the machine. The agent looked up, confirming that her face matched the photo, and waived her through. Sterling did the same, however, when his passport scanned through the side, the machine registered an audible alert and the light flashed red. The agent looked at the message on the computer screen. Sterling started to scan his passport again when the customs agent said, "Sir, you need to wait a moment. Someone will come to assist you." Taylor looked behind her to see two men grabbing Sterling's arms. Sterling shouted to her, "Don't miss your plane. I will catch up with you later."

The men maintained a tight grip on Sterling's arms until they reached a room halfway down the hallway. One man pulled a keychain from his belt and unlocked the door. "Have a seat. Someone will be with you in a moment," said the taller of the two agents. They shut the door and Sterling heard the key turning as bolts secured the metal door. He was locked in the room. Sterling had a seat at a small table. A tubular metal bar stretched the length of the table. It was clearly used to secure handcuffed suspects to the table. Thankfully Sterling was not in handcuffs, but this was no doubt an interrogation room and he was not free to leave.

Thirty minutes later a slightly balding middle-aged man in a gray suit opened the door. "Greetings Mr. Sterling. I am Agent Trout with the FBI Miami office." Sterling couldn't help but be impressed that the FBI figured out his money laundering scheme so quickly, yet he offered a simple, "How can I help you Agent Trout?"

The FBI man explained that this was a courtesy interview on behalf of the Bahamian Police Department. "Do you know Felix Mercado?" Sterling didn't actually know Felix's last name, but assumed they were talking about the banker. Felix was so cautious and secretive that he didn't share his full name. Sterling replied, "I might have met him. I met a man named Felix. Not sure of his last name." At this point evasion seemed like a bad idea so he might as well answer questions until he got an understanding of what they wanted.

The agent asked a dozen questions about Sterling's business in the Bahamas and his whereabouts last night. It seemed like an odd line of questioning. They didn't seem to have any questions about the shell companies or account irregularities. Sterling explained where he was the night before and they asked if anyone could verify his whereabouts. Sterling provided Taylor's name and also suggested they could check the security cameras at the hotel. He and Taylor mostly hung out near the hotel pool except when they were in their room.

The agent wrote notes on a legal pad. He said he would get the information to the Bahamian police so that they could verify his alibi. Finally, Sterling said, "Alibi for what?" Trying to take measure of Sterling, the FBI agent said, "We found your business card in the pocket of the late Felix Mercado. It seems you were one of the last people to see him alive." Sterling's face went white, despite his efforts to maintain his composure. Sterling managed to say, "I didn't kill him. I am his lawyer." For most lawyers these statements would be mutually exclusive although Sterling wasn't beyond making an exception.

The agent explained that Sterling was not free to leave, and that they would have someone check on his alibi. Sterling knew he hadn't killed Felix. Susan sent him to bribe the banker, not to kill him. It didn't take Sterling long to realize that Buster's conspicuous absence from the flight must be linked to the banker's death. Buster had been skeptical of Felix's willingness to keep his mouth shut, and apparently sought a more foolproof method of securing the banker's silence. Sterling wouldn't shed any tears over the loss of Felix, but he didn't want to get wrapped up in some kind of murder investigation.

Sterling could only imagine what Taylor must be going through. She watched him get dragged off by two customs agents. He tried to send Taylor a message, but the phone didn't seem to catch a signal inside the metal box that was his interrogation room. He assumed that was by design. Anyone stuck in this room effectively disappeared from the grid. Alone with his thoughts, his mind wandered. He had to ask himself if working for the gang was worth the legal hassle. He loved the money they were paying him, but he didn't want to go to jail.

Two hours later the door opened. Agent Trout directed Sterling to complete a form listing his address and phone number. "Your alibi checks out. We will be in contact with you if we need any additional information."

Sterling again attempted to pass through customs, and this time he did not have a problem. He had missed his flight but at least he was not under arrest. He checked his phone and a frantic Taylor Jane had sent him a dozen text messages and left three voice mails. He tried to call her back, but she did not answer. She was probably in the air heading home. Sterling changed his flight plans and found a flight home scheduled for the next day.

When Taylor's flight landed in Chicago, she gave him a call. This time Sterling was able to pick up. He explained that the client he had visited in the Bahamas ended up dead. The dead man had Sterling's business card in his pocket when he died. The police asked him questions then let him go. Taylor had a lot of questions, and Sterling promised to discuss it with her when he got home. It occurred to him that he had the keys to the G-Wagon in his carry-on bag. She said she would catch a cab back to his place.

Sterling arrived home the next day. Taylor gave him a hug when he walked through the door. She had ditched work because she was so worried about him and just needed to see him get home safely. He was happy to see her. The thing he feared most about getting arrested for some bank fraud charge was the prospect of not getting to see her.

Although Taylor was happy to see him, she still had some questions. She was not stupid, and like Sterling, she noticed that Buster did not travel back with them. Taylor asked, "Did Buster kill the banker guy?" Sterling paused too long. Finally, he said, "Not that I know of." Taylor burst out, "What kind of fucked up answer is that? You don't know? That means you are also not sure if he did it or not, right?" Sterling didn't respond.

Taylor had emotional whiplash having gone so quickly from total bliss to feeling like she didn't even know this man. What kind of business was Sterling handling in the Bahamas? Who takes a trip to the Bahamas just to spend half an hour fixing a paperwork problem. Suddenly all she thought she knew about this man was in doubt.

"What are you into Sterling? What kind of work do you when you are not defending people?" Sterling started to talk about his duty to maintain confidentiality. Taylor grabbed her purse and car keys, ready to speed away from his house. "Wait Taylor. Fine if you want to know, I will tell you," said a desperate Sterling. He then asked, "OK, how much do you want to know?" Taylor replied, "I need you to tell me everything."

Sterling knew this could take a while and would be hard for Taylor to process. He invited Taylor to have a seat on the couch, and she agreed. Sterling told her everything. Meaning everything except how he murdered his own client and about how he and Susan Maddox had frequent liaisons before he and Taylor were back together. But to his credit he did tell her about his work setting up the money laundering operation, about his tax evasion and about how his business thrives on envelopes full of cash from the Crips.

After his mostly full disclosure he lowered his head apologetically and asked seriously, "Is that too much? I love you but I can understand how knowing the truth could force you to leave me." For a moment, Taylor considered leaving, but there was something disarming about how he placed enough trust in her to tell him the worst things about himself. What he had done was terrible, but he was willing to let her make a decision about their future knowing what he had done.

She said, "You are right, that is a lot to deal with and if you were anyone else, I would walk away. But I love you. And I want to be with you." Sterling nodded his head in agreement. Taylor continued, "But, I don't want to worry that you are going to prison or that you will end up dead. I can't worry that our child will be at risk because of who you represent. I will stay with you, but only if you end your association with the Crips. I mean 100% done. Are you willing to do that? Can you go legit and just rely on the legal part of your law practice to make an honest living?"

If it was anyone but Taylor, the answer would be no. He had grown accustomed to the perks of living better on more. He had convinced himself that he was better off alone, that is until Taylor came back into his life. Sterling didn't need time to ponder his options. He said, "Taylor, I love you. I want to keep you. I am done. I will let them know tomorrow if that is OK." Taylor, relieved that he agreed to her demand replied, "Thank you Sterling. I love you. Yes, tomorrow is fine." She gave him a big hug.

For Sterling, it just felt like the right decision. He couldn't picture his life without Taylor. He had grown to love her like no one else. He saw them having a life together. He saw them growing old together. He even thought they might start a family together. This is what he wanted. He would go legit if that is what she needed from him.

Chapter 66

The next day, Sterling set up a meeting with Susan Maddox at the gallery. He updated her on the trip to the Bahamas, but she seemed to already know the situation. Sterling assumed that meant Buster somehow made his way back to the United States.

Wasting no time, he dropped the bomb and told Susan, "I am out. Thank you for all you have done for me. I am no longer available to provide your organization with legal services." Susan replied, "Oh look sugar, we can do a better job of shielding you from anything messy. You are a gifted lawyer, and we value your services. We need you to stay on until Tricky gets out of prison, then you can go. How about that?" Sterling held his ground. "I am out. Going to get out while I can. I love Taylor, and I need to do what is right for her, and maybe even for our family if we get to have a child together. Good luck Susan."

Sterling opened the door and walked out of her office. Mrs. Maddox didn't yell at him. She didn't threaten him. She just watched as he walked away. It was over.

Bottom-line is that no matter how much money he lost by dropping the gang as a client, he had to cut ties with the Crips. He could not risk losing the love of his life. He didn't ask Taylor to change her mind and let him keep working for the Crips. He knew she would leave him if he crossed that line.

Sterling was in no danger of going broke. His house was paid off and so was his dream car. He socked away a lot of money while working for the Crips. He knew he was going to spend a chunk of that money on a ring for Taylor. She stuck with him, and he wanted to propose before she changed her mind. The only question left to resolve was timing. It wouldn't be long. He was sure of that.

Sterling focused on building his legitimate business. He made good money even when he only devoted half of his attention to that side of the business, and now he would be able to double that income. Even so, the income he lost from representing the Crips would be impossible to replace with hard work alone.

Chapter 67

When the Army granted Taylor's request to be stationed at Ft. Lewis, she was under the impression that she would serve a three-year rotation. That was pretty standard. She was about halfway through that three-year tour, and her next duty station was not even on her mind. To the extent she thought about the future, she thought of Sterling. He had come so far since his days of overt narcissism and profound arrogance. She had asked a lot of him. Sometimes she asked him to change to suit her needs. Some issues were simply non-negotiable for her, like making him give up the illicit side of his law practice and agreeing to have a child with her. Sometimes she would ask him to change just to test his resolve. He never failed to rise to the occasion and give her what she wanted.

Sterling knew he had changed his life significantly to be with her, even going so far as to plan a reversal of his vasectomy so that they could have a child together. He gave up his lucrative, but dangerous, business because she asked him to. He never failed to do what it took to please her. But what he got out of it was far more important to him. He got Taylor.

Staring at her transfer orders, she was in shock. The Army was transferring her to S. Korea. It was going to be a one-year PCS (Permanent Change of Station). How would Sterling react? Would he wait for her? She couldn't even say where her next duty station would be after she got back from Korea.

She scheduled an emergency meeting with S1 (personnel) to discuss her options. She updated a stack of Army forms while she was there and waited patiently for a chance to plead her case. She wanted to stay at Ft. Lewis. Her concerns were elevated up the chain of command, until she was able to secure an audience with G1. The officer in charge of JAG assignments explained that they were plugging holes and filling positions of highest priority, and right now that meant a year in Korea. There was no way around it, unless of course she resigned her commission. She would then receive a bill from the government demanding that she repay a large portion of her incentive pay she received when she became an officer. She lacked the money to pay the ransom.

Taylor could barely make it through her duties that day. Time slowed to a standstill. She left early and drove to Sterling's house in a daze. Sterling wouldn't be home for three hours, maybe more. He was working hard trying grow the legitimate side of his practice. She was pleased that he made that change but now it didn't seem to matter. Soon she would be heading overseas.

She poured herself a drink. Not the Chardonnay which was her go to drink. She needed something stronger. She pulled a bottle of Stoli out of the freezer. Filling the glass up about three fingers, she downed the glass of vodka in large gulps. The combination of freeze and burn coated her throat. She poured herself another, but this time took a seat in Sterling's leather recliner and sipped her vodka slowly. Her anxiety level neared panic level. Hopefully the alcohol would kick in soon.

Three hours later, Sterling came through the door. He found Taylor leaning back in the recliner. She didn't get up when he walked into the living room. Looking at her puffy face, he could tell she had been crying. She grabbed paperwork off the side table and held it in the air for Sterling to see. Sterling approached and reviewed her transfer orders. He was familiar with PCS orders and noted that the Army was sending her to Korea for a year. The news was nearly as devastating for him as it was for Taylor. They were on the verge of getting married and starting a life together.

Sterling asked, "What are your options?" She explained she didn't have any. She already chased the issue up the chain of command as far as she could. "Would you consider resigning?" asked Sterling. She explained that she couldn't because she owed too much money to the Army. "How much?" asked Sterling. "Ballpark, about $40,000," said Taylor.

Taylor could hear Sterling walking a few steps. She turned her head in his direction and saw him open the kitchen drawer near the coffee machine. He retrieved his checkbook and wrote a check payable to the US Army, in the amount of $40,000. He handed her the check. "Problem solved," said Sterling, giving her a smile. Taylor frowned and said, "I am not a charity case. Besides, I don't even have a job here. I can't just quit my job."

Sterling asked Taylor to put on a coat and take a drive with him. "I really don't think a drive in your fancy car is going to fix this," said Taylor. "Humor me," replied Sterling. They loaded up in his fancy car and headed downtown, eventually pulling into the parking garage of the Wells Fargo building. "Follow me please," said Sterling. Taylor wasn't in a mood for games but got out of the car and followed him.

They made their way to the 6th floor. He pulled out his key and opened the outer door leading to his law office. He walked Taylor over to his spare office and invited her to sit in the chair in front of the glass desk. He said, "You are not a charity case, so how about a $40,000 signing bonus with the firm?" Taylor said, "Sterling that is super nice of you. I love you but I don't want to work for you." Sterling replied, "I am not offering you a job. I am asking you to be a full partner. It will be our office."

The look on Taylor's face was priceless. Sterling presented her with an option that solved all of her problems. Even better, he did so in a way which made Taylor feel valuable and appreciated. He didn't do it out of pity. He treated her like a first round draft pick and even paid her a signing bonus. He convincingly laid out how they could build the dominant military defense firm in America.

Taylor had strengths that he lacked. Her empathy and kindness could fill gaps in Sterling's case selection. He generally turned down clients who he thought would demand more compassion than he could convey. Plus, unlike Sterling, Taylor could handle matters which required overnight travel. Sterling was pretty much chained to the Seattle-Tacoma area during weeks with his kids. He was still not on sufficiently good terms with his ex-wife to count on her to take care of the kids if he was away. With Taylor on board, Sterling was sure they could more than double the firm's current caseload, leading to greater efficiencies and higher paying clients.

Sterling's offer wasn't based solely on Taylor's value to his law office. An equally important consideration was his fear of losing her. He assumed they could weather the storm of a one-year separation while she completed her duty in Korea, but he had seen many examples of couples who didn't survive being apart. Time, distance, distraction, and loneliness conspire to tear people apart. Sterling was going to make sure that Taylor would be around for their wedding.

Taylor reached out her hand so they could shake hands on the deal. With Sterling clasping her hand, Taylor said, "I accept your offer, partner. Now, let's discuss who gets the big office with the wood desk and who gets the small office with the glass desk." She smiled, sure that Sterling knew she was joking. He offered her a full partnership in his law firm and paid her a $40,000 bonus so she could afford to resign from the Army. She wasn't going to press her luck.

Chapter 68

The next day, CPT Taylor Jane reported to work and advised the Army that she would not be going to Korea. She submitted her resignation packet. Quitting the Army is more complicated than serving the boss with a two-week notice. It would take some time to process her resignation. The Army estimated she would receive a discharge in about six weeks, maybe more, but at least she would not be heading overseas. She had enjoyed her time with the JAG corps. With a few notable exceptions, she loved the experience. Now the prospect of leaving the Army to work with the love of her life had her on cloud nine.

CPT Jane's colleagues weren't surprised by her decision to join Sterling's firm. As part of casual conversation, she had shared with her friends the status of her relationship with Sterling. He even joined her for some family events on post. Most of her friends were supportive of her decision, but Sterling maintained an unflinching group of detractors. He rubbed some people the wrong way. Some expressed their concern to Taylor. She knew Sterling had faults, but those were largely under control. Setting aside their misgivings, her friends planned a going away party for her.

Sterling also had plans he needed to set in motion. He called Susan and asked if they could rent the art gallery for their wedding. Susan could not have been more gracious and offered to let them have the wedding at the gallery at no charge. She asked to review some details with Sterling at her office and he agreed.

Sterling greeted Susan at the gallery, and they sat down in the office. Susan asked Sterling about the recent changes in his life. Sterling admitted that he was surprised that he had fallen in love so hard. But it felt right. He knew that Taylor was the one. Susan waived her hand over her face as if to cool herself from the heat of Sterling's passion. Sterling himself was shocked as he ran down the list of all the ways he had changed his views because of the love of a good woman. Susan took in the sight of a changed man. She wondered to herself if Tricky ever felt that way about her. He surely didn't feel that way about her now.

Susan gave Sterling the option of a couple dates about six months out. Taylor might decide she wanted more time to plan a proper wedding and if so, he could make changes, but at least for now he had something planned. He made note of the dates, hoping that Taylor would accept his wedding proposal and they could set a firm date. He didn't yet have a ring for her, but after she agreed to join his firm, which would soon be their firm, he knew he would propose very soon. They would be partners in love and in business.

Chapter 69

Having agreed to turn down the type of business which brought illegal money into the firm, Sterling needed an alternative source of income from legitimate clients. Gang money made him comfortably well off financially but that was now behind him. He hadn't been accepting sex offender clients recently because he found gang clients less morally objectionable than perverts. But he made a commitment to Taylor, and he wasn't going to violate his agreement. Gang clients were bad, but sex offenders were good. What kind of fucked up world was he living in?

Shortly after resigning as corporate counsel for the Crips, an accused sex offender sought Sterling's services. This wasn't a good time to be picky about his client selection. Sterling needed the money and accepted the case.

Stone Turner was accused of raping his eight-year-old stepdaughter. Sterling agreed to represent him in exchange for a hefty fee. If convicted, Mr. Turner would go to prison for the rest of his life and lose his job as a senior bus driver with the Pierce County Transit District. Mr. Turner maintained his innocence. Sterling pushed the man, advising that if he admitted his guilt, he could be eligible for a sentencing alternative which focused on treatment instead of prison, but his client steadfastly denied violating his stepdaughter.

Sterling wasn't easily offended. He represented criminals for a living. But sex offenders were a different bread. It was a sickness that couldn't be treated. The only effective deterrence short of incarceration was old age. Statistically sex offenders became less of a threat to society if they were 60 or over. Not coincidentally that was the age in which men in general observed a noticeable decline in sexual activity. Unfortunately, his client was about 20 years away from reducing his risk of recidivism. He was almost certain to keep violating his stepdaughter unless he was stopped.

The case had previously been handled by the public defender's office. His client assumed, like many criminals, that the public defender's office lacked the skill to defend him. In reality most public defenders are as good as private attorneys. Sometimes they are better. They get the benefit of repetition. Private attorneys could devote more hours to their client's case, but public defenders knew their way around the courtroom. Sterling was the complete package, having both experience and the willingness to devote countless hours to his client's case.

By the time Mr. Turner decided to hire Sterling, trial was right around the corner. The judge was unwilling to grant another delay and forced Sterling to commit to a trial date one month away. It was a tight schedule, but Sterling could do it. His level of experience gave him the tools to quickly understand the allegations and to formulate a defense.

The more Sterling researched the case, the more it became obvious that his client was guilty. Sterling participated in a victim interview. Sterling hated these interviews. The last thing he wanted to do was to force a young victim to recount the worst day in her life. But Sterling did it. It was his job. The child victim, Renee, told Sterling about how her stepfather placed his private part inside her private part. She said he did it a "whole bunch of times" when her mom was out of the house. When asked to describe the private part of her stepfather, she said it looked like a monk wearing a robe over his head. As Sterling forced the visual into his mind, he realized the child nailed it. The hooded cloak would look like a penis from the perspective of a child. Sterling knew his client was guilty. Sterling managed to shield his realization from the prosecutor.

After the interview, Sterling tried to gaslight the prosecutor by claiming that the child was off-base, and that the prosecutor didn't have a good case. Sterling tried to negotiate a settlement. The young prosecutor, not knowing what she had, offered Sterling a five-year sentence for his client. Sterling pretended to be disappointed but internally he was thrilled. His client deserved life behind bars, but it wasn't Sterling's job to decide what is fair. His job was to secure the best deal possible for his client.

Sterling presented the offer to his client. His client declined the offer. He recognized that it was a good offer. It was a far better offer than anything he got when he was represented by his public defender. But he could not take the offer. Any conviction would deprive him of his retirement with the government. Sterling pointed out that any outcome short of a long prison sentence was a good outcome. His client recognized the benefit but just couldn't admit that he raped his stepdaughter. He had so consistently proclaimed his innocence that he couldn't change course. His wife needed him to be innocent. If not, then she was the woman who failed to protect her daughter. She stood by her man, and he couldn't let her down. It was better to risk a conviction than to admit what he did.

Mrs. Turner did more than just stand by her man. Child Protective Services (CPS) took custody of Renee. The government agency refused to release the child back to her mother until Stone Turner was out of the house. Mrs. Turner refused to kick her husband out of their home. She simply refused to believe that her husband had committed such an unspeakable act. She loved her child, and knew her daughter usually told the truth, but it was easier to believe the child was lying. Money was a consideration, but CPS authorized a housing allowance so that Mrs. Turner could move out of the home and care for her daughter. Mrs. Turner declined CPS's offer, instead allowing her child to live in a foster home pending trial.

Sterling hated both of them. He hated his client for committing this crime and he hated his client's wife for not protecting her daughter. Part of him wished the prosecutor hadn't offered a five-year deal. His client deserved to go to prison for the next couple decades, then he should get a lifetime of probation and registration as a sex offender. Thankfully his client had the bad sense to turn down the offer, thus increasing the odds that he would get the sentence he deserved.

There was a competitive streak in Sterling that motivated him as much as his duty to provide his client with zealous representation. Simply speaking, Sterling didn't like to lose. Gearing up for trial, Sterling approached the case as if he was a juror. When Sterling first took the case, he wanted to believe that his client was innocent. He assumed that the jurors would also want to believe his client was innocent. The evidence against him was the testimony of the child, and some inconclusive evidence from a child rape exam suggesting there was some damage to the child's vagina, but there was no sure way to know what caused the damage.

Sterling worked hard on preparing the trial. He read every word of every police report, forensic examiner, and medical report. By the date of trial, Sterling was ready to provide zealous, although not enthusiastic, advocacy.

Arriving in Pierce County Superior Court for trial, Sterling and the prosecutor engaged in two days of grueling jury selection. Each juror completed an initial questionnaire. Some of those questions focused on whether they themselves had been the victim of sexual assault. Three of the 44 potential jurors answered that they had. Following individual questioning about their ability to be fair and impartial, each admitted that they would not be fair jurors. Another four jurors answered that because of the nature of the charge, they could not be fair or impartial. They were also struck for cause.

Eventually the pool of remaining jurors sat through jury selection, leaving a final jury of 12 jurors plus 2 alternates who would be available to replace any juror who became sick or otherwise had to be excused.

The prosecutor's opening statement was persuasive and informative. It outlined how Mr. Turner repeatedly raped his eight-year-old stepdaughter. The child disclosed the abuse to a classmate who then told a school counselor. The counselor was a mandatory reporter, who then told law enforcement. A child forensic examiner questioned Renee, who gave a graphic description of her abuse at the hands of her stepfather. Medical evidence would corroborate damage to the child's vagina. In all, Sterling was impressed with the prosecutor's opening statement.

Sterling had more trial experience under his belt than most attorneys earned in a lifetime. He found that going to trial gave him credibility in negotiating. His adversaries always knew that he was willing to back up his plea negotiations with a very real threat of trial. He never backed down. No one could intimidate him. The "go big or go home" approach meant that sometimes his clients paid a big price for going to trial. More often they got to go home at the end of the trial. This time, Sterling hoped that his client's decision to roll the dice would result in a conviction.

Sterling's opening statement poked holes in all of the prosecutor's evidence. He undermined the child and her testimony, pointing out that her description lacked critical details and was fuzzy as to timelines. The medical evidence was inconclusive. His client would take the stand and testify as to his own innocence, and his wife, the mother of the child would also testify that she never saw anything that gave her concerns about how her husband interacted with his stepdaughter. His opening statement was more like an argument, but the prosecutor didn't object so the judge let Sterling keep going.

The trial proceeded mostly as expected until the testimony of the prosecutor's medical expert. Nurse Practitioner Antonia Diego testified that she knew exactly how the injury occurred. She said the injury could only have been caused by a male penis entering the child's vagina. Sterling knew it was impossible for her to be so sure and made it his mission to tear her apart on cross-exam. She admitted she wasn't there when it happened, didn't see the actual penetration, there were no photos of the actual penetration, and the injury could have been caused by insertion of any number of objects, including by the child herself. Two dozen similar questions followed. Sterling may have pressed too far when he asked if she was attempting to add "psychic" to her curriculum vitae. That question drew a sharp objection from the prosecutor, which was sustained by the trial judge. But the point was made. 45 minutes of cross-exam later, an exhausted witness had to agree with every challenge Sterling made, then managed to blow any remaining credibility by sticking with her original claim that she knew exactly how this happened.

Despite the substantial evidence against his client, Sterling thought he did a good job of pointing out holes in the prosecutor's case. After getting his juices fired up during cross-examination, Sterling was starting to believe that he just might be able to win this case. He had mixed feelings about the prospect of winning the trial. His client didn't deserve to win. He deserved prison. But Sterling liked to win. His moral compass gave confused readings.

Sterling's closing argument found him writing on butcher paper for the jury to track along as he attacked the prosecutor's case. He pointed to his client and told the jury, "This man deserves to have a fair trial and the jury's decision will have lifelong impacts." As he listed all the shortcomings of the prosecutor's case, he made eye contact with each juror. Several of the jurors nodded almost imperceptibly as he spoke. They might not like his client, but they liked Sterling's passion and commitment to presenting a persuasive defense.

After a full day of deliberation, the jury still had not arrived at a verdict. The judge excused the jury and instructed them to return for a second day of deliberation. The next day, just before the lunch break, the judicial assistant called the attorneys, instructing them to come to court. He did not say whether the jury had a verdict or a question. Sterling rushed to court and arrived at the same time the jail deputies transported his client to the courtroom.

The judge announced to the parties that the jury advised the bailiff that they are hopelessly deadlocked and unable to reach a unanimous verdict. The judge advised the attorneys that he was going to bring back the jurors to read them a jury instruction. The so called "dynamite" instruction was meant to avoid the jury giving up too quickly. The judge would ask the presiding juror one question, "Is there a reasonable probability that the jury could reach a verdict in a reasonable amount of time?" The presiding juror responded, "No your honor. We cannot agree." Given that the jury deliberated for a day and half, no one could claim that they gave up too quickly. The judge dismissed the jury and thanked them for their service.

The judge announced that he was declaring a mistrial based on a deadlocked jury. Mr. Turner would remain in custody pending the prosecutor's determination as to whether she would retry Mr. Turner. The judge invited the attorneys to speak with the dismissed jurors if they wanted to gain insights as to their thought process during deliberations. Sterling and the prosecutor both agreed.

Most of the jurors remained in the jury deliberation room to speak with the attorneys. It was not mandatory, and they were offered a chance to leave, but most of them wanted to stay. Sterling thanked the jury for their consideration, then asked the only truly relevant question, "What was the split?" Sterling needed to know how many jurors voted to convict, and how many voted to acquit. The jury foreperson responded that the jury was split down the middle. Six in favor of convicting and six opposed. The six who opposed said they simply couldn't imagine anyone committing such a horrible crime. Sterling himself wished that no one could commit this kind of savage act on a child, but Sterling knew to a near certainty that his client did exactly what the prosecutor accused him of doing. Sterling thanked all the jurors, explaining that he genuinely appreciated how seriously they discharged their duties to be fair and impartial. He meant it too. Underneath his cynicism, he believed in the system of justice.

The prosecutor needed to run it by her boss to decide if they would retry the case against Mr. Turner. That was office policy. The Chief Deputy Prosecutor usually made the decision as to whether a case would be retried following a hung jury. The prosecutor was not required to try the case again. Usually, the decision to retry a case was based on the seriousness of the offense, and the split of the jury. Sometimes a jury would split 11-1 in favor of convicting. This usually happened when a single holdout refused to be persuaded. When that happened, the prosecutor would usually retry the case.

An even split left the prosecutor's office with a tough choice. The conventional wisdom held that if the prosecutor can only convince half of the jury, that is more than just a statistical aberration. Better to move on to the next case. Sterling had not been a prosecutor in nearly three years, so he wasn't sure about their current policies.

Sterling demanded the soonest possible setting for his client's retrial. Prosecutors tended to wait until the last minute before dumping a case. This extra time keeps the defendant in jail. By moving up the timetable, they would need to make a decision sooner rather than later. The judge granted Sterling's motion for a trial setting one month away.

Sterling visited his client in jail. His client was thrilled with the outcome of the trial and was feeling fairly confident that the prosecutor would not risk a second trial. He was probably right. Sterling held out hope that his client would end up in prison. Sterling thought about the child, Renee. If her stepfather won the trial and went back home, the odds were good that the CPS case would be dropped. Renee would likely be sent home. Her mom was not a protective factor in the home. The child would no doubt endure years of abuse. Renee would learn that it does no good to seek help. Sterling could only imagine how she would turn out as an adult. He hoped she would get the therapy she would need in order to deal with so much abuse.

A week later, the prosecutor called Sterling to let him know they were dismissing the case against Mr. Turner. Sterling thanked her for the courtesy of the call and assured her that she did a good job during the trial. She thanked him for his kind words, although the tone suggested she was skeptical about his sincerity. Sterling wanted to tell her that his client was guilty and should be retried and sent to prison, but if his client found out he did that then Sterling would lose his law license. Sterling knew he just needed to use this case as a learning experience. The lesson was not to take sex offender cases unless he had no other way to support himself. This was the one time that Sterling believed he used his powers of persuasion for evil instead of good. He just felt dirty.

Sterling wished he could persuade Taylor to let him resume his duties as corporate counsel for the Crips.

Although it would make life easier for him in terms of money, he didn't want to expose Taylor to the potential for physical harm. Given his earlier experience with Jamal, he knew that representing gang clients could be dangerous.

In addition to the risk of physical danger, Sterling wanted to shield Taylor from the risk of the IRS discovering that his firm took in a lot of cash. That was a risk he had been willing to take, but he was not willing to expose Taylor. Ultimately, he just had to close that chapter of his life, no matter how profitable or exciting.

Chapter 70

The ACLU invited Sterling to their annual Giants of Justice Awards in Atlanta, Georgia. Sterling was a nominee for their highest award based on his successful defense of a truly innocent client, LTC Carter. He was a longshot to win the award, but even a nomination was a great honor and could help boost his reputation in the legal community. The timing was good. Sterling needed to bump up his marketing. Sterling and Taylor needed to grow the legitimate side of his law practice. He had nearly forgotten how hard it is to earn an honest living. When Taylor completed her Army duty, they could expand their law practice quickly with the right exposure.

The timing was good for another reason. On the heels of his successful defense of an accused sex offender, Sterling needed an event like this to cleanse his palette. He knew it was his job to represent people accused of crimes, even if that crime was a sex offense. His mind had long ago come to terms with the fact that guilty people are entitled to representation no less than innocent clients. Still, he wasn't feeling good about helping his sex offender client avoid a conviction. Part of him feared that by helping his client to avoid a conviction, he enabled his client to continue his efforts to rape his eight-year-old stepdaughter. This weighed heavily on him. But thinking about LTC Carter reminded him that there are truly good people who need a good lawyer.

Taylor wanted to join him for the award show, but she had a trial scheduled for that day and Judge Anderson did not agree to her motion for a continuance. Judge Anderson didn't understand why anyone would nominate Sterling for an award, and he was even more surprised to hear that CPT Jane found something attractive about that jackass. Judge Anderson wasn't going to change his docket just to make life easier for Sterling.

Sterling offered to let Taylor borrow his car while he was gone if she agreed to drop him off at the airport and then pick him up when he returned. She didn't care that much about his car, but she knew it meant a lot to him, so she pretended to enthusiastically accept his offer. She wished him luck and made him promise to update her on the status of the award. It wasn't the type of award which was broadcast on national TV, so watching the event was not an option for her.

Taylor dropped him off at the airport early in the morning then she went straight to work. The trial she had scheduled for that day was a theft case. The Army called it a "green on green" crime in which a soldier allegedly stole money from a fellow soldier in the barracks. Such crimes were considered particularly egregious because the morale of a unit hinges upon the trust of the men who fight together.

The prosecutor's case against Private Daniel was pretty solid, but not perfect. It was based on circumstantial evidence. Her client was the only one in the room when the money was stolen. He wasn't caught in the act, but the victim entered the room and noticed his wallet was on top of his bed instead of in the drawer where he always put it. The alleged thief was the only other person in the room. The alleged victim checked his wallet and discovered $80 missing. A shouting match ensued between the two soldiers, drawing more and more soldiers to the area. Eventually the defendant's peers bullied him into emptying his pockets. He had $85 in his left pants pocket, suggesting he already had $5 then added the $80 from his buddy's wallet. He denied stealing anything, claiming instead that the money in his pocket was his own money.

PVT Daniel's proclamations of innocence rang hollow with his unit. His commanding officer requested an investigation and prosecution of PVT Daniel. The JAG office moved ahead with the case, and PVT Daniel faced a court-martial.

For CPT Jane's client, going to trial wasn't a bad idea. The prosecutor's offer was so unattractive that it couldn't get much worse following a conviction. The prosecutor would agree to six months behind bars if PVT Daniel entered a plea of guilty. The maximum was only 12 months. By going to trial, CPT Jane gave her client hope that he could avoid serving a jail sentence at the Regional Confinement Center at Ft. Lewis. PVT Daniel did not want to plead guilty. He had told his parents that he was being unfairly prosecuted, so he decided it was better to risk a conviction than admit his guilt. If convicted, he could always blame the system for failing him, while maintaining his standing with his family.

Leading up to trial, the prosecutor, CPT David Bohn, treated CPT Jane as a solid professional. Most opposing counsel got along with her. Unlike Sterling, CPT Jane saw no percentage in provoking her adversaries. She consistently secured good deals for her clients and part of her success was simply being nice. But not every client's case can be settled, and CPT Jane's client PVT Daniel was one of them. PVT Daniel's commander had no use for a soldier who steals from another soldier. The commander needed all of his soldiers to trust each other and have each other's back, and he pushed hard for the prosecutor to make an example of PVT Daniel. Consequently, the prosecutor's plea offer was harsher than average. Despite CPT Jane's efforts to present mitigating information ahead of the trial, CPT Bohn would not budge. It probably didn't matter, since PVT Daniel had no intention of pleading guilty anyway.

CPT Jane was nervous. This would be her first trial without a co-counsel to assist her. Her only other trial was months ago, and she was mostly there to learn while watching the Senior Defense Counsel conduct the defense. During that previous trial, CPT Jane handled a couple witnesses, and she was in charge of presenting the closing argument, but her co-counsel did the heavy lifting. CPT Jane usually settled all of her cases, and generally didn't need to go to trial to secure good outcomes. This case couldn't be settled. CPT Jane wanted to prove that she is a solid trial attorney. She and Sterling were going to be partners in his law office soon, and she wanted him to know that she could handle the stress of trial.

During the trial, the prosecutor presented his case without any showboating, hyperbole or dirty tricks. He called his witnesses and presented evidence for the jury to consider. He didn't disparage PVT Daniel, except in the sense that the evidence suggested PVT Daniel was a thief.

CPT Jane's performance at the trial was excellent. She had a firm grasp of the facts. She presented a compelling argument. No one saw her client commit any crime. Soldiers often carry cash so the fact that her client had money in his pocket didn't prove anything. The cloth wallet didn't lend itself to fingerprinting, so it was hard to prove who moved the victim's wallet from the desk drawer to the bed. During closing, she argued that the evidence simply didn't support a conviction beyond a reasonable doubt.

Unfortunately, the jury didn't see it that way and they quickly convicted PVT Daniel. The jury sentenced him to four months in jail. In that sense, CPT Jane beat the offer. She won. The prosecutor got less than the six months he had offered as part of a plea bargain. Sometimes defense attorneys need to qualify their victories. It might not be an acquittal, but it was better than her client's next best option of simply pleading guilty and getting more jail time.

PVT Daniel thanked his attorney for her hard work. He was happy to be done with this matter. He could serve his time in jail and move on. He would no longer be in the Army since the jury also sentenced him to a bad conduct discharge, but at least he could soon put this behind him. He could also insist to his family that he was unfairly convicted of a crime he didn't commit.

CPT Jane was more disappointed in the outcome than her client. She invested a lot of work into the trial. She convinced herself that she could win. She fell into that sense of trial psychosis in which her efforts at persuasion made her believe in the strength of her case. Thankfully, despite the loss, CPT Jane got to go home at the end of trial. Her client did not. MP's escorted her client to the Regional Confinement Center for in-processing.

It was a long day for CPT Jane. In a single day she picked a jury, argued the case, received a jury verdict, argued sentencing, and received the jury's sentencing findings. Judge Anderson pushed the jury to complete the whole case in one day, keeping them working until they were done around 6:00 pm Pacific Standard Time. Looking at the time, she knew Sterling's award would be coming soon. The ACLU event was scheduled to end at 9:00 pm Easter Standard Time, but it typically ran long. Attorneys were not known for short acceptance speeches. She gave Sterling a call just in case he was done. He did not answer, so she left a message.

Dragging herself to Sterling's G-Wagon after the trial, she was ready to go to Sterling's house, which would soon officially also be her home if she was reading the tea leaves correctly. On the drive home, she took a moment to reflect on their likely pending nuptials. She wondered when Sterling would propose. They had talked about it in general terms. He even had her look at engagement rings during their recent trip to the Bahamas. Their two lives were quickly joining as one and the clock was ticking. She wanted a ring on her finger.

After a thirty-minute drive battling I-5 traffic, Taylor arrived at Sterling's house. She stopped in the driveway with the transmission still in drive. Her foot was on the brake. She sent her right hand digging into the center console feeling for the remote control to open the garage door. Sterling always parked in the garage. He didn't want his beautiful car exposed to the weather or catch the attention of thieves. Parking in the garage also made it easier for Taylor to get into the house. She would usually enter the house through the door of the attached garage.

Out of the corner of her eye she saw movement to her left. A man quickly made his way toward the driver's door and pulled on the handle. The locked door did not budge. Another man approached from the passenger side. The man at the driver's door raised his hand and slammed his fist on the window but the glass held firm. Taylor nearly panicked. She managed to push the button on the remote to open the garage. She took her foot off the brake and inched forward but the garage door wasn't moving fast enough for her to press the gas. In her confusion, and being unfamiliar with Sterling's car, she wasn't able to get the SUV in reverse.

The man on her left raised what appeared to be a gun. Instinctively Taylor tried to duck out of the way. A flash lit up her peripheral vision. The shot barely missed her head. Glass shattered as the window exploded, leaving shards of glass in her hair. She screamed as the man redirected the gun. She saw another flash coming from the barrel. That was the last thing she saw. A small hole entered the left side of her head, and a much larger hole appeared on the other side of her skull, spraying brain and blood matter inside the vehicle. CPT Taylor Jane's lifeless body limped forward, resting on the steering wheel, pressing on the horn. The G-Wagon inched forward, coming to rest in the garage with the engine still running.

Chapter 71

Sterling watched patiently as the awards were handed out to hard working attorneys who defended the rights of those both wrongly accused and rightfully accused. He began to wonder why he attended this event in the first place. He was honored to be nominated, but he knew he was a relative newcomer to the world of advancing civil liberties. If it wasn't for his media tour after securing a victory for LTC Carter, very few people would even know he existed. His mind wandered as the event handed out award after award. His mind was on Taylor.

Sterling needed to put a ring on her finger. He wanted to make it official. He decided he would return home after the awards, pick up a ring, then pop the question. Maybe he would get a bottle of good champagne and throw the ring in the flute before handing it to Taylor. He would wait and see how long it took her to find the ring. He quickly rejected that plan. He didn't want the ring to get sticky. Instead, he could take her outside near his pool. They would take in the view of Commencement Bay, and he would get down on a knee and ask her to marry him. Yes, that was a better plan.

At long last the event's highest award received its place for consideration. Sterling forced himself to put a pause on his proposal plans. Sterling mentally prepared himself for the moment when someone else in his category earned the award. He tried to focus on smiling and clapping for the winner. He wanted to appear gracious even in defeat.

Against all odds, Sterling won the Giants of Justice award. The camera panned to his face, which displayed an authentic expression of disbelief. He was shocked to hear his name. He stood slowly and made his way to the stage. Taking a position in front of the microphone he thanked the ACLU, but mostly he thanked the love of his life, Taylor Jane, for inspiring him to be a better man. He spoke of the importance of holding the government accountable and forcing prosecutors to uphold the Constitution. He thanked his client for having the confidence in him to move forward with a risky strategy designed to expose the dangers of ego driven paper pushers in positions power. He ended with his favorite expression, "Let's do justice!" The audience stood and applauded. A more humble man would blush but Sterling basked in the glow of his unlikely victory. He wished to himself that Taylor could have shared the moment with him.

Sterling stepped off the stage wishing that there was a redeye flight from Atlanta to SeaTac. He moved off the stage behind the curtains and considered taking the most efficient route back to his chair in the audience. There were no additional awards to be handed out, so Sterling did not need to return to his seat. The event was done, and Sterling found himself lost for a moment.

Offstage, reporters gathered to interview award winners. Sterling captured the highest award and consequently drew the largest number of reporters asking for a comment. The pretty blond from MSNBC approached Sterling and asked if he was going to celebrate his victory at an after-hours party. Sterling never planned to win, so celebrating wasn't on his radar. CNN, being based in Atlanta, went out of its way to ensure the winners received a VIP invitation to the ballroom of the Remington Hotel. The media company also extended invitations to reporters from every network except Fox. It didn't really matter since Fox didn't cover the ACLU award event.

Sterling would have preferred to ditch the party but considering that he won the coveted Giants of Justice award, he couldn't exactly blow off the after-hours party in his honor. One of the interns assigned to the ACLU event helped Sterling to secure a cab to the party. Making his way to the Remington Hotel, he found himself rubbing elbows with actual stars. It wasn't an event for A-listers, so stars like Brad Pitt and Jennifer Anniston were absent, but Megan Fox and Ryan Reynolds made an appearance. Sterling was never one to be star struck. The actors enjoyed his ability to engage them on a personal level. For a moment, he thought Megan Fox was flirting with him, but that was probably the alcohol talking. Sterling tipped back a few drinks, more than a little proud of himself for winning the prestigious award.

He gave a few interviews to the reporters who tracked him down at the celebration. Eventually the attractive blond from MSNBC made her way to the event. The cameras were off when she approached him. She appeared to have abandoned her role as a reporter, instead mingling as a fan. She congratulated him for being a pillar of justice. Even off duty, she skillfully engaged Sterling in conversation. Not that it was difficult to get a few words out of him. He was riding on the high of winning the award. Their eyes locked and she raised her glass. Reflexively, Sterling did the same. The reporter shifted her vision slightly, trying to subtly determine if Sterling was wearing a wedding ring. He was not.

She smiled to herself and asked him if there was someone special in his life. Sterling snapped out of his trance. For a second, he had considered inviting her back to his hotel room. But then thoughts of Taylor brough him back to reality. He loved Taylor and was not about to be seduced by a beautiful and famous reporter. He responded, "I have an amazing woman at home. When I get back, I'm going to ask her to marry me." A disappointed, but flirty smile on the reporter's face hinted that she might be willing to overlook Sterling's display of commitment. Sterling politely excused himself. He suddenly wanted very badly to be home.

Tracking down the ACLU intern, he secured a cab ride back to his hotel. Despite ditching the party early, it was already well past midnight EST. He was ready to be done for the night.

He retired to his hotel room, only then noticing a voicemail. It was from Taylor. She said, "I love you so much! Win or lose, you will always be my Giant of Justice." He smiled when he heard her voice. He called her phone to report the good news of his victory. Taylor did not answer.

Minutes later, he called again. Still no answer. Sterling grew concerned but hoped that Taylor was caught up in some Netflix series and just didn't see his calls. He had to take into consideration the three-hour time difference, figuring that Taylor might still be working on her trial if it was set to go into a second day, although he would be surprised if it took more than one day. Sterling attempted to sleep but he couldn't stop worrying about Taylor.

Sterling's phone rang about 0300 EST. "Thank goodness," he said to himself. Turning on the desk lamp, he picked up his iPhone. Looking at the screen he did not recognize the number. He answered the phone and said "hello." The man's voice on the other end said, "Is this Preston Sterling?" Sterling replied, "Yes, who is this?" "This is Detective Marshall with the Tacoma Police Department. Do you live at 1532 Ridge Cliff Road?" Sterling recognized his own address and said, "Yes, why do you ask?" The detective replied, "Do you own a 2007 Mercedes G-Wagon?" Again, Sterling replied, "Yes, I do." There was a long pause and the voice at the other end asked, "Do you know a dark-haired female, 28 years old, name of Taylor Jane?" Sterling's heart stopped. What the hell happened to Taylor, he wondered. Sterling was tired of the question-and-answer game and asked, "What the fuck is this about? Put Taylor on the phone." Another long pause, then the detective replied, "I have some painful news to pass on to you. You might want to brace yourself."

Chapter 72

Sterling raced to the airport arriving about 0400. He scheduled the first possible flight back to SeaTac, almost getting himself arrested when he demanded a sooner flight that did not exist. Leaving ATL, he arrived at SeaTac about noon. He paid a cab driver an extra $200 to race him to his house. Sterling shouted obscenities at the cab driver trying to get him to move his ass. Arriving at his home, he observed a tow truck taking away his G-Wagon. He exited the cab and the cab driver left quickly, happy to be done with Sterling.

An exhausted looking man in a crumpled suit approached Sterling and held out a hand. "I am Detective Marshall." The man had been up all night but wanted to stay on scene long enough to brief Sterling on the case. Sterling shook the man's hand and asked for an update. The detective explained that the case is under investigation, but neighbors reported hearing a woman scream. They saw two men approaching Sterling's G-Wagon, then they heard shots. Police responded to find Taylor Jane unresponsive with a gunshot wound to the head.

Sterling's heart sank. Was this a random attack? It seemed unlikely. Sterling knew some violent people. Did someone kill Taylor in retaliation for something he had done? Did one of Jamal's relatives find out about Sterling killed the Jamal and they extracted revenge by killing Taylor? It was Sterling's vehicle, so did they think Sterling was in the car and just accidentally shot

Taylor instead of Sterling? The wheels were turning inside Sterling's head when he realized the detective was still talking. "So, Mr. Sterling, can you think of any reason why someone would want to harm Ms. Jane?"

Sterling answered the detective's questions in a generally honest manner. Truthfully, Taylor was the most wonderful person he had ever known. She was the love of his life. He couldn't imagine anyone wanting to hurt her. Detective Marshall completed his questioning and had Sterling fill out a form with his contact information. Sterling was becoming familiar with this type of form.

When the police cleared out and let him enter his home, Sterling charged his dying iPhone and called the only person he thought could help. Susan Maddox answered the phone. Sterling told her what had happened. She relayed her sympathies. Sterling asked if she had any idea who would want to harm Taylor. Susan paused, then asked if he could meet her at the art gallery. Sterling agreed to meet her then realized the police had just towed away his car. Thankfully he couldn't part with his trusty Camry and had it in a storage unit a few miles down the road. Sterling dug the keys out of his safe then called for a taxi to take him to the storage unit. Despite being covered with dust that mysteriously made its way into the storage unit, the Camry started without issue and Sterling drove to the gallery to meet Susan Maddox.

Sterling was caught between equal amounts grief and rage. Entering the gallery, Sterling walked to the back office. Susan gave him a hug and invited him to have a seat. She said, "I am so sorry Sterling! I know how much you loved that girl." Sterling thanked her but could only manage a blank stare. He asked her, "Is there any chance Tricky did this?" Susan turned her head for a moment, then looked at him and said, "That was my concern as well. Word on the street is that Tricky found out about our past relationship and put a hit out on you. I thought I was able to cancel the order, otherwise I would have warned you. My guess is that they thought it was you in the car, and accidently shot Taylor."

"Ah Jesus!" said Sterling. "Why didn't you tell me?" Susan replied, "Like I said, I thought I had it under control. I never thought he would go forward with such a stupid plan." Sterling looked at her, with dark, cold eyes and said, "I am going to kill that mother fucker." Susan said, "Don't be silly. He is in prison. Who would you get to kill him?" "Fuck! I don't know. But I bet I can find a way," replied Sterling. "Sugar, I bet you could. You are a smart lawyer. But give it some time. He will be out of prison eventually. Take your time." Sterling was in no mood for patience. "I am going to find a way to get that asshole." Susan took a breath and said, "You do what you got to do. But don't go yapping about it. This needs to stay between you and me." Sterling nodded and left the gallery. He was going to kill Tricky. He was going to kill anyone involved in Taylor's death.

Susan's revelation about Tricky putting out a hit on him stabbed Sterling's heart like a dagger. It was Sterling's fault that Taylor died. It should have been him. They must have thought he was in the G'Wagon when the vehicle pulled up to his house. They shot the driver of the car assuming it was Sterling. But he was not sure how to proceed. Maybe the police should handle this but how would he explain it? Could he tell them that he was the corporate lawyer for the Crips and met Susan as part of the money laundering operation he set up for the gang? No, like Jamal, this was a matter Sterling needed to take care of himself. He would kill Tricky.

Chapter 73

Despite his tough words to Susan, she had a point. Sterling had no idea how to organize a hit of a gang leader inside a prison. He would need to consult with an expert. Contrary to Susan's request that he only speak to her, Sterling reached out to the only gangster he trusted. He called Buster, who agreed to meet him at his law office.

Sterling arrived at the office first. In his trance, he somehow wasn't expecting to see his receptionist working at the desk. She greeted him, seemingly oblivious as to what had happened to Taylor. He ignored her greeting and told her to cancel all of his appointments. He then said, "Cancel all of my appointments for tomorrow too." She replied, "Will do Mr. Sterling. Is everything alright?" Before her question left her mouth Sterling slammed the door leading to his office. She got to work cancelling his appointments.

Buster came to the law office about an hour later. Sterling met him at the door as his receptionist was starting to tell Buster that all appointments were cancelled. Sterling waived her off and invited Buster to chat in his office.

With the exception of Sterling's receptionist, pretty much the whole world knew what happened to Taylor. Buster expressed his condolences. His expression conveyed actual sympathy. Buster enjoyed their flight to the Bahamas sitting next to Taylor and had formed something of a bond with her. Sterling thanked him for his kind words.

Sterling took a moment to ask how Buster made it out of the Bahamas. Buster smiled and said, "I thought you would figure out that I killed Felix. I managed to catch a fishing trawler bound for Key West. I bribed the skipper to drop me off." Mystery solved, Sterling moved on to more pressing business.

"I am going to get back at Tricky for what he did to Taylor. I need to know how to kill him while he is in prison. I am willing to pay you for your expertise if you will help me as a consultant. I don't expect you to personally get involved." Buster gave Sterling a confused look. "First of all, you don't need to pay me to help you. What happened to your girlfriend is fucked up. She was a great woman and I know how much you loved her. Second, and most important, why do you think Tricky did this? You think that man cares about you banging Susan?" Sterling did a bad job of trying to hide his surprise, and Buster laughed out loud. "Wait, you thought it was a secret you was banging Mrs. Maddox? Shit, everyone knew you were hitting that. Susan didn't exactly keep it secret. In fact, she often joked about sleeping with the hired help. In fact, I was supposed to be her ride home the night of your office warming party. Susan said she was going to stay behind to keep you company, so I waited in the car until she was done. If it means anything, she said you are hung like a horse." Sterling tried to compose his thoughts.

After a long pause he said, "So then why am I not a dead man already?"

Buster took a moment to consider his response. He said, "Tricky doesn't care. Sometime during his prison sentence, Tricky switched teams." Sterling's look of confusion prompted Buster to connect the dots for him. "Look, Tricky don't like women no more. But he likes money. You helped him make lots of money so that means he likes you. If you also kept his wife from complaining about being lonely, then that was just a bonus. There is no way he killed your girlfriend. You are the goose that lays the golden eggs."

Sterling believed Buster but this revelation left him more lost than ever. "If it wasn't Tricky, then who killed Taylor?" Buster replied, "Fuck if I know. Maybe some crack heads looking for drug money. Maybe it was just random. I don't know. Good chance we will never know. Sometimes you just got to move on."

Chapter 74

After Buster left his office, Sterling did not simply move on. He couldn't move on. He continued to press law enforcement for an update. They promised to call him if there was a break in the case. Sterling never fully developed patience. It wasn't a skill he possessed. Detective Marshall went out of his way to be nice to Sterling, but Sterling still cursed at the glacial pace of the police investigation.

Exhausted, he went home and drank himself to sleep. The next morning, Sterling didn't go to work. He stayed home despondent, spending most of his day drinking and trying to figure out who to kill. A knock on his door brought him to his feet. Two men dressed in Army uniforms were at his front door. They claimed they were there regarding Taylor's death. He invited them in with as much enthusiasm as he would have for visiting Jehovah's Witnesses.

SFC Gardner explained that he and SGT Phillips were there as part of the Army's Casualty Assistance Program. They explained that shortly prior to her death, CPT Jane designated Preston Sterling as the beneficiary for her death gratuity. The SGLI benefit payable to him was $100,000. They asked him to complete some paperwork to receive the benefit.

"Unbelievable," said Sterling to himself. Her generosity made him feel even worse. He spent his life pursuing money until he met Taylor. Then money took a backseat to love. Ironically, her death brought him money he had come to value less than her, which he received only because of her love for him. He would trade the money for her life any day.

Sterling completed the paperwork then invited the Army guys to leave. He had no use for them. Although not fit to drive, an intoxicated Sterling jumped in his dirty Camry and made his way to the office. He wanted to see if he could make any progress on finding Taylor's killer, and it wasn't going to happen just sitting at home drinking. His receptionist greeted him and expressed her condolences. By this time, she heard about Taylor's death. He thanked her then directed her to cancel all of his appointments. She gave him an odd look and told him he didn't have any appointments set for the day. She had already cancelled them all. He thanked her again, then fired her and told her to leave. She stood up, wondering if Sterling was joking. He was not. He shouted to her, "Get the fuck out! You are fucking fired!" She grabbed her phone and her purse, not bothering to shut down the computer. She walked out of his office. Sterling knew that she had done nothing wrong, but he needed to lash out and she just happened to be at the wrong place at the wrong time. He would need to call the temp agency to send a new receptionist. Firing her didn't make him feel better. Then again, it didn't make him feel worse.

Sterling needed access to the police reports. He needed to see for himself what evidence was available. He managed to bribe the records clerk into giving him a copy of the police report. She emailed him the preliminary report. The rest of the paperwork had not yet been filed by the detective. Sterling read through every detail three times but didn't find any concrete evidence identifying the killer. The only witnesses were Sterling's neighbors. They started watching through their windows after they heard Taylor screaming. The report noted that the witness statements were nearly identical. They both saw two men outside Sterling's vehicle. One man shot the gun into the driver's compartment, then both men fled on foot before entering into a getaway vehicle of unknown make and model.

Chapter 75

Susan Maddox gave Sterling a call. She invited herself over to his office, but he declined. She came anyway. The reception area was empty, and he opened the outer door when he heard her knock. She walked in, shutting the door behind her. Sterling walked away from her toward his office without saying a word. He really wasn't in the mood for company. She followed behind him and sat in a chair across from him on the other side of his mahogany desk. She offered him a drink from a bottle of bourbon she pulled from her bag. He accepted.

Sterling said, "I spoke with Buster. He encouraged me to leave it alone and to look elsewhere. He thinks Tricky didn't do it." Susan gave him an odd look, then said, "Well, I'm not sure Buster is taking into account Tricky's jealous streak." That seemed like an odd thing for her to say. Buster seemed to suggest it was generally well known that Tricky was now gay. Sterling's brain was in a fog, so maybe he just wasn't understanding her correctly.

Looking to change the subject, Susan looked at the police report on Sterling's desk. She said, "Now don't drive yourself nuts reading the police report. Those three guys who killed Taylor will probably never be found. Sometimes bad things just happen to good people." Sterling's brain froze for a moment. Something Susan said was setting off alarm bells in the part of his brain reserved for sniffing out bullshit during trials. It took a moment for that part of the brain to open the gates and let the rest of the brain in on its little secret. The police report only noted two suspects. How did Susan know there were three killers?

Susan inadvertently looked at Sterling's face. She knew she had said too much, but she didn't know if Sterling heard her comments or knew enough to understand the significance of her words. Not seeing any sign that he registered the meaning of her statement, she said, "OK hun, I know you are in a tough spot. If I can do anything for you, just let me know." She turned and started to take a step toward the door. Sterling's hand was already reaching under his desk, feeling for the Glock holstered inside a carrier he bolted to the interior side of the desk near his knee.

Before she could reach his door, he launched his body upward, grabbing Susan by the throat. He shoved her up against the wall and held the Glock at the side of her head. Flashes of rage bounced through his head. She was trying to speak but he could not focus on her words. He could only focus on the image of Taylor's face burned in his memory. Susan tried to talk but Sterling's hand around her throat prevented her from uttering anything more than a grunt. She couldn't breathe. Sterling continued to squeeze. Darkness began to press in from the sides as her field of vision narrowed.

Sterling snapped out of his trance long enough to decide he should shoot her instead of choking her. It seemed a better response to mirror Taylor's death. Loosening his grip, Susan struggled to say, "You are right, I killed her." Sterling loosened his grip even more. He leaned his mouth near her ear, and said, "I know, and now I am going to end your life." His finger pressed along the trigger. Susan grunted, "I did it for you."

He knew he should just shoot her right there on the spot, but curiosity got the better of him. Or maybe he just wanted to give her a chance for the traditional courtesy of an opportunity to express her last words. "Susan, what the fuck are you talking about? You killed the love of my life as a favor to me?" Said Sterling through a clenched jaw.

Susan looked at him and said, "I know you. I know you better than you know yourself. You have a gift. Who else could have risen to the top the way you did? How did you get there? It wasn't by following rules. You are a killer, both literally and figuratively. You have great instinct and an unparalleled ability see through bullshit. I have never seen anyone with such a complete grasp of the law and human nature."

Susan paused, and said, "But, you fell into a trap thinking that you could change your true self. You gave in to Taylor's demand to have a child with you even though you knew you wanted to be done. A man doesn't get a vasectomy if in his heart he wants more kids. You gave up the most profitable side of your business just because she was uncomfortable with the work that made you the bulk of your money. Never mind that she probably enjoyed your house on the hill and your Mercedes. You were about to give away half of your law practice to her just to make her a partner.

She didn't earn it, you did! You let yourself be reduced to the status of a neutered dog tethered to some fantasy that the love of a good woman will set you free from your sins. Let me tell you something that you should already know: Your strength is your ability to embrace your sins. You tapped into the part of yourself that is unique. Tell me honestly that you could be happy playing house with that girl? Sure, maybe for a month, even a year. But long term? You know where you would end up. You will be divorced again, broke, and maybe she will even use your past against you as blackmail in the divorce proceedings. What if you got her pregnant, then you are stuck with another set of child support payments and a second baby mama taking you to court every year. You were ready to give away everything you worked hard for and for what? Sterling, you know it and I know it. I saved your life." A silence filled the room.

Sterling squeezed her neck again, this time pulling her face close to his. He sat the gun down on his desk and used his now free hand to join the other around her neck. He leaned in within an inch of her face before pressing his lips against her lips and loosening the grip around her neck. He reached his hands around her waist, and she did the same to him, locking in an embrace. After a long kiss, Sterling pulled away slightly. Susan smiled and said, "Are you ready to get back to work?" Sterling locked eyes with her and said, "I'm back."

-THE END-